M000194429

West Along the River

Stories from
The Connecticut River Valley
And Elsewhere

Copyright © 2011 David Brule

ISBN 978-1-60910-615-7

All rights reserved. No part of this publication may be reproduced, stored in a retrieval system, or transmitted in any form or by any means, electronic, mechanical, recording or otherwise, without the prior written permission of the author

Printed in the United States of America.

Cover photo by Monique Brule

Cover design by Lynn Stowe Tomb

Booklocker.com, Inc.
2011

West Along the River

Including
Village Sketchbooks,
And Travel Notes from Ireland,
France, and Brittany

David Brule

For Arthur and Shirley Brule

*whose small house above the Narrows
on the Connecticut River
provided warmth, love and inspiration.*

Table of Contents

Foreword

The river of the title is the Millers River, known to the native people of the region as the *baquog,* or the *papaguntiquash.* This river flows west along the woodlands of the family homestead, then abruptly north to its confluence with the great Connecticut River on whose banks nestle the homes of many of those in this book. We were born, worked, and lived within sight of the river, as did 12,000 years of native populations. For many of us, the river is a pathway for exploration of the natural world, adventure, imagining and dreams. The stories in this collection attempt to evoke the spirit of those who have lived on its banks, and of the wild things that inhabit that world.

This book owes its existence in part to David Detmold, Lyn Clark, and my wife, Monique.

David is the editor of the *Montague Reporter* in whose pages, starting in 2005, many of these stories have appeared. David has the gift of encouraging us to tell our stories and then provides the means by which we can share our tales.

Lyn Clark, also of the *Montague Reporter*, and an author herself, provided the guidance and experience to enable me to bring these stories to publication in the form of collected essays.

My wife Monique has provided patience, artistry and understanding, in accepting to make a home for us in this old homestead along the river.

WEST ALONG THE RIVER – 2005

A Winter Morning Walk (*February*)

January snows drift into February, still light and powdery even after days on the ground. Easy walking to the river, sometimes directly along the traveled and packed path, or other times off on an angle taking a new route to the water's edge. Tracks appear, this one an errant coyote, good stride until it intersects our own path and mixes in with snowshoe, boot, house Siberian and squirrel traces.

The river, beyond the birch and alder, moves along brightly and silently in the frozen morning mist. Some days under dark skies and snow-filled air it moves sullenly, slurrying partly frozen liquid snow on its surface; but this morning it's bright and steaming at 0 degrees. Trees along the edge are frosted with inch thick lace on every branch and twig, that falls away with even the faintest breath. Calendar days indicating January or February mean nothing here, just winter unchanging for the time being.

The swift running river is open and free of ice drawing wintering black ducks and goldeneye up-river from the frozen Connecticut. They line the shore of the island basking or feeding in the early light. They will be gone at the least sign of intrusion, ever wild and wary. On the cliff at the bend, long icicles hanging over rock faces glisten in the frost. Otter sign—tracks and slide marks—criss-cross the snow-covered surface. Memories of a glimpse of three of them, playfully loping over this spot years ago in their hunch-backed and humping scramble, shooting a wild glance over a shoulder and gone in a wink. Missed them this time, although they did leave their tracks behind. On a winter morning walk such as this, few birds other than the ducks are present. Still, from somewhere overhead the calls of wintering robins drift down, and up on the mountain is a red-tail on his perch in a lightning-killed tree, catching the warming sun, breast feathers fluffed to the southeast.

1

Bright days in February unlock the snows; the river rises and pushes through channels in the woods usually unlocked only by the spring freshet. And this year, February has seemed mild, encouraging the first hooded merganser, dandified male, here to fish in the swift currents rushing by the cliff face. Even the first red-winged blackbirds have been coaxed up the valley and now deck the trees around the yard, the first migrants following the glacier's retreat, the first of millions , literally, to flow back into our Northern veins swelling the woods and river with color and song. But spring is a chancy affair, and snows will yet drive the blackbirds to the feeder and the Cooper's hawk back to the yard, as last week when he sat on the picket fence, a burning eye fixed on the terrified flock of English sparrows huddled deep in the brush pile, usually chattering and fighting like rag pickers, now frozen in silence not daring to blink. The hawk, finally discouraged, left to scour the marsh, later to leave the darkening woods to the great horned owl, that tiger who prowls the edges of our settlement at dusk, already his booming voice calling in the dark pines at the foot of the mountain, reminding all of his night territory, of his intention to mate and nest in these February woods.

Waiting for the Call *(March)*

The first of March arrived with fleecy, all-day snow. The Farmers' Almanac calls this St. David's Day; if this were Wales, my editor and I would be celebrating in pubs by the singing sea. But here it's a good day for a ski along the river at French King Rock. The woods are empty of sound, hushed by the falling snow.

The landscape could draw Claude Monet out of doors one more time to turn out a variation on *A Road to Honfleur under Snow*, a grey leaden sky with all contours softened.

Skiing in slow motion down the trail, quiet dark water slipping past the rock, black and white birds on the river. Glide and stop. Carefully lift one ski then another to the side to avoid the first snow striders taking priority on the trail. These are hardy leggy insects making their slow early spring way across the whiteness. Going who knows where? Could they be the first signs of spring coming?

Growing up on the banks of the Connecticut, in a house above the Narrows, winter meant the river frozen solid from the town to the French King Bridge, the sound of its icy booming at night sometimes reaching right into the house. Spring in those days was on the way by March 17th when the current eroded the ice at Red Rocks, with the first mergansers trying their luck fishing in those depths. Or many a spring came with the first robins by March 10th, or the grackles calling from the towering white pines of the Shady Rest. But up here, living on the Millers on abandoned pastureland-gone-to-woods, a different sign ushers in spring. The song sparrow can tune his pipes at the edge of the garden, the robin and cardinal can tell us to cheer up from the top of the willow tree, but just a single syllable at dusk in the empty woods confirms that winter's grip is loosening. Not very musical, just a nasal *peent* tells you the first woodcock is back, ready to strut and show off for his first-choice female, modestly hidden in the birches, waiting to be impressed. That one syllable call is followed by silence. Then, high up in the air, a faint twittering (no other word for it) makes its way to the ear as the proud male reaches the height of forty or fifty feet and begins his spiral descent to land back where he started, only to begin strutting again, preparing to repeat his performance.

Moving north in early spring, the woodcock takes his chances. Needing soft ground and worms willing to move to the surface where he can get them, perhaps he depends on the Almanac's predicted Full Worm Moon in late March to keep himself from perishing. Many times in the past, several woodcocks have collected beneath a great white pine after a late snow and managed to tide over there until the skies cleared.

Years ago, grandfather Abe hunted these little game birds down below the house in the pasture in the fall of the year, but now for two generations they have had safe haven here along the river, when elsewhere they've been severely reduced in number.

One day last spring, Dawn from next door brought me one of these birds which must have succumbed to the strong desire to move north ahead of his time. The light had gone out of his eyes, his limp body fit into the cup of my hand. His long bill, carefully designed for probing the earth, gave him a rather eccentric wall-eyed look. His plumage was the color of autumn leaves.

Such a long journey to undertake just to have it end here, betrayed by our own capricious New England March. Yet this month, looking out over the snowy woods and the frozen frog pond at dusk, we find ourselves impatiently awaiting the cocky little life-affirming call that will soon reach us, signaling a new beginning out there beyond the garden.

Something about May *(May)*

There's something about the month of May, when the cycle of nature and the cycle of family and community events intersect more often that other times of the year. May always seems memorable, a month of anniversary dates. Along the river, the flow subsides, and although it's still bright, clear and cold, it's not the mad rising river of March and April.

The first tree swallows burst upon the scene with their cousins the chimney swifts, clearly thrilled and excited to streak up and down the river, in the pure joy of flight with clouds of insects spurring them on.

The First of May brings the fiddlers, the Morris teams, and the maypole dancers to the common in Montague Center, to celebrate the ancient pagan rites and to welcome in the spring. The First of May is always a day of celebration in our family: it marks the birthday of our family patriarch, Abe, born in this house on the river before the turn of the century, when this homestead was a farm and the woodland was an open pasture. He became a fixture in the village of Millers Falls, and to this day, just to mention his name to some of the older residents here conjures up a vision of his wool cap and corncob pipe, both stuck at a jaunty angle, along with a dozen tales of his adventures.

May 3rd brings the swifts, as faithful to their date in the valley as the swallows of Capistrano. By the 5th come the hummingbirds, shivering a little in their jeweled feathers; then the wood thrush, beginning its fluting deep in the woods, a voice with no body for now. By May 10th, a number of anniversaries converge. For those of us who grew up in the 50s, May 10th was Audubon Day. And on that date, in Mrs. Keough's fifth grade, a thin and prim lady came to class and took us on a field trip (a rare thing in 1957!) to Arcadia. The lady was Pearl Care of Erving Center. She provided the spark. After visiting Arcadia, with its barn full of swallows, and the woods filled with rose-breasted grosbeaks and Baltimore orioles, my friends and I were hooked on birds for life!

Back home, imagine our surprise when we saw the same birds in our own trees! They couldn't have been there the day before! Of course, they were, but we didn't know how to see them. Mrs. Care showed us how. Interestingly, in other towns, a few special individuals were performing similar works of inspiration: Gerry Bozzo in Amherst, Bob Coyle in Athol, and Alan Richards in Deerfield inspired a lot of young people to make nature a fundamental part of their lives. The natural cycle and the human experience intersect, and May is the best time to see that conjunction.

So now, May is in full swing: the oriole is out and about *"sportin' in them baseball clothes of his"* (according to J.W. Riley); the woodpeckers are drumming and nesting; the pair of geese over in the marsh clamor by, low over the house in the morning and evening; the male cardinal carefully selects a seed to bring to his mate, who modestly waits for the favor; the redtails swoop and dive toying together with a branch that may eventually find its way to the nest; the titmice have discovered that a shedding Siberian is a great source of bedding and so have begun collecting tufts of Husky hair from the grass, giving them a strange bearded look as they gather up this innovative nesting material.

Within this life-affirming activity, a sad note passes through the family in mid-month: we lay to rest our father Arthur up in the Highland Cemetery, overlooking the Millers valley. The mournful sound of Taps echoes through the graveyard and rises on the spring wind. Another of the dwindling generation of millions who fought in the last war has passed on. May is full of these intertwined events, and we add a different kind of anniversary to our spring rituals.

May unfolds, as the other "firsts" succeed one another: the first chipmunks (very rare this year), the first lilacs (blooming a full three weeks earlier now than years ago, what with the climate change), the first cook-outs, as we tune up for Memorial Day. So now, close to the end of the month, we're poised on the edge of summer, with frost still at our heels, and lots more yet to unfold in the woods and river just beyond the yard. More feathered arrivals have yet to appear, and it'll be a while before the blackpoll warbler—the last scheduled arrival—will call from the pines to signal the end of the May migration and open a new phase, the raising of the next generation in June.

Knee Deep in June *(June)*

Tell you what I like the best
'Long about knee-deep in June,
'Bout the time strawberries melt
On the vine—some afternoon
Like to jes'git out and rest,
And not work at nothin'else.

June just happened this year, popped open like an umbrella, after a long damp cool May. Deep, green vegetation turned the woodlands rainforest-like, with bejeweled birds calling and swooping through the green canopy. Trees and grasses crowd to the river's edge, water now laughing full and bright over the warming stones.

Sometimes though, you just have to be patient with June. Tropical heat can send you indoors where it's dark to sit near the fan. A walk to the river is a mission of mercy for the dog who needs to stand in the pool of icy spring water to soak his fur—his panting making circles and waves spreading out from his submerged belly and back.

Just as quickly the heavy weather can break, and did, one afternoon, as the front moved through, twisting and turning branches, huge trees swaying and bending under turbulent skies. The temperature plummeted. In just a few hours we were contemplating whether or not to tap into next year's woodpile and fire up the stove again!

June is the month of new life. All the inhabitants of the river and woods are raising young. This year's generation of muskrat and beaver paddle around with the grown-ups, tadpoles keep an eye on the cannibalistic bullfrog. The redtail has a hard time holding onto his favorite sunning perch, with bluejays and redwings dive-bombing to get him to leave their territory. The permanent residents already are bringing their young to the feeder; the downy woodpecker gives his youngster a lesson in how to whack a dead branch just right. The resident dinosaur, a snapping turtle, retraces prehistoric steps to the exact spot in the floodplain where our garden now is, to lay eggs.

Flowers are everywhere: wild blue flag, autumn olive, multiflora rose, mountain laurel, domestic roses of the garden. The explosion of renewal and exuberance of the cycle is impossible to inventory. Pick anytime of the day to walk out and down to the river, and you'll not be disappointed. In the early morning the concert of birdsong is as stimulating as the first jolt of coffee of the day. In the afternoon, the warming sun coaxes off the jacket, the bees hum loudly in the flower bank, emerald green dragonflies glitter, the vireo endlessly recycles his song. In the dark, the wood thrushes echo their best vibrato and ornamentations. The heron rows home through the darkening air, bats tumble about and whip-poor-wills question the night. Just about the best time of the year for a body to be alive and thriving!

But when June comes--
Clear my throat
With wild honey! Drench my hair
In the dew! And hold my coat!
Whoop out loud! And throw my hat!
June wants me, and I'm to spare!

(Poem by James Whitcomb Riley 1849-1916)

7

The Pause in the Season *(September)*

The change in the season is subtle at first. You notice it in the way the shadow falls across the grass, the way the crickets chant louder, and the cicada buzzes like a saw through metal; the way the katydid ratchets up her song in the heat. The quality of the sunshine has been exquisite, pale through the faint fog in the morning, warm bright and uncomplicated through the day, golden in the evening—the kind of early September days you wish could last forever. The busy days of July and August are fading. In the woods and along the river, most creatures are moving about in a relaxed way, feeding, visiting, trying to send the young they've raised out on their own, trying to get them to shift for themselves. Dozens of waxwings hawk for insects along the banks, or chug down the dogwood berry crop; phoebes and other flycatcher cousins sally forth and return to the same perch, yellowthroats are masked no more, as their feathers change. There is little territorial imperative now, just leisurely eating, moving ,and loafing, very little song, just chips and stutters, a few echoes of springtime arias. It's time to bulk up rather than flirt, court, and fight.

The season was summed up in a snapping turtle just yesterday morning. She had pulled herself up onto a rock ledge just out of the river to sun. Her huge shell looked like a small boulder, probably close to forty pounds and the same number in age. This prehistoric relic was fully stretched out in the sun, long neck as thick as your forearm, with a blunt fist for a head, her formidable claws curving out from broad bear-like paws, her eyes opening and closing like a contented cat lolling in the gentle September sun.

The pause of the season, happening now, is very ephemeral, maybe lasting a few days or a week. Some years it doesn't happen at all: due to the weather, you just go crashing into the next season and before you know it, you're looking down the barrel of late autumn, without a chance to enjoy the bounty of the season. This year has been different, a pause worthy of a 19th century engraving of rural felicity where man and beast can loll about and loaf, before dealing with the reality of the coming lean seasons.

Birds sprawl akimbo in the warm grass, garter snakes drape in twos and threes in the tangle of the morning glories, wood stacked to catch the sun of the day dries all by itself.

Gathering on the River *(October)*

Come with me down to the edge of the river through still-green maple and birch. We'll push the battered canoe in, walk it through the shallows, shove, jump and glide into the river channel flowing barely two feet deep in early fall.

The river bends sharply and runs suddenly north at the cliff face. To our right is the edge of the Sokoki lands and to our left along the cliffs begin the Pocumtuck lands. This river, the *baquag* (the Algonquin name for the Millers River) separated the lands of these two ancient valley tribes.

The water's surface is sun-dappled in the late morning, stones golden just below as we glide over them. Kingfisher rattles at the bend, Osprey wings over and pivots in the air on sharp pinions, spotting a lazy sucker lying near the surface. The river's Old Man— Great Blue Heron—rises up reluctantly and flies upstream, giving us a wide, wary berth. The *baquag* enters the Long Blue River on the way to the Great Falls at *peskeompskut* .We drift through red shale canyons lined with pines. Just above the ancient plunge pools, the river widens and a low, insistent tattoo-beat of a great drum reaches our ears like distant thunder. Pull the canoe up the sandy silt shore and walk up through the pine trees and step into the Wissatinnewag Gathering of 2005. Quiet noise of a large number of people murmurs, then a high ancient song sung in a tongue we have never heard in this valley becomes clearer. The words we don't know, but the lament and exhortation in the voice all peoples can recognize. The language is Cheyenne, not the Sokoki or Pocumtuck of the River People, but a High Plains language. No matter, listeners are enthralled and drawn to the songs under the pavilion by the river. Here, the first harvest gathering of native peoples and their allies has attracted many friends, most gentle and respectful of this place. The song evokes the 10,000-year history of peoples on this river and at the Great Falls.

This is land where dinosaurs walked and left footprints just over there on the ridge, this is where peoples of all nations came to fish in the spring, this was a place of pilgrimage and peace, and this is where the 10,000 year truce was shattered in a desperate, vicious act of genocide, which remains a mere footnote on the pages of Manifest Destiny. The songs evoke all this if you listen, and the Friends of the Harvest, the dancers and story-tellers are helping turn a heavy page of history. Will this also help the restless spirits that inhabit this place to be a little more at peace?

Feast on the River *(October)*

A week after the Tribal Peoples' gathering we approach the same site, by car this time. We pull off the French King Highway and nose down the blacktop along Barton Cove. The day is gray and cool, mist lifts from the water. Just over the last rise, and spread over the flat sandy terrace on the Connecticut, the noise rises to greet us and grows louder. The summer isn't over 'til the Schuetzen Verein throws its fall clambake. Spread out before us is a sprawling, animated scene. A huge tent is filled with long tables the length of it and lined with benches where hundreds of people will chow down shortly. In all, close to seven hundred devotees to the steamed clam will mark the real end of summer. Under the pavilion, hundreds more socialize and await the arrival of the first round of clams.

The fire is already roaring and the stones to hold the heat to cook the clams and lobsters are shattering in the blaze with a popping sound as the split. The club members in charge of the bake are lining up in regiments waiting for the timbers to be pulled away and the stones mounded. Before long, the bucket brigade forms from the Ipswich Co. truck and the clams start the short journey to the bake pile. A bed of seaweed is laid down, and then the clams, lobsters and more seaweed are tossed on the baking rocks. The teams pull the sodden canvas tarps over the mound and then we wait.

Fragrant salty seaweed boils, shock white steam escapes here and there from the wet tarps. The last round of quahog appetizers are shucked , the last of the hot dogs wolfed down, and people head to the tables, excitement building. The feeding frenzy is about to begin. There's festival excitement in the air, the talk and laughter builds under the tent in anticipation of this traditional feast that brings hundreds of people together once a year to mark the end of summer. Hurrying servers start carrying bowls and utensils to all of us who are waiting patiently. Wise-cracks abound amidst the jovial and business-like bustle of the club members assigned to the tables. The chatter rises, the good-natured ribbing picks up since most of us know each other here, although there are strangers from as far away as Boston and Greenfield. Many, many of us are part of clans, extended families, former teammates, classmates, and neighbors. Many here form the backbone that keep our community running—firemen, policemen, nurses, teachers, post office workers, repairmen, selectmen, all of us neighbors, really. The food keeps coming: squads of men who are serving us move through the tables: rapidly dispensing bags of clams, baked potatoes, hot melted butter for dunking the clams, corn on the cob, and lobster. The good-natured banter rises as people gorge and to hell with the diet today and who cares about cholesterol!

When you're finally stuffed, there's no other word for it, you push back from the table and think about another beer. It's time for conversation, chatting with cousin Tom Gessing, or with old classmates, taking a break with Benny Rubin, or shooting the breeze with Steve Bassett, Brian San Soucie or neighbor Bob Miner. It's mostly small talk: the news, the weather, the passage of the years. You're in the after-glow of good company and a big meal. In a while, real world obligations will impose themselves, the inevitability of Monday morning will dawn upon us, but in the meantime, we're having our last blast of summer.

As for me, before long, I'm up and moving, thinking about school on Monday, and in the mood for a quiet walk after all the excitement. I take a quick look in the club kitchen where my father Art, a life-long member, always assigned himself KP duty, working on pots and pans. As he got older he preferred that task, saying that after 40 years of working at Dickie Williams' garage, his hands were finally clean. This is the first clambake he has missed, now that he rests beneath the grass in the Highland Cemetery.

The walk out on the peninsula to the Bear's Den plunge pool is good for the digestion, gets the sluggish blood going, the head clearing. The sound of the crowd and the clang of the horseshoe pitch fade. Late afternoon sun glows from the west. The summer is just about over. Long live summer!

November Tasks (November)

For a lot of us raised in New England, November is supposed to be a dark month. Probably all those paintings and renditions of Pilgrims in their grey Puritan cloth on the way to church services in Plymouth set the tone for this month. Sunny warm days, of course, are always welcome as are those of early morning frost on the pumpkins, the fading chrysanthemums, vapor rising in the cool air from the warmer river.

The floods of October that had sent such a roar up from the river for weeks have now faded. The rushing sound reaching our back porch has changed to that of the wind through leaves still clinging to branches before that last graceful flight to earth as the month ends.

November seems to signal a return to fundamental things: fuel for winter, clothing that will keep us warm, and in New England there's a turning inward, a tightening of the family circle, chastened by year-end ritual, and gatherings of friends. Things, like the colors outside the window, get simpler.

Down here on the Flat along the Millers, November brings its tasks, ritualized in practical considerations that bring real world and the spiritual world closer together, blurring their borders. Oftentimes you can pass from one to the other without much effort. Bringing in the wood is one of those tasks. Left stacked and drying for the last two years, it needs to be brought up to the house where it'll be easy to get to when the snow piles up.

Here wood gets stacked in a circle. The woodpiles look like the Irish monk beehive huts found on the Dingle Peninsula, or those that Lionel Girard spent years exploring and studying throughout our region. The circle is aesthetically and spiritually pleasing - it represents the cycle of life depicted frequently by ancient Celtic peoples and Native Americans alike. On the other hand, circular wood piles are practical too. Air circulation rises naturally through the top of the stack, convection playing its role in the drying. Taking apart the stack, and the familiar rumble of wood tossed on the porch, is part of the November cycle.

Inside the pile you find snake skins, shed some time back in August, warm wooly bears in a tight ball, stiff spiders still guarding their cocoons, chipmunk and mouse nests. The wood comes from many places: some oak was felled by beavers in the pasture years ago, and some oak was killed by the last gypsy moth plague years ago, brought down from Wendell by Bert Damon, who has long since passed on but whose memory is stirred by the sight of some of his old gnarled oak knots. Our old climbing tree from my parents' back yard is in there, cut down and split by Walter Carlisle and Monsieur Vincent, wood even from John Zywna's old woodlot in Gill. When you burn wood, you get it where you can, you make it last, and you never have enough.

The other practical task that links the past and the present, the natural and spiritual, is putting up storm windows. I'm probably one of the last oddballs in town to be still wrestling with wooden frame storm windows, but I wouldn't trade them for all the aluminum screen/storm combinations in the Northeast. Twice a year, I'm up on the ladder washing and hooking, or unhooking windows way up there, close to the parts of the house that you could take for granted, if you didn't have to get up there to check things out.

Perspectives are different, like a bird's eye view, and you get to look close at the outsides of your home. You see where the mud daubers put their nest, cracks in the shingles where nuthatches have whacked open sunflower seeds, interesting ladybug shells and other insect debris. The storm windows are house relics bought just before the war by Aunt Pete and Uncle Johnny when they lived here. Pete and Johnny are long gone, but handling their storms brings me back in touch with them.

The windows are efficient, to a minor degree. Even though they don't stop Jack Frost from creating his lace swirls and geometric arabesques in January, with their aged wood, now an amber-ginger color, they are beautiful just in themselves. And when they're finally up, fastened tight, when you're inside looking out, only muffled sounds now reach you, where just before you could hear the wind, bird calls, and the trees swaying.

Standing up here on the roof, I watch robins fly down the sky, draining the last colors from the landscape with them. They leave behind them the Pilgrim drab and signal the coming winter that has formed the character of those who dwell in these regions.

> *"It will be long ere the marshes resume,*
> *It will be long ere the earliest bird,*
> *So close the windows and not hear the wind*
> *But see all wind-tossed"*
> - Robert Frost

WEST ALONG THE RIVER - 2006

Counting Winter Birds *(December)*

The winter sun is a pale traveler through these parts in late December and early January. It barely clears the treetops, the valley rim, the steeples of our villages. The landscape is done in tones of brown and gray, and now some white, since the latest snow. But there are brilliant yellows, reds and blues just outside the window, adding zest, life and animation to the scenery. The evening grosbeaks are back. Years absent, they clamor at the window feeder, robust and cheery, visitors from the North bringing their hearty disdain of the cold and noisy celebration of the fine social gathering in the yard. The cardinal is a scarlet brush stroke in the snowy landscape, adding balance and an echo of the reds in the holly and barberry. The clan of blue jays, twelve strong, occupies the porch feeder side by side in the pale blue frost hanging in the air of a cold morning.

Chickadees seem to be everywhere this year, investigating every nook and cranny in the woods, leading titmice, nuthatches and woodpeckers in noisy bands through the trees.

One snowy morning along the river a fierce predator appeared, a mink, racing his way over stone and ice, in and out of the swift water, knifing through snow banks like a laser-guided assassin. He covered every inch of territory likely to produce a meal. His actions seemed frantic, driven apparently, by raging hunger, but I'm sure that most days are the same for him, high metabolism needing lots of fuel. He was into the current, without a glance at me, and in an instant, gone.

Further along, the gift of a bluebird in a winterberry tree. Soft summer blue, in the company of decorative and faded goldfinches, he lingered along a finger of the river before melting quietly away.

With so much activity in the natural world, in spite of the year's end and the cold, a certain part of our human population participates in the bird watchers' equivalent of the Polar Bear Club—the Christmas Count. On the designated day in late December, birders make an attempt to count every bird in the district during a 24-hour period. This tradition was established around the turn of the century by a group of conservation-minded Bostonians wishing to change the ignoble practice of hunting clubs that made a yearly attempt to *kill* every bird in the district in a 24-hour period. So the Christmas Hunt was slowly turned into the Christmas Count, and has since spread across the country.

For years, I covered my designated area with two retired ladies, Peg Wert of Gill and Eleanor Sheldon of Northfield. The three of us conducted our count in Millers Falls, Erving, the Millers River and Mineral Mountain, up the Connecticut to Northfield Farms. We did this by car, snowshoes, and sometimes by the seat of our pants, going down icy meadows not in the way intended. The women were merry company and we counted a lot of birds, although I would speculate that the highlight of each count (for our team) was the stop at the end of the day down here at the homestead on the Flat in Millers. We'd thaw out by the glowing cast iron Glenwood C cook stove, and Monique would prepare some hot spiced wine in the best French tradition. After a few sips, the ladies' cheeks would take on a reddish glow, and their eyes would sparkle behind the bifocals as the day's adventure began to seem more comical to them.

Eventually, we headed out to the car in the dusk, flushed with the warmth both inside and out. I drove my companions to their homes, our windows rolled down to listen for owls in the fading light.

We counted birds again this year, my son and I, covering the Peg and Eleanor Memorial Route along the Millers and the Connecticut. I'll admit to secretly invoking the ladies' heavenly intervention, to see if they couldn't use some of their influence up there to send some birds our way on this dreary day. I'd like to think they pulled a few strings with the One in charge and got it to rain bluebirds in Northfield (nine to add to our count!) and send a wave of horned larks lilting across a rolling field in the late afternoon.

By Count Day's end, Mark Fairbrother, our district compiler, reported we had managed to tally 55 species of birds, and close to 8000 individuals. He was happy to report that Pat Carlisle had found the totem bird of Turners Falls by locating two bald eagles on that crucial day! In all, species and individual totals were just about on the average for our last 30-years' worth of record keeping.

With our lists filled with names like Iceland gull, Lapland longspur, and snow bunting conjuring up images of Arctic landscapes, taiga and tundra, other softer summer-sounding names like bluebird, hermit thrush, and Carolina wren added a current of warmth to the close of Count Day. As did one last glass of spiced wine and warming icy feet on the oven door of the Glenwood C.

Spring Almanac *(May)*

The way I see it, the Romans had it wrong. They named January after the two-faced god Janus, blowing both winter and spring anytime he felt like it.

That may be fine for those who dwell along the Mediterranean, but here in New England, we know where we stand in January alright; it's March and April who are the hypocrites. Often it's warm enough to coax out the early mosquito and frog in the warm evening rain, but it also freezes us solid at 18 degrees many a night. It keeps the maple sap pumping but freezes it into sweet icicles that hang from the branch.

With the increasing light, birds are encouraged to tune their pipes, and the song sparrow earns his name, by piping sweetly from the bare lilac. Even the shrill jay tries his nearly musical yodel, but he's no match for the redwing and his *oak-a-lee*. The yard is still frozen and gray, but fills with music in spite of the icy wind and coming snow squall.

The frigid feast of St. Patrick comes and goes with the March wind but nature seems to take no heed of the Celt, and vice-versa. One week later, sun brings out the first green from the ground, spears push up through the early morning crusted earth. The birds that have depended on us all winter for daily sustenance reward us with song. Those same sparrows have tunes that are becoming more clear and liquid as they call from several places around the yard at once, their cousins the tree sparrow and the whitethroat add their notes to the March chorus. The blue jay clan, once 30-strong during January, has thinned to 10 or 12, but they still crowd the feeder, cheek by jowl as they work on the seeds they've chosen. Geese trumpet in the marsh, crows pump their call from the tallest pine, head and shoulders stretching. Red-wings huff their scarlet shoulder epaulets to impress the others. By mid April, sparse flowers appear. Tree swallows are moving north over the river, goldfinches changing from drab faded green to gold, with a jaunty black beret over one eye. The osprey is coming along the river, pivoting on one wing when a fish rises to the surface. In the dusk a pair of wood ducks pass in slow nuptial flight over the house and through the trees.

But oh my, when May arrives! Especially this year! The mild winter brought the spring birds up while the winter visitors were still sticking close to the feeders. Tree swallows and rose-breasted grosbeaks telling their winter cousins: no rush, you stragglers, but here's your hat and there's the door! Make way for spring!

As everyone can see, this May has been exceptional in the simultaneous flowering: forsythia and daffodils still linger while crabapple, cherry, peach, dogwood, lilac, quince, azalea, shadblow, violets, trout lilies and trillium have all come into bloom at once. We won't see this happen too often in a lifetime. The Baltimore oriole and blue jay are sporting about in "them baseball clothes" of theirs, the wood thrush is fluting in the glen near the frog pond, the catbird is meowing from the burning bush. Titmice have come right up on the back porch to gather tufts of freshly shed Siberian husky fur to line their nests; the phoebe is already incubating under an eave of the cabin in the woods.

This is also becoming the year of the Jack-in-the-Pulpit. This quiet woodland plant is popping up all over, with Jack the pistil quietly surveying his patch of earth from under the graceful curve of the hood of his pulpit.

So far however, the greatest gift this spring has been a pair of wood ducks who have decided to nest in a hollow tree between the yard and the pond, and visible from the living room. From time to time we see them, perched in a tree and peering at us duck-like as we move around the yard. We take care not to look at them directly, preferring to let them feel they are invisible, perched high up on an oak branch. The male is a stunning dandy with reds, blues and greens, stripes, spots and bars, and a demure crest at the back of his neck. This brilliant and gentle duck was driven to the edge of extinction during the last century, but 50 years of restricted hunting have brought it back. Any day now, ducklings will climb their way up out of the hollow of the tree and make the thirty foot jump down to the ground, to scramble off to the pond with their mother, and later to the wider Millers moving slowly just the other side of the trees. In the meantime we wait patiently for more migrants that should be moving in after this rainy spell, bringing bright song and exotic rainforest color to the glowing emerald woods.

A Walk on the Wild Side *(June)*

The confluence of two rivers was sacred ground to Native Americans. The sacred and the mystical still mix in those places today. The *baquag,* now known as the Millers River, enters the Connecticut on the very edge of Montague township. Erving land begins a little more than a stone's throw away on the other side. The land on both sides of the river has little changed since the Pocumtuck and Sokoki fished and hunted along these banks. The old footpath that led from Pocumtuck lands (in Deerfield) to the village of Squakheag (Northfield) was used for thousands of years by peoples native to this place. When Europeans first came here, the path led into hostile territory, at the edge of the known world. White men and Natives died on this path and at the mouth of the Millers. Captain Beers led his men to slaughter at the hands of the fierce Sokoki a few miles north in 1675.

After King Philip's War, the path became part of the stage route bringing Montague to Boston. It's now a quiet country road which saw its heyday during the stagecoach era, when Durkee's Tavern offered hospitality to wayfarers, days when riverboat traffic used the locks through the French King rapids, and at the turn of last century when log drives jammed the Connecticut.

One Sunday morning this wet month of June, a small band of hikers stepped off the edge of the freshly-mown lawn of the last house on the road and into the wilds, for a ramble up Mineral Mountain, as guests of the Waidlich family. Most of us hikers were members of the Millers River Watershed Council, out for an energizing jaunt along the Millers corridor, on private land that has been set aside and protected from development forever by the Waidlichs.

Henry Waidlich was born, grew up, and raised a family with his wife Betty on this farmland at the mouth of the Millers. Henry's father, John, came here in 1925 and gradually bought up 400 acres of field and woods. Years later in 1988, Henry and his brother Joe decided to set the land aside under a conservation restriction, in perpetuity.

Henry and Betty were founding members of the Watershed Council in the1970s, when the Millers was a foul, polluted stream that poured a putrid brownish green current sullenly into the bigger river. Now the Millers flows clean and noisily to its appointment with the Connecticut.

Which brings us full circle to our intrepid band of hikers slipping and sliding along the path this wet June day. Bird calls are sparse in these rainforest-like conditions. Ovenbirds insist on calling, "Teacher, teacher, TEACHER!" louder and louder; the Towhee tells us, "Drink your TEA;" a red-eyed vireo warbles endlessly; otherwise, the only other sounds are the various exclamations from our group over finding red efts everywhere, off to become newts! Here and there are rather pale, sun-deprived Jack-in-the-Pulpits, and plenty of coyote scat. Fortunately, or unfortunately, the mother bear and her cubs, the bobcats and the accidental cougar apparently give us a wide berth, although the last hiker in our file keeps a wary watch behind. We traipse around vernal ponds, slide past lovely rock ledges covered with primitive lichens, peer uninvited into a red-tailed hawk's nest.

All the while, the ancient river rushes past below us on the other side of the pine woods. From a high aerie above the river, we try our best to scour the streets of the village of Millers Falls far below. But try as we may, we have an impossible time orienting our vision and none of us recognize the landmarks from that height and angle, even though several of us have lived there for more than 30 years!

We loop homeward through a boulder-strewn ravine, cool under the last towering hemlocks. This gap feels like the site of some cataclysm that split the ridge above us, leaving high rocky ledges and slides on each side of the path. In fact, we are on an ancient fault line where the prehistoric super continent of Pangaea began pulling apart and drifting, more than 400 million years ago. The fault line we are standing on did not split deeply enough, but 100 miles east of here that part of Pangaea would eventually wind up as North Africa!

Actually, we're quite content to be here in Massachusetts, thank you, and like horses headed to the barn, we're moving quickly down the gentle wooded slope to the other mountain of sandwiches awaiting us in the Waidlich kitchen.

We've accomplished our objectives. We've gotten acquainted with a wild and protected part of Montague only a few miles from our citizens' comfortable living rooms, we've energized our inspiration to cobble together a green corridor along the Millers, and we've worked up an appetite for those hard-earned sandwiches!

Sundays in the August Garden *(August)*

I've got to be the laziest and most unreliable gardener in town. I can't be counted on to water things on time; I can barely remember to get out and pick salads or basil while the cool dew is still on them. And forget about the weeding! The flower and vegetable garden achieves a state of colorful anarchy and riot when I'm in charge.

What I am good at, though, is just sitting and appreciating the work of other gardeners. Especially on a Sunday. The Old Sabbath still brings people to church, but down here on the Flat, church bells don't seem to drift this far like they used to. On the other hand, the warming Sunday sun does make its way slowly into every nook, cranny, and garden corner. It's Sunday in the parlor, Sunday in the kitchen. Early morning piano concertos drift through the rooms and up the stairs where it's too hot to sleep. Sunday sun on the bookshelves, on the old dog's warming fur. It's coaxing me out the kitchen door at 7 a.m., out onto the back porch, to do some serious garden contemplating. And although the house is empty this month, with the others off visiting family in faraway places, I'm far from alone in this idle porch-sitting and contemplation.

The first visitor is a female hummingbird, young and demure, probably raised in a tiny nest in the hemlocks in front of the house. She hovers over my page, impertinently looking me in the eye, then moves off among her flowers, drawing in her breakfast. That cheeky catbird meows from the bamboo tutor for the honeysuckle. This one has me trained to supply her with her favorite treat, pieces of peanut. The song sparrow tribe who take care of this garden winter and summer move purposefully through the green depths of the flower stalks. The garter snake eases himself up onto the deck and slips under a random board thinking he's concealed while warming in the early sun, but one big loop of him sticks out, although head and tail are invisible.

The black hornets that nest under the porch slip back and forth between the weathered boards, back from harvesting caterpillars from the flowers and chain-sawing them into bite-sized green pieces to bring into the nest.

With all this activity, comings and goings, it's difficult to keep mind on matters! Forget about reading or writing or even sitting and thinking. "Sometimes I just sits and thinks, sometimes I just sits," as the folk saying goes. Which is not a bad idea of a Sunday. We all need a truce once a week. The Middle East is afire, there are mad bombers in England, murder and mayhem in New Orleans. Right now, for a few hours at least, that sweet hummingbird is more important, so much depends on the catbird who's waiting for her treat, and the dog wants a walk.

Along the river, the doe and her fawn have left perfect tracks in the damp sand, and the monarch dries his wings on a warm stone— wild creatures providing wisdom and respite…and we can get back to saving the world and fighting the good fight on Monday. Today is a day for cultivating peace of mind, for letting the Sunday into our thoughts.

That's exactly what the day and the garden are for.

The Marie Rose *(September)*

The season has come to its yearly pause once again. In the garden, woods and along the river, all seems to be at rest. Birds are no longer pressed to court, sing and fight or raise young. This year's generation of young creatures is learning the ropes, starting to build fat reserves before they plunge headlong into winter.

A special case in point is the young hawk, an accipiter, probably a juvenile Cooper's hawk, who has regularly visited the yard and fields. He seems as hapless and as determined as Henry the Chicken Hawk in the old Sunday comics. This youngster comes around regularly, but the chickadees and the blue jays have always tipped off everyone in the neighborhood within earshot.

Poor Henry has hung around in plain sight—on top of the fence post, the point of the goose house, in the apple tree over the birdbath. He just can't get himself a break. At one point a squirrel sat a few feet away from him shaking his tail in annoyance, while this hawk just sat there, wondering where breakfast went, his head feathers in a permanent cowlick, with a baffled look to him and a big question mark over his head.

I saw him again up in the field on Mineral Mountain, eyeing a flock of nine crows that were walking idly around, hands folded behind their backs in crow fashion, carefree in the new-mown hay despite the determined young hawk glaring at them. They flew up into the trees at the far end of the field when I stepped out into the clearing, and so did our Henry! He flew into the flock to perch and look around, and the crows couldn't have cared less! Maybe he was lonely, maybe he was hungry, but I could tell from his strained look that he felt he just could get no respect! Even the crows didn't want to bother themselves with mobbing him or trying to make his life more miserable.

Down closer to the garden, our female hummingbird continues her friendly visits, perching on her arched stick among the flowers, although we are getting nervous. With cold not far away, we hope she's thinking about moving south ahead of the frost. She's got thousands of miles to go soon, and thousands back before she visits our flowers again next year.

Which brings us to the subject of roses. Our last flowering rose is called the "Marie Rose." None of us in this house can pronounce the name without thinking of the only person we ever knew whose name was Marie Rose.

She lived in a small hamlet of ten houses up the lane from Monique's family's farm in Central Brittany. It was many a time in the summer that we walked up the *chemin creux* to the cafe Marie Rose kept. A *chemin creux* is literally a hollow lane - an ancient farm wagon-sized passage. On each side of the lane are five-foot earthen hedgerows topped with centuries-old stunted oak and chestnut trees that form a canopy over the grass-covered wagon-path. The lane is really a sort of tunnel, dark green and cool in the day, either mystical or nightmarish at night, depending on your frame of mind at the time. And whether your imagination transforms hedgehogs and glow worms into *korrigans* (the Breton version of nasty leprechauns) or the *Ankou* (the Breton Grim Reaper)....we always chose to take the lane in broad daylight, so we were reasonably safe.

Oftentimes, Monique's grandmother accompanied us up to the Marie Rose cafe, and it was always pleasant to listen to the two women chatting softly in the language of their region. They were first cousins, and both well into their 90s. Marie Rose was the elder, a few years shy of 100. The cafe was really a large kitchen at road level, so when you were seated inside you could watch the occasional dog, cat, tractor or neighbor passing by the open door out there in the sunshine. In spite of being close to 100, Marie Rose made it a point of honor to serve her customers herself at a little round table. She always wore a long black dress and a grey apron with small flowers on it, sparse hair up in a chignon, and wooden shoes (*sabots*) on her feet.

Sometimes she would just wear the felt liners, which were quieter, but not as comfortable as *sabots* in wet weather.

When we were seated at the table, she stood barely at eye level with us. Age had bent her over, but she was still standing, and proudly capable of serving us our coffee. (Although she usually gave me permission to go to the counter to serve myself a bowl of cider, while she socialized.) The two women chatted, as ancient cousins would, about family, about incidents long ago, both merry, with twinkling eyes. The world's events had swept over them and their village in their long lifetime: they had survived two World Wars, the Nazi occupation, the IIIrd, IVth and Vth French Republics! But the weight of history and personal chagrin never intruded during those afternoons in the neat little cafe.

Of course, finally one summer when we came back to the farm, Marie Rose was gone. But one evening on a walk along the small canal that runs along the farm, I heard the clipping of shears and there were hedge tops falling down on the path from the overgrown shrubs. Presently a small weathered Breton face appeared from the greenery. I recognized him, and he, me. We exchanged small talk about the weather, and the season, as you must do if you are polite, before getting to what really is on your mind. Finally, I said something about Marie Rose, his aunt. And in a poetry only country folk can use as natural everyday speech, he said simply, "*Un soir, elle s'est éteinte, comme une fleur.*"

"She faded out, like a flower, one night."

I know that, from what we have seen of harsh seasons and death, many of us would choose just such an ending if we could.

> *"Tis the last rose of summer,*
> *Left blooming alone,*
> *All her lovely companions*
> *Are faded and gone;*
> *No flower of her kindred,*
> *No rosebud is nigh,*
> *To reflect back her blushes,*
> *Or give sigh for sigh ... "*
> *Thomas Moore (1779-1852)*

So our last Marie Rose of summer is still on the stem, but before we let that 18th century poet draw us into an autumnal melancholy, wait! There are a few buds optimistically forming just now. And so who knows, before the frost comes, they just might make it!

Seven Thousand Years on the River *(November)*

"We have been here," Tonupasqua would say. And then she would drop her words and roll her right hand over and over in a circular pattern, extending her arm as she did so. The gesture was time, that time goes backward on occasion, forward on others... it simply is."
          -John Mitchell Hanson
            Ceremonial Time

Robins fill the late November woods, bringing the season to a close. The first here in March, they're the last to leave, gorging themselves on this year's unusually abundant winterberry crop that lends its holly-red brilliance to the somber landscape. November is always the season of reflection. The riot of color is gone; things get simpler outdoors; the mind dwells on remembering: All Saints' Day, the Day of the Dead, Veterans Day, Thanksgiving.

Before beginning preparations for the festive season of December, if you live here, close to the river in any of our villages situated on ancient sites near water, you can see back into time past, if you like, and if you know how.

For example, down here on the Flat, with the leaves all down, I can see far into the woods and conjure up my great--grandfather's fields along the Millers, before the great floods of the 30s, when the land was clear. But that only goes back one hundred and thirty years. If you look further back, you see the terraces formed by the prehistoric river in this part of the original Erving Grant. One side of the river has a corresponding level on the other side where our river has cut down through the earth. Our house, and our neighborhood, sits on the edge of an ancient 5 to 10,000-year-old terrace plainly visible in the bare November woods.

Local historians tell us this part of our region was still empty of Europeans in 1800, not yet settled by whites, unlike other parts of the valley, although meadow lands along the Millers had been cleared by native peoples, probably the Sokoki and their ancestors, thousands of years before.

Regardless, it came to be that houses were built on this terraced flood plain known as the Flat on Ervingside. This house went up in the 1870s, setting in motion, for the purposes of this story, a curious chain of coincidences involving a dog, a lilac bush, and a grave.

Shortly after his house was built, great-grandfather Judah planted lilacs at the edge of the bank facing the river, which was also the edge of the backyard and garden. One day, a hundred years later, when it was our turn in the family history to live in this house, an unexpected key turned up that opened the door on a vision of this land more than 7000 years ago. It happened that a beloved first dog died unexpectedly, and was sadly laid to rest under the lilacs Judah had planted. Our dog had loved to find cool, green and shady escape there from the heat of the day, and so it was natural to bury him in his favorite spot. Digging down through the roots of the lilac, we came upon a curious find: a spear-like projectile point, and a gnarled ball of glass with sand and debris imbedded within. After finishing the burial ceremony, I showed our find to an archeologist friend who promptly identified the point as a spearhead, probably dating from 4 - 5000 BC! Our archaeologist friend speculated the glass ball was lost at the same time as the point and was probably the hunter's personal talisman - a ball of glass formed by lightning striking a tree and sand thereby creating this misshapen ball.

And now, holding this point, chiseled and shaped by a hand thousands of years ago, something mysterious happens: I'm hurtled back in time at dizzying speed, houses and gardens fall way, the veneer of a mere 300 years of European presence falls away, and I'm standing where he stood, trying to see what he saw. What was he looking for the day he dropped his spear and good luck talisman? Elk, great Grizzly Bear, mastodon, deer? The river could have been raging or calm as it is today this November. Perhaps he saw canoes slipping quickly down this current coming from the sacred mountain of Wachussett on the way to the Great Falls to fish. What language did they use to call out to each other on the river? I wonder if his people's children jumped and swam at the cliffs on the bend of the river like we do. Perhaps he was a sachem or a poet, a hunter or the hunted or all of those. Did he die here on the bank of the river 7000 years ago? That's unknowable, but through lucid wondering, somehow you can see.

With a bit of imagination you can try to see backwards, to get a glimpse of what went before, to see how we fit into this river culture. When you look at our landscape here, and let the building and roads with their streetlights drop away before your eyes, when you see the undisturbed rock outcrops, the flood plains and the dunes, you become attuned to the experience of this valley.

The river runs around and through our community. The river is the reason why many of us are here; it's what drew the human race here more than 12,000 years ago. We still look up to see the wild birds flying high over our main streets as they have since the glaciers faded back north. We still get a primitive feeling from the call of the wild geese flying over parking lot and the library to get from one part of the river to the other. Yet, in our villages we eat, work, and sleep and it is rare that we ever think of those who have walked here before in ancient times.

The Jurassic and Pleistocene lurk just a mile from the center of town, and it wouldn't take much for nature to reassert itself, to push up through the asphalt and concrete once our civilization has run its course. If you can imagine that, then the passage of time has a different feel to it, you see where you fit into the scheme of things, what your own place is in the landscape. Then again, that may just be the mood brought on by peering into the past at the end of the month of November.

Christmas in the Old House. *(December)*

Going home for Christmas is the phrase on everyone's lips at this time of year, even though it's oftentimes only in thought, and even though describing home is not so easy anymore. If you really can go there, you are lucky indeed. With the havoc, imperatives and opportunities of modern life sending family farther and farther away from its roots, it does seem that this season, which celebrates the origins of the religion of peace and love, inspires memories of childhood when invariably times seemed gentler and simpler. The memories of Christmases past call back together the scattered members of the family, both living and dead, however briefly. The yearning to go back to simpler times is strong in all of us at Christmas, when the year pauses,

The nights are wholesome, no planets strike,
No fairy takes, no witch hath the power to charm,
So hallowed and gracious is the time.

Our heart strings are tugged by old airs and Christmas carols, scenes of snowscapes, holly and evergreen trees. Getting home for Christmas is on everyone's mind, whether in war or peace time, and if only in your dreams.

Here in the old family house on the Flat, the knock and clamor at the door on the last Sunday afternoon before Christmas renews the generations-old tradition of pulling the extended family back to the homestead, if only for a few hours. First to arrive is cousin Tom and two grandchildren, Ryan and Sarah, visiting from California. Tom has special status in Millers Falls: not only was he the long-serving postmaster for the town and one of the unofficial mayors of the village, he's also the last to have actually been born in this house, and so is always given particular deference when he visits. Maybe some day we'll put up a plaque. Right after him and in short order, the house fills up with uncles, aunts, cousins, sisters, brothers, in-laws, daughters and sons, stepchildren and grandparents all under one roof again for a short while. The dog lifts his wizened old head briefly, figuring that's the end of his plans for a quiet Sunday snooze. With the Glenwood C woodstove fired up and heaped with potluck dishes, the kitchen table piled up with desserts, wines and whiskeys, the excited talk and Christmas greetings fill the house to the rafters, rising up to the spirit world high in the attic. Tom's wife Joan sails in with arms laden with poinsettias and a smile warm enough to heat the farthest corners of any room.

I'm sure you know how the rest goes, for the scene is repeated in households all over in our villages. Stories of generations past, exploits of ancestors who spent their lives in this house are re-lived. Adventures, jokes and mishaps are repeated and shared round the rooms of the house as the noise level rises. The generations mix, the children romp with new toys and cousins they rarely see, the adults get noisily caught up in the past few months news. Grand octogenarian Uncle Rusty, a guest of honor among honored guests has come back on his annual Christmas visit to his parents' home here on the Flat, his wife Dot and his sister Shirley (my mother!) visit for hours sitting just out of the maelstrom swirling around the room. A particular favorite moment happens when young Ryan and Sarah remark after having met Rusty that they hadn't even known they *had* a great-uncle! At that point, I bring the children face-to-face with the family portrait of Judah and Elizabeth Smith looking sternly and confidently out at them from the 1880s.

So here was a new generation face-to-face with their ancestors, their great-great grandparents who had actually lived in these rooms! They were introduced to their forebears, they now have a connection to this place, and that is the main point of the family gathering, to renew a sense of place. Their eyes seem to shine with the new knowledge.

Before long though, the children all head out to the woods along the river like all the children down the one hundred and thirty years of our family before them, happy to escape the confines of the house and the adults, off to skim stones on the quiet river, their joyful shouts and laughter echoing and ringing through the river valley. Then, like at all family parties, the tide of hilarity slowly subsides with the coming of dusk. We gather in smaller groups near the woodstove and fireplace to bask in the feel that only the warmth of family can provide in this season. Gradually some groups drift out the door, into the gathering cold, among cheery shouts of "Merry Christmas!" The house grows quiet again, the old dog that has slept through the clamor and riot opens his eyes and stretches (Are they gone? He's wondering.) Host and hostess collapse into the nearest chairs with a warm whiskey before tackling the dishes. Christmas tunes come back on the stereo to encourage with the clean-up. The Spirits that dwell in the house give satisfied sighs, and I swear that the dignified old Gent in the holly-framed portrait has a brief Christmas twinkle in his eye.

King in the Woods *(December)*

The sun rises bright over the rim of the hills on the last day of the old year. Time to count birds in the valley, something a group of us have been doing together for the last 33 years.

Using Montague as its center, the group fans out to cover a range of habitats in a 20-mile circle. Some of the census takers have already been up since dawn, thumping on trees and calling owls that've been out all night hunting. Some of us, on the other hand, get up leisurely, with that cold sun, and begin counting over a steaming cup of black coffee while sitting on the frosty back porch.

It's handy having juncos and sparrows pecking at seeds on the ground nearby, moving from one foot to the other on the frozen ground. Easier to count. A cluster of cedar waxwings wheeze and undulate by, 24, no, make that 25 of them. The counting has started so we need to get some exactness into our estimates. Some counters like to head off early in the car, scoping out favorite spots near open field or water. I take a low profile approach. I finish a second cup of coffee. I'm already counting up to 15 blue jays and a couple of woodpeckers, without breaking a sweat!

Time to head down through the woods to the Millers, now steaming in the first rays of the sun. Black ducks slip through the air just the other side of the birches and alder. One, two, three, just like that. This counting is easy! Feeling pretty smug about my rising tally just now.

Down on the bend, the summer kingfisher rattles up the river as he does in all seasons, but luckily, this is Count Day, and he showed up! Walking and pausing along the open water rushing by, a dusting of snow on the shore, there comes a faint wisp of a call from the warming hemlocks on the sunny side of Mineral Mountain. I just hold still and wait. The wisp becomes movement and a golden-crowned kinglet materializes and pirouettes on a bough hanging over the water twenty feet away.

This is a small mite of a bird, barely the weight of two pennies in his pale greenish suit and brilliant yellow-striped crown. Indeed, in some cultures he is called the Firecrest, or the little king - *le roitelet* - because of his gold crown which runs from the base of his beak to the back of his neck. He got his name, according to various Celtic and Woodland Indian legends, when there was a dispute in the bird world in the early days of creation.

It was the bragging of Eagle and Raven that started it all. Each claimed to be the strongest and each claimed to be the one who could fly the highest. To prove this, Eagle and Raven began flying higher and higher in dizzying circles. What neither of them noticed, however, was a small mite of a washed-olive colored bird who hopped on Eagle's back at the last minute. As they drew nearer and nearer to the sun, Raven dropped out because he was getting too hot, but Eagle kept on going long enough to beat him. But the little greenish mite of a bird riding on Eagle's shoulders actually got higher and closer to the sun than the one who was carrying him. He got so close to the sun that he scorched his head, which left a golden stripe blazed upon him! That's why this smallest of birds became kinglet by when we meet him in the woods.

So, at this rate, my counting day starts off in a fine way, what with meeting a king and all! A few minutes later, the red-tailed hawk casts a wild eye on my side of the river from the top of a tall pine on the mountain. He and his mate control this part of the valley during the day. He's just warming his back in the early sun, getting ready to take over the day shift from the fierce tiger of the night, the great horned owl, who's off for a quiet snooze now until dusk.

Winter has been easy for the predators, hawks, owls and foxes that don't have to deal with mouse and vole tunnels under the snow. With this brown winter, their food supply is plentiful and scurrying about in the open, ready for the picking.

I add a few more familiar birds to the list, but things are slowing down. Or maybe the coffee is wearing off. Neighbors across the Flat, cousin Annabelle and Ernie Lucas, let me know who's been at their feeders, and we compare notes on the hawks raiding the yards this year. Ah well, time to give in and get into the car to take the Peg Wert and Eleanor Sheldon Memorial Bird Count Route, through the fields, along the river and eventually up to Northfield Farms.

Peg from Gill, and Eleanor from Northfield, were my regular count companions for years, and the ladies did their best under much harsher conditions than those of today. As I've mentioned in earlier writings, I'm convinced that the best part for them was the hot spiced wine waiting for us at the end of the day, sitting around the Glenwood C cook stove, chuckling about the adventures and misadventures of our day, trying to make sense of the random lists we'd kept of the things we'd seen. They are both with us in spirit today, but this time even their intervention from up there in the firmament doesn't send anything special our way. The lack of snow, the monotony of farms turning from cornfields and dairy cows to sterile, flat turf farms stretching as far as you can see, produce nary a horned lark, snow bunting nor sparrow on that bleak plain.

Later in the evening, Mark Fairbrother confirms that we're headed for a banner year however, with 10,579 individual birds (give or take an English sparrow or two). With 64 species, that's quite respectable! We're up to 23 red-bellied woodpeckers this year, when back in the 70s there was only one in the state, and that was down here on the Flat! Nearly created a birder's riot that year, with cars coming in from Boston, with hordes of listers staked out at our feeders. But that's a story for another time.

This year, Pat Carlisle, from atop her aerie over the Narrows spied an unexpected great blue heron on the shore and made sure the eagles were accounted for. The ravens checked in too, and were added to the tally. But in spite of the mighty eagle and powerful raven, the one who was high up at the top of my list, again besting both eagle and raven, was the plucky little king I met in the cheery woods, bright and early in the morning.

WEST ALONG THE RIVER - 2007

Sundays on the Ice *(February)*

If you ever felt you could walk on water, now's the season for it. Once the liquid-solid boundary is passed at 32 degrees, instantly ice crystals form. If that temperature is held below 32 degrees long enough, there you go! You've got water to walk on.

Granted, we all know all too well about ice around here, but how many of us venture out onto the new landscape formed by that frozen water? Luckily enough for those solitary walkers who prefer to meet as few people as possible while out on a ramble, adverse conditions and severe weather is the best time to be out, and the tundra-like conditions on the frozen cove suit us just fine.

Sunday has brought me to the Cove, for the above reasons. Out on the ice there are a few hardy souls. You don't need to be Polish, Russian or French Canadian to be fishing through the ice in this weather, but it helps. Something in the DNA triggers the ice-fishing urge: a mixture of patience, perseverance and a little madness keeps guys out on the windswept ice on a Sunday like this, waiting for hours for a quarter-pound perch, or bass, or maybe a walleye, to go for your shiner!

Standing out here before heading off on my walk into the woods, something brings to mind a winter long ago in the past, maybe 1959, when it seemed like all of Turners Falls was out here on the ice. That year the river froze over from the dam to the French King Bridge and beyond. So one Sunday, down to the river we drove, my father, my sister, and I. The DeSoto was left near the abutment across from Doc Cassidy's, where the Boat Club buildings were, and down the wooden ramp we went, out onto the river, and across to the Cove.

We hadn't gone far before we saw a dapper gentleman gliding effortlessly by, skating backwards, waving and smiling. My father pointed out Harvey Welcome, locally famous for his flawless skating and performing dog. Easily he sailed by on the bare windswept ice, reappearing with his wife, the couple now waltzing as gracefully across the surface as anyone on the floor of a ballroom. We made our way to the Cove, I gliding and flopping as best I could on ancient hockey skates, while my sister tripped pertly across in her new high-lace figure skates. Once across, we skated from ice fisherman to ice fisherman, my father seeming to know everyone, although I can't be sure now, since he talked to anyone and everyone so easily, whether he knew them or not! But it didn't really matter; everybody was eager to talk about the ice, their luck, and the weather.

We explored the Bear's Den on skates this time, instead of in the rowboat we used to keep tied up below the house at the Narrows. There was a blazing fire in the middle of the Cove on a little birch-tree island, where we stopped to warm up and chat some more, while other skaters criss-crossed the Cove or played hockey.

The ice that day was three feet thick, but we knew better than to try to continue up the river through the Narrows. Just the thought of the treacherous currents there and the 140-foot deep dark water was enough to make you want to speed back to the shore and walk home! My father claimed to have skated up the river from Turners to his father's camp just below the French King Bridge one time before the war. We sort of believed him, but didn't care to try it out just that Sunday!

Back here in '07, a visit to the ice shanties is just my starting point. My afternoon goal is a walk along the peninsula that sticks out into the river. There's something about the silence and solitude of the towering pines out there, where the pale sun and winter light filters down through the branches. Cathedral-like awe and silence is broken by the occasional faint voice of the persevering kinglet or the lonesome call of a crow.

This walk takes you out along a bedrock ridge that forms the spine of the peninsula. The Cove side of the ridge has two cuts with steep circular sides, one of which we used to call the Bear's Den, and the other the Quarry. Thirteen thousand years ago, this was the site of twin waterfalls, the ridge having formed a barrier over which the Connecticut had to flow, creating these circular plunge holes. Later on, at some point in time, the river broke through at the Narrows, a quarter mile further out, and the plunge pools became isolated from the river.

These pools came into public prominence when in the 1840s Professor Edward Hitchcock of Amherst College began collecting dinosaur tracks from the site, eventually amassing over 10,000 prints that can now be found at the Pratt Museum and in other museums around the world. Out beyond the plunge pools and the eagles' nest and the fishing shanties is the submerged site of the native peoples' encampments. They arrived on this site at about the same time the twin falls had fallen silent, when Lake Hitchcock waters were already rushing through the gap in the Narrows. Dozens of tribes came to the Falls to fish and camp for the next 12,000 years, the truce grounds only being violated by the massacre perpetrated by Captain Turner's forces in 1676.

Regardless, the sweep of history here might as well be the sigh of the wind through the pines. You can't help thinking that if there are sacred places in our Hidden Landscape, then something must be going on out here. There's a certain light, a sound in the trees, the lay of this prehistoric land, the lonely booming of the frozen river that gives the solitary hiker the sharp sense of being in the presence of a benign ancient force.

Be that as it may, the path and the cold keep you moving through the pine grove, out to the point. From there, you can see the rooftops on Carlisle Avenue, the street just across the river. The path leads up around the point, overlooking the eagles on their island, while headlights move along Route 2, and the last fisherman trudges back across the ice, going home. Once back down to my starting point, I take one last trek out to the center of the ice field to watch the sun go down in an orange haze behind the silhouetted steeples of St. Mary's, St. Anne's, and Our Lady of Czestochowa.

A Morning Along the Sawmill *(May)*

People who live along a river are lucky. And luckier still, I suppose, are those who have the sense to appreciate it! Lucky is the river, too, if there are people nearby willing to organize and fight to protect it. Rivers are powerful, capable of destroying any obstacle in their path to the sea. Rivers are fragile, too; they can be abused, poisoned or killed, if their neighbors aren't vigilant.

Saturday, May 26th, the sun peeked up over the rim of our valley, spreading green light, reflected from two-week old late May foliage, through yards, woods, rushing water. Down went the morning cup of black coffee, up the street we went, through Millers Falls and off to our sister village of Montague Center, where river people were gathering to walk the length and width of the fields and floodplain that make up the Sawmill River Access Area.

Down at the end of North Street lie 36 acres of grasslands, historic flood plain forest, and wet meadows, saved in the late '90s by a concerted community action led by the Friends of the Sawmill and the Montague Grange, a far-sighted landowner (the Garbiel family) and a little help from the state Division of Fisheries and Wildlife. This morning, brilliant New England warblers of grassy meadows and river margins called, as the group started out; chestnut-sided, blue-winged, and yellow warblers were staking out nesting territories. Would the bobolinks, indigo buntings, maybe grasshopper sparrows be there too?

The walk was led by Colleen Sculley and Chris Polatin of the Montague Grange. Mark Girard, a landowner with the Sawmill River for a front yard, lent quiet commentary about every nook and cranny, hillock and boggy depression on the parcel. He, as others, had gained this firsthand knowledge through years or mowing, cutting, walking and living along this winding river.

The Montague Grange recently received a $10,600 grant from the US Department of Agriculture Natural Resources Conservation Service—represented this morning by Diane Petit—to restore and preserve the grasslands habitat along the Sawmill. These meadows, hayed and farmed for generations by the Garbiels of Montague Center, had been acquired as part of the Montague Wildlife Management Area, but since pasturing and mowing have ceased, many non-native invasive species have gained a foothold and are threatening the habitat. The names of the culprits are familiar:

Japanese knotweed, Japanese barberry, as well as some other species that are gentler-sounding and sweeter-smelling but just as relentless—for example the honeysuckle and multiflora rose. These escapees from gardens, aided by unwitting conservation-minded groups who, years ago, placed them everywhere in the belief that these species provided food, cover, and erosion control, are now out-competing native species. Along with burning bush and autumn olive these vigorous non-natives are taking over the Montague meadows. The grant will finance control and eradication efforts, and add further research data in the fight to minimize the negative impacts of the invaders.

A stone's throw from the common, the grass flows and shimmers as do the limpid waters of the Sawmill meandering through town on its way to the Book Mill and the Connecticut. Tree swallows surf the waving grasses, warblers call from the willow banks and sycamores, vesper and song sparrows haunt the secret corners and margins of this place. And if you're lucky enough to live in the village, all you have to do is step out your back door and into this timeless meadow.

At day's end, back home on the Millers, the shadows lengthen in the rainforest-green woods. Our river still swirls noisily from last week's rain, but the fluting of the wood thrush echoes and floats over the current's voice. Off on the hill, the young owl is getting hungry and impatient, hoping his parents will wake up to come and feed him. A doe steps gingerly out along the shore to nibble at sweet new grass. Greenwood depths here, while out along the Sawmill, golden light covers the old river pastures. And thanks to the Montague Grange river-keepers, bobolinks and indigo buntings crisscross the fields, joyous and secure in their ancestral home.

Back on the River *(September)*

It's Sunday afternoon. The old wooden rowboat, chained to an alder bush in a nook above the Narrows has been waiting alone all week. First in, the dog. Impossible to make her wait, she loves a boat ride. She takes up her spot in the little bow seat; we have to squeeze past her. She leans a little to let us past, but not much, scrunching down to hold her claim. Next is sister, then my father, who will do the rowing for the time being. The chain with its familiar rattle drops into the bottom of the boat. The oars set in the oarlocks. With one shove from me, the boat glides effortlessly from the shore, free of the bushes, pivots gracefully away downstream, and we're on the river again. It's 1957; it's Sunday. With every pull my father gives on the oars, the boat leaps ahead briefly. The rings left on the water by the dripping oars mark our progress through the Narrows, until they fade ...

And now 50 years later, I'm in my own boat, alone. The new kayak's sleek hull glides on the glassy surface of the Connecticut like a glistening otter. Back on the river, after a long absence and years spent on the shore, the same unique river smell of sand, mud and water stir distant primal memories imprinted decades, or even generations ago. The old river still flows through these parts on the way to the sea, as it has for 20,000 years. The water this late autumn day is still dark and warm, although the air is cool enough to give rise to small wreaths of fog in the early morning air. I'm skimming over the sunken, hidden canyon of the Narrows, where 90 years ago log drives choked the river. Now it's still and empty, no voices or shouts, just the fading patter of ducks on the water as they lift up in front of the boat.

We entered the secret lagoon of the Bear's Den that Sunday in '57, when Barton Cove looked different from what it does today. The woods in those days closed around the pool of the Den, leaving just a small passage large enough for the rowboat to slip through without grazing the soft mud inches below. *The boat comes to rest near the shallow cave on the shore, and out jumps my father to have a look. Sister and I push the boat back out onto the surface of the enclosed pond to poke around and practice rowing. Before long, my father's stretched out on the bank to catch a quiet Sunday snooze, while we turn in figure eights in the boat like the whirligig beetles speeding away from us on the surface.*

Looking back to those days I can't help but wonder what was going through his mind on those Sundays spent in the hidden lagoon. Just little more than ten years returned from the War. And to find himself back in familiar surroundings on the river on a Sunday afternoon with his two kids and a snug warm house up on the Hill just beyond, overlooking the river, my mother expecting us all back shortly. Having survived hundreds of bombing runs in the Pacific, dozens of kamikaze attacks on his carrier, the *Ticonderoga,* explosions, violence and death, three years on the sea and thousands of feet up in the air in one of those flying rattletraps, coming in to the carrier on a wing and a prayer. All that mayhem and fury, and just now catching forty winks on the quiet river bank, his hat over his eyes, legs straight out and hands folded, asleep and far from the War, and for that matter, far from the job he came back to at William's Garage.

Nowadays, there are still some of us who go down to the river in this river town, or who still look up when the ancient calling of passing geese drifts down from the sky. When you pause and think of it, this river has run through our lives all this time. Some of us know this; others barely see it. Our town is almost surrounded by it, water on three sides.

We wouldn't be here if not for the river. This site drew the Native peoples here more than 12,000 years ago, long before the first white settlers appeared. Then, even after, the Great Falls drew generations upon generations of immigrants to farm and work in water-powered factories. For some of us now, this river runs through our veins. It's a constant, a place to come back to, a thread running through our lives.

There's still a river subculture around here, but it seems to be fading. Years ago, on any given morning, you'd see two or three cars parked at the foot of Ferry Road. Old guys, sitting and smoking and looking at the water. Yet even now, if the mood strikes you right, you could go down to the shore just on the edge of town, and take a closer look at this long river that comes down through the North Woods, a ribbon through New England, to wrap itself around our town. It brings a whiff of tall trees, deep snows, history, and the tundra beyond its source. Some of us know this; some of us are not conscious of its presence. Some who do come down to the water love to race over the surface, thrilled with noise and speed, and the need to get somewhere fast. Some fight over it and its banks, use it, appropriate it for selfish reasons, foul and abuse it for corporate profit.

And others, like myself, just like to paddle, fish, or poke around on a quiet sunny morning or blue dusk, to find some peace, rest and renewal, like my Old Man asleep on the shore that Sunday years ago back on the river, just after the War.

Creatures in the House *(October)*

We lived in the city once. Not just any city, either. The City of Light, *la Ville Lumière*, that is Paris, with its bright cafés, museums, concerts, bookstores and cinemas. The city of *joie de vivre, savoir vivre*. But in spite of all that, I found myself scrutinizing the Eiffel Tour for a glimpse of the fierce little falcon who lived in the steel girders,that touch of the wild that reminded me of my Connecticut River Valley home. I was making frequent trips to the Impressionist museum, then located in the *Jeu de Paume,* before the *Musée d'Orsay* opened in the 80s. The Jeu de Paume was smaller, more intimate, and I found myself lingering before the snowscapes of Monet, Pissarro and Sisley, with pangs of homesickness and longing for the country, for the familiar beauty of snow-filled woods, the graceful slope of blanketed fields.

During those years in the city, we had discovered Konrad Lorenz, an Austrian naturalist and animal behavior specialist, and we wanted to try out some of his experiments. What Lorenz did, in addition to many technical aspects of his research, was to live in close association with his animals, not as master but as a fellow creature, to get to know them and what motivated their actions and behavior.

The European-American notion of taming the wild, of pushing back the Wilderness, of fighting a war on nature to promote our concept of civilization was, and still is, a driving force in our culture, a key feature of Western civilization—to dominate nature, as opposed to living in harmony with the natural world. This all sounds pretty familiar these days, but in the 50s and 60s, it was cutting-edge thinking and very appealing to the country people we were, exiled in the city, even if that city *was* Paris. So when we saw our chance to make our way back to Millers Falls to settle into the old family homestead on the Flat, we booked passage on an ocean liner and moved back to the Valley, fully intending, among other projects, to emulate Konrad Lorenz, to bring more animals into our lives, to learn more about the creatures that lived just outside our kitchen and living room. As it turned out, some of these creatures actually came *into* our kitchen and living room.

Our first experiment was with ducks, flying mallards to be exact. Some of my 7th grade students were raising ducklings, but their parents determined that they had too many and wouldn't I want to raise a few? We jumped at the chance to try out Lorenz's theories, especially to see if the ducklings would imprint upon us as their parents, in spite of our lack of feathers. So that weekend the ducklings moved into our kitchen, next to the kitchen table, where they lived in an improvised warm box incubator for a few weeks, where they ate while we ate, and observed us chatting, drinking coffee, writing and so on.. This worked fine, their clever eyes picked up everything, and we learned their various ways of communicating with us through voice tones, eye contact, and posture. Then one day, they found a way to push open the cardboard flap on the box that separated them from us, and turning this flap into a drawbridge, down marched all five ducklings onto the table, triumphant, and pleased with themselves! They made a bee-line for our food dishes (er, rather, our plates) assuming their "parents" were willing to share with them. That was the signal that it was time for them to move out. But it also began years of wonderful adventures with these beautiful and intelligent animals, and besides, they did know how to fly! In the mornings they left their hutch in the garden, and flew to the Millers River, several hundred feet away through the woods. And when we spent time on the deck for coffee and a book, they flew in, circling the house at the level of the upstairs bedroom windows and landed on the porch (often barely missing us) to sit with us while we chatted. They apparently liked to listen in to our various conversations. They settled under our chairs, beaks under wings, with contented murmurings and slept. They never actually came back into the house, but they lived outdoors in a small hutch not far from the door. We were thrilled with our success in following the Lorenz example, and thus began years of close association with animals, both wild and domestic.

One of our wild brethren who made it into this old house was a female opossum. Somehow she found an abandoned pipe that led from the small creek beyond the yard to the cellar and by following her nose, she made it into the cozy cellar for the winter. I should have known when vegetable peelings that we had tossed into the compost the day before mysteriously began reappearing in a dark corner near the furnace. When one evening we heard scratching at the cellar door, and opening it a crack, looked into the impudent eyes and fierce bared teeth of the lady opossum, I knew we had a new boarder. Instead of investing in a Havahart trap, we waited to see what would develop and what we could learn from this opportunity. By investigating every corner of the crammed cellar, we found her nest, and believing correctly that babies were on the way or were already here somewhere probably in her pouch, we let her finish out her child rearing. Later in the spring that pipeline to the opossum luxury suite was sealed up!

A notable experiment in our pursuit of rural felicity and insights into the nonverbal world of animal behavior involved geese. We acquired goslings, one male and two females of the Pilgrim variety. The gander of this particular breed is snow white, and ours was promptly named Martin, since every gander in Brittany and provinces beyond is a Martin, and not a François, for example. The two females were a demure soft grey, and were named Josephine and Lizzie. The three of them lived together in a small A-frame shelter and earned their keep by pulling weeds, dandelions, trimming the grass in the back yard, walking and inspecting all corners of the property, ready to alert the rest of us if any intruder approached. They thus emulated their forebears who saved Rome from its enemies millennia ago, by raising the alarm as the invaders approached the outskirts. I'm sure that the Miners and Staffords next door on the Flat did not always appreciate Martin and his noisy honking, especially at midnight if a raccoon was moving around the yard, but gradually the geese became part of the micro-habitat at this end of the neighborhood. They too spent time with us on the porch, coming to sit with us and enjoying the conversation on the warm boards in the sun. Martin always kept himself between us and his mates, but did wait expectantly for me in the evening at his front door, for his ritual of conversation in soft tones, his elegant neck curved, as I scratched and tickled him first under one offered wing, then the other, my fingers deep in that wondrous down.

Of course the day came when Martin's last mate, Josephine, died. We were in the kitchen, then looked up to notice his head peering through the screen door like a periscope to see us. The communication was clear. He wanted to come in, which he had never done before. So in he came, quiet and subdued and needing company. He had climbed up the stairs of the deck from the now empty yard, followed us through the kitchen and into the living room, and sat quietly with Kevin, murmuring a bit, clearly lost and in mourning.. Now as everyone knows, geese do defecate when excited and we had been vaguely concerned about goose poop on the floor, but that's easy enough to clean, and his loneliness was our first concern. Eventually, he gathered himself up, went back outside to bathe, and only then did he evacuate. Slowly, he resumed the last years of his life with a new younger companion.

Over the years, we have held Open House for a variety of creatures: some seeking to get in, some coming in by accident and eager to get out. One case in point was a blue jay who came in the open parlor window while I was painting the walls. The visit was unusual in that he came in backwards, tail first, because his head was in the cat's mouth. The young cat didn't quite know what to do with this brilliant bird who was furious and terrified, and not ready to go quietly! The confused cat got a strong dose of animal/human communication from me in the form of a string of expletives that my mother would be shocked to find out I even knew, and sensing correctly so that the gift to her humans was not appreciated, the cat released the jay who went back out the open window, the right way this time, head first, and pell-mell to a nearby tree to berate the cat using jaybird talk to continue the list of curses I had started. It may be that cats have nine lives, but this bird probably had lucky stars, and may well remember his trip into the house even to this day.

The long list of visitors to the house includes chipmunks, flying squirrels, grey squirrels, shrews, garter snakes, robins, even a ruby throated hummingbird! Some were not always living, like the owl in the icebox, but that's another story. The ones we raised, including generations of dogs and cats, all eventually taught us to communicate with them. And although it was never a question of spoken language, we all learned with patience to read each other's signs, and although we didn't really talk with the animals, on a different level there was a definite transfer of information between us. And most of them have communicated more honestly and clearly than many of the humans we know!

WEST ALONG THE RIVER – 2008

Ice Fishing on the Arctic Circle *(February)*

Just when we were thinking we'd have an early spring, with the February thaw at the beginning of the month, a blast of frigid weather blew down from the plains of Quebec with 0 degree temperatures and swirling white-out conditions. And now, in the last part of February, it's still up and down in the 50s with its promise of another roller-coaster plunge into the teens. Such is New England weather.

This has been the Winter of the Jay here in Millers Falls. Every morning they pour out of the sky, some 30 strong, flooding the snowscaped garden with blue. Waking from the sea of pines on Mineral Mountain, and from the marsh island grove they come, brash and bold in the steel grey cold of a February morning. Others may boast of their redpolls and grosbeaks, but we can boast of our jays. The very spirit of winter here on the edge of the woods—clannish and jaunty survivors, flashy and proud—they wing in like clockwork, resilient and undaunted by the cold and icy rain or the snow squall, they bob and leap over the corn on the February snow crust.

These winter thoughts plus an occasional hour spent on the H. D. Thoreau journals from Walden, put me in the mind for a saunter, as Thoreau took daily. So it's off again to Barton's frozen Cove for a late afternoon's winter walk. Standing out on the ice among the fishing shacks, with the sun going down over the windswept tundra surface of the Cove, and the sweep and sway of the lofty pines on the far shore, suddenly I hear, welling up from the frozen landscape, the tinkling sound of the balalaika, the rising chorus of the theme from Zhivago that echoes over the emptiness. My saunter comes to a halt, and I catch myself beginning to want to rise up on my toes to dance and spin in a waltz when... Whoa! Stop the music! This isn't a movie; this isn't Karelia; it's only the frozen Cove.

But it's already too late, my Thoreau saunter has turned into a train ride through the dark, plunging into northern Russia. Somewhere in between the *glasnost* and *perestroika* of the 90s, I wound up on

47

that train on the Murmansk-St. Petersburg line, whistling through the Russian winter night, with legendary Russian teacher Jude Wobst of Leverett and twelve exchange students in what was becoming the post-Soviet Union. We were on our last leg of a journey to Karelia, with jet lag pulling us deeper into hallucination. We had bunks on the train, but we couldn't sleep: we were traveling in a car with an itinerant gypsy circus, so the night was filled with music, performing dogs, cognac, and hilarious stories in an incomprehensible tongue! The only break in the action was a sudden halt in the middle of nowhere because our car was suddenly full of smoke.

We all piled out onto the windy steppe lands wondering if in this corner of Russia, the Cold War was alive and well and we were about to be transferred to Siberia, or worse. It turned out that a grandmotherly peasant woman (a *babushka*) had felt it was time for tea and had fired up her samovar in the corridor sending the smoke through the car that stopped the train.

Back into the smoky car we went, the gypsy *joie de vivre* recommenced, with more stories and dance. And this was only our first day in Russia!

Days and weeks flew by that February. Nights filled with music and dance, days were taken up by classes at our partner School #17 in Petrozavodsk, the capital of Karelia. At one point in our month-long stay, my hosts determined it was time for me to go ice-fishing. Being in Karelia, whose nearest neighbor is Finland (indeed this region has changed hands so much over the centuries that most people speak both Finnish and Russian, just in case), ice fishing, even if we were near the Arctic Circle, appeared to be a little less weird than the other things they had had me do so far, so I figured, why not?

I headed north with my new friends. (As if you could go farther north! You mean there's more?) We were already closer to Murmansk than I thought was necessary. We made our way in the Russian-manufactured car through the frozen emptiness to a small village set in the vast whiteness on the edge of a lake. On go my Sorel Arctic Pack boots, my good-for-30-below down jacket, a heavy wool ski hat made in Quebec, union suit underneath all that, and off we go? Not so fast, *tovarich!* My Russian hosts felt my clothes were not suitable for the climate, so, off came Sorel boots, my good-for-30-below down jacket, my French-Canadian ski hat. They let me keep my long johns, though. Onto my head was placed a huge Russian fur hat (with the ear flaps loose, of course, and ready to flop in the air with every frozen step). My down jacket was replaced with a big sheepskin affair, and my Sorels became knee-high *valenki*. These were thick felt peasant boots that actually were fun to wear in the freeze-dried snow. Thus clad, out I went onto the frozen lake.

Slowly it dawned on me that my jovial hosts were laughing and gesticulating in a Russian I couldn't understand, but I was beginning to get the point. They were totally attired from head to foot with the latest hi-tech Arctic gear, ready for fishing in the frozen North, and I looked like a survivor from the 19th century or at least ten years ago, which is just about the same, in Russia. After walking a half mile out on the ice, and after the hilarity had died down, we checked the various fishing holes where lines, and even nets, had been sitting for a while. We jigged and re-baited, sat on pails, caught a few perch-like fish and some unappetizing sucker-like things, declared it a good day on the ice and went home...to the sauna. Something I hadn't expected. So for the next hour, I burned in searing dry heat, got flailed with stingingly refreshing birch branches by the other guys (was this a kind of revenge for us winning the Cold War?), then a heart-stopping roll in the snow. By then the sun, which never did get more than a foot over the horizon, was slipping even lower, and I was ready for a drink. I figured I had earned it.

So back we trudged to the wooden cottage in the wooden village where the women had spent the day drinking tea, telling stories, and waiting. Like horses to the barn, my hosts headed to the warm kitchen and the vodka. So, alternating cups of tea and glasses of homemade vodka, along with pickles and pirozhki, the rest of the afternoon slipped by, and eventually we headed back, a few miles south, to what was at that time considered civilization.

The sequel to the fishing adventure came a week later at our farewell ceremony. I had practiced my speech in Russian for weeks. Never one to fail to grasp the obvious significance of the moment, I realized who I was giving my speech to. They were Russians, recent

Communists of some shade or another, and they were my age, with children in our program. I evoked growing up in a small town on the Connecticut River in the 50s and 60s, growing up under the fear of nuclear annihilation. My Russian counterparts grew up under the same fears too. Only, where I was haunted by Russian Communists, they were convinced the Americans would one day come to kill them. Yet, I was stunned by the fact that there I was, talking to them in my halting Russian, of how important it was that we were all there in that same room, and that having feared each other all our lives, we had been finally able to discover that we had shared the same fears and now shared the same hopes for the future of our children. It was as though the door had been opened and we could see into the room that had been closed for so long.

What were the odds that we would meet face to face in a schoolroom, after a lifetime of Iron Curtain, Brinksmanship, a policy actually called MAD (Mutually Assured Destruction), the Cuban Missile Crisis, Krushchev assuring us "We will bury you!" and those grim-faced party leaders on the Kremlin Wall, with their parade of missiles on Red Square? Yet there we were, talking about the new peace, making plans, embracing new friends for life.

From there, we went straight to the Stalin-era train station, still adorned with the hammer and sickle, clouds of smoke and noise rising up as we boarded the train for Moscow. Our new friends ran alongside the train as we pulled away, waving and blowing kisses, just like in the movies...

Those images fade in slow motion, I find myself back on the ice alone, wind and snow squall rising. Dusk is falling on the Cove; there's just me out there among the fishing shanties, as the eagle settles in a bare tree on the edge of the ice and a few crows head for the shelter of the pines for the night. Walking back to shore, with the Russian vision still in my head, I think of our two countries again, now run by two angry little men, when what we need are giants. In the gathering dark, I swear I can hear the distant sound of a door closing.

Spring Home-coming *(April)*

This has been an unusual April: good for curing firewood and nest-building. The first task pretty much takes care of itself and the second takes a lot of know-how and the right genes. The phoebes took care of the nest-building part. The same pair, or their look-alikes, have set their nest-cup under various eaves here for years. This April, they've set their '08 edition on a shelf under the wood shed roof, working at it all morning every morning, and taking it easy in the hot afternoons. These are grey, soft-spoken New England birds—modest yet voracious in their appetite for mosquitoes. So of course they are welcomed with great ceremony when they come home in April. I like to think that they, like me, share the sense of place here. I like to think that their ancestors first nested in my great-grandfather's barn when it went up in 1872. They most likely watched Judah with their sharp bright eyes as he took out the horse in the morning and brought him back after a day's work at dark. I know that when the barn fell down in 1972, they moved across the road to Stafford's abandoned garage. And when that was torn down, they moved back in with us, finding the woodshed to their liking. They went about nest-building early this year, encouraged by the unusual warm temperatures.

They finished just around Patriots' Day, no doubt timing this to coincide with the anniversary of the Shot Heard Around the World, and when the last runners in the Boston Marathon crossed the finish line, they quietly celebrated their new nest built to phoebe specifications.

We've inherited a flock of 30 redwings who have lingered here, mooching cracked corn and gurgling all morning draped in the pale-green-budded trees. They're good musical company to keep oneself entertained while hauling the afore-mentioned wood from the overgrown pasture along the river.

A lot of us are used to felling our trees in full winter so that by early spring we can get to the wood-drying part in the warmer weather. To drop my supply of trees I use a Stihl Farm Boss 290 (bought at Sirum's down the road in Montague), a Swedish bow saw (same handle for 25 years, new blade from time to time) and three beavers. The beavers came with the place, and my grandfather Abe introduced us one evening when I was 11. We went down to the edge of the pasture and sat on a log at dusk to wait. A bird flew up the river making a rattling racket. "Kingfisher," said Abe. A winnowing call came from the pines on Mineral Mountain. "Screech owl," said Abe. Then two dark blunt heads floated purposefully down the river. "Beaver," said Abe, out of the corner of his mouth, in between draws on his corncob pipe. At that, he got up to go back to the house to his glass of Narragansett and the Yankees-Sox ballgame, both in progress. So, like with the phoebes, the beavers and I have developed a relationship. They knock down trees and limb them, I cut up the trunks they can't use. Or, I fell the trees, and they move in at night to remove the limbs, depending on which trees either of us want. When their trees get hung up, I pull them down so they can continue their work. They're into American Hophornbeam this year. We'll see how that burns this winter. Between us, we're clearing the sunny south side of the river bank, and new grasses and plants are moving in. Even the deer and the geese are pleased.

Otherwise, there's only one junco left from the crowd that spent the winter. He's a hard one to dislodge from the comfort and free meals in this warming yard, but soon he'll be off, maybe moving up to Wendell for the season, where we might meet him in a tall pine up there this summer. His flock of snowbirds treated us to many a concert in the April mornings before leaving, delightful liquid warbling and trilling, in exchange for having kept them plump and well-fed during this past record-breaking winter. The brown thrasher has already dropped in, this genuine northern mockingbird bursting forth with his birdcall imitations every bit as well as his southern cousin. Another old-fashioned looking bird, the towhee, dropped in too. As beautiful and eccentric-looking as anything that Jean-Jacques Audubon ever painted, and I don't have to shoot him to observe his coloration like old Jean-Jacques used to. Binoculars are a good substitute for the gun.

The three Canada geese raise a racket all day long from the marsh, honking and trumpeting in the springtime and pre-nuptial silliness. The three of them are going to have to work this one out before they get serious about starting a family. There's no *ménage à trois* in the goose world. Their trumpeting up and down the river echoes with the wail of the trains that pass through Millers Falls then along the edge of Lake Pleasant and the Montague Plains. Sometimes geese and engine whistles are in harmony, but more often they ring out in post-industrial dissonance.

So with the phoebes safely ensconced in their ancestral home, the stage is set for the gaudier crowd coming home soon: the orioles, the tanagers, the rose-breasted grosbeaks. We'll take it as it comes, one arrival at a time.

Late at night, a strange pinching and burning on the skin. The first tick! Pinched painfully off and crushed between thumbnail and forefinger. Yep...Spring has come home to the valley.

Late-Summer Almanac *(August)*

Every summer day is a good day at this house on the edge of the river. Writing this in a lilac arbor under green branches and blue sky, no rain for a change. A noisy family of wrens inspects the fence nearby, cardinals and jays bring their families into the yard for food and a bath. Sure, there are always the summer chores: either paint the porch, bring in wood for the winter, repair the roof, get the car inspected, or, pick up some sweet corn for roasting over the campfire tonight, and schedule the afternoon in the hammock, for example.

Some lazy days start with efforts to outfox the big grandfather bullfrog who lives in our pond. He spends his mornings sitting at the base of the big oak tree on a nice emerald moss cushion a few feet over the pond. Everyday I try to sneak up on him and every day he sees me coming and pulls off an Olympian dive into the pond leaving a perfect ring on the surface and nary a watery plash. I'm concerned for him though; we spotted the Loch Ness monster in the little pond, that Jurassic survivor of a snapping turtle that could come up on our froggy dodger like Jaws from the depths. Not today though. He has glided home safe underwater to the base of the yellow river iris where he'll spend his morning cannibalizing pollywogs, probably his own offspring. Outwitted by the batrachian again.

In a cove along the river two young female kingfishers practice their fishing techniques from a log jutting out from the shore. They don't seem to be too serious about it, splashing noisily into the water several times in succession before returning empty-billed to perch and preen in the welcome sun before diving carelessly into the river again.

A pair of dapper yellowthroats, masked, sleek and yellow-green, are working themselves to the bone to feed a monstrous baby cowbird who follows them everywhere pleading for more food. Reminds one of any number of teenagers in any given family. It would almost be comical if not for the fact that it would be preferable that were feeding their own baby yellowthroat with his sweet warbler voice rather than this illegitimate offspring slipped into their nest. The female cowbird deadbeat parent is probably now off gallivanting and hanging out with others of her tribe, free from ever having to raise her own children. Let someone else do it.

July seems to have been one tropical rainstorm after another. The edge of the woods has become a wall of green. Rainforest growth has put up an almost impenetrable tangle along the river's edge. High water has erased the shoreline and minnows swim in grassy underwater forests, where brilliant cardinal flowers glow beneath the surface. Mushrooms and mosses seem to feel content and at home to be growing on the back deck. Soggy blue jays enjoy the bird bath under a drenching shower.

In early August the rain seems to have stopped. On one of these dry mornings, I spot twin fawns moving daintily along the spring in the middle of the woods. Actually they are already spotted when I see them. They are all legs, like new-born colts, large eyes and ears, backs still dappled as with snow or apple blossom. Born a few months ago, they are moving through our woods, munching on touch-me-nots, sprouts and shoots growing from oak and maple stumps. Like magic, they disappear behind their mother into the foliage, in an instant.

Other sunny days bring hummingbirds and bees to the flower garden. The bees are all of the bumble variety, the honeybees are totally absent this year, more than likely under severe assault from evil viruses and blight affecting their hives. Luckily the bumble bee continues his job, visiting flowers and bringing pollen from one to another. Deep inside the foxglove he goes, and then stumbles his way good-naturedly out the chute and, a little bit tipsy, on to the next flower tavern. Curious-looking hummingbird moths move among the blossoms too, some imitating the colors of pink bee balm and coral columbine, one other totally disguised as a bumble bee complete with a bumblebee suit in yellow and black stripes. The hummingbirds themselves move among the blossoms or alight on their bamboo perch an instant, before launching a vicious attack on another hummer intruder.

During the second week in August, a violent wind storm bursts upon the town, with hail hammering off every surface. The hail shreds the forest greenery, riddles leaves of rhubarb, and pock-marks melons and fruit from Millers to Wendell. A walk through the woods in the aftermath is strangely brighter now by light reaching the forest floor more easily through broken branches and missing leaves.

Since then however, evenings in early August have been dry. Taking a break from the Red Sox game—it's the seventh inning stretch around 9 o'clock—time to lie down on the back lawn and wait for the bats, instead of going bats over the frustrating game going on inside. The high peak of the old house and its ridge line run north to south, now silhouetted against the twilight sky. The peak often serves the dove who spends her time up there calling to the nearby woods in gentle fluting. She watches our comings and goings with inquisitive eyes fixed on the familiar household activities. Sometimes a jay sits on the peak on the lookout for seeds that seem to spring from our hands. More often than not a squirrel watches us, inquiring eyes focused down the twitching nose with the impertinent expectation that I will do something for him. Once even a gentle wood duck had her favorite perch up there. Once a whippoorwill, too—maybe related to the one that had called all through the Depression and the War, as my mother tells it. That peak has sailed on through the blizzards of 1888 and 1978, the hurricane of '38, like the prow of a ship, neither flood nor storm has gotten the best of her yet! A roof over dozens of lifetimes of family in those 140 years. You think about things like that while lying in the grass, looking up through the fireflies, and waiting for bats. Sure enough, the four of them come tumbling out into the sky from who knows where. They tilt and whirl, pirouette and chatter, tease and almost collide but not quite. Cleaning the air of insects as they go. It is said that their babies accompany their mothers on these wild hunts, clinging on tight throughout the roller coaster ride. Such joy in seeing our bats back again, especially since there were dire warnings of disease, disorientation, and death in their winter caves. But ours made it back to their summer homes again.

The stars pivot over the house, the bats move on to another spot on the river. Time to get up out of the grass to see if the Sox will pull it out in the bottom of the 9th, once again.

The Kitchen at Christmastime *(December)*

When the days get shorter and darker, and the calendar tells you there are just a handful of days left in the year, the kitchen in most houses takes on a special importance. But when, like us, you have chosen to live in your great-grandparents' house, there's more than just cooking that goes on in the kitchen. There's the weight of history and tradition tossed into the bargain.

Three women have been in charge of this kitchen over the past 130 years. There's great-grandmother Elizabeth, and grandmother Hannah, who split the first 100 years between them, and now my own Monique has taken over for the last 35. None of the generations of men folk, by the way, have ever done much in the way of cooking, and I'm no exception to the tradition. I'm a terrible cook, although I do like to eat! I'm more in charge of the parallel dimension of this homestead kitchen, as you will soon see.

Over the years, the earlier generations of males in the house brought home venison and rabbit, partridge and woodcock, trout and bullheads to the kitchen for the women to fix up. As for me, I bring home the groceries, having no inclination or need to spend time in the woods and fields blasting away at wild creatures. And that's that.

Our house was new in the 1870s, and it's apparent that it was built up around the kitchen, with function in mind. It's a bright place, facing south, southeast with two walls of windows that bring in both sunlight and ·moonlight. In December, and especially if there's snow, the Cold Moon lights up the room well enough so that you could read a newspaper by moonlight.

Invariably, guests arriving here have always been channeled into the kitchen by any one of the three doors that lead to the heart of the house, where the heat and light are, where the aroma of cooking roasts and baking pies leads. One of the other doors leads to the parlor, open now, but which was for most of the house's existence almost always closed except for occasional social gatherings, oftentimes wakes or funerals.

Most deceased family members went from the parlor to the cemetery. Also, there's a small room off the kitchen usually reserved for birthing, being sick, or dying. After the dying part, the next stop was the parlor, and so on. So, of the three rooms, this kitchen has always been the source of heat, light, food and life.

The three women who have run the kitchen over their long reigns have had their challenges, especially at Christmas time. Like trying to keep dishes and platters moving from stove to kitchen table among 20-25 family members busy chatting and drinking.

Grandmother Hannah had her hands full because when she was in charge the family had grown, and all her children had had children and we all went over the river and through the woods for Christmas dinner. There were so many of us that we had to eat in shifts at the kitchen table.

The experiment with putting some of us youngsters to eat at a flimsy folding card table in the parlor didn't work out. Imagine dealing with rambunctious and over-excited grandchildren plus their noisy new toys, pop-guns and cap pistols, crying dolls and windup trucks with sirens, plus platters of food eventually winding up on the parlor rug.

In those days, first served were the fathers, mothers, uncles and aunts who had just gotten off work, or who were headed for work. The tool shop and the paper mill didn't shut down for the 25th. Aunt

June had to report to her nurse's duty at the Farren also, so those on shifts had priority.

Of course, the whiskey and beer for chasers were the workingman's drink of choice, before, during and after the meal, so that once the first shift of adults had been served, a sort of lovely fatigue set in that caused the uncles (Johnny and George) to feel a need for some quiet time to recuperate before going back to the factory. They made their way to the room off the kitchen to catch a snooze and digest.

Then it was the youngsters' turn at the table, and our chance to fill up on turkey, stuffing, and, cranberry sauce amid the clatter of dishes being washed and refilled for us, our noisy chatter, breaking toys, and the adults' wreaths of cigarette smoke.

The kitchen throughout its earliest days had the simplest of facilities: the sink, the stove, the ice box. Originally the sink hosted the pump, which drew water up from the well in the cellar. Aunt Pete told many a story of an electrical charge that followed the water line up the pump during a thunderstorm and reputedly knocked one of the ancestors across the floor!

I stay away from that sink in a storm to this day, even though the hand pump is long gone. The stove and its oven have undergone multiple incarnations. When Lizzie was in charge in the 1880s, it was a wood stove, long since departed from family memory. Later it became a coal stove where my mother and her brothers and sisters warmed their feet after the cold walk home from school. That was replaced by a gas stove.

Mention the gas stove and up pops the image of my uncle Sammy Semaski, driving down our street in his big red Mackin's truck in the swirling snow. Sam delivered gas for the stove and fuel oil to this house, making sure my grandparents Abe and Hannah were always well supplied. He was a jovial man, probably the best-natured man in Millers Falls. He was one of those big round uncles you sometimes have, always a big smile and a gentle laugh that only certain Polish can have. His face creased all over when that smile came on, his eyes crinkled in laughter. It's nice to think of him this Christmastime.

By the way, that gas version of the stove was replaced when we took over. We installed a big electric stove inherited from grand-uncle Doug Smith, the one he had bought built to last in the early 50s. It did indeed make it to the middle 90s, when we once again replaced it with a more modern version, sadly not at all built to last, or at least it did—until just one day over the warrantee.

We twinned the electric stove with a restored Glenwood C wood cook stove, and the cycle from Lizzie to now was complete: we have both electric and wood-burning stoves these days.

So as I was saying, when you inherit an old family house, you get more than just the walls. Stories, histories and spirits of past Christmases crowd into the old kitchen and it's my job to keep track of them,

You never know who's going to turn up unannounced from those old Christmases, maybe cigar-smoking, smooth-talking Joe Conway shows up, with a good deal on a newer version of a life insurance policy, or maybe fire insurance, or some such.

Maybe Father Mac makes his way to the light, eager to trade jokes with our grandfather Abe, who himself always puts in an appearance on Christmas Eve, his face beaming, glowing and flushed from the Christmas cheer he'd been partaking of at the Tool Shop party. Unnamed Kerry Irish relatives of Hannah crowd in, on the way back to Ireland and tired of sleeping out in the barn.

Then there's the smiling young man I've only heard about; he was before my time. His name was Rudy, and he came of age just when Gene Autry began singing about that Red-nosed Reindeer of the same name. The story goes that my mother and her sisters teased him about the nose and the song until he blushed. He was a young Marine then, at Christmas, and soon gone off to fight at faraway Bougainville in the Pacific, never to return except in the memory of an old photograph and of course, that song.

Even Cousin Pat may come down from tending bar at the Red Lantern up the street. He brings hilarious, infectious laughter, and tales of hunting, that proved to be his undoing. Another uncle, with that tragic hint of lonesome Hank Williams honky-tonk hanging in the air around him, drifts in. Thin features, shy smile and sharp eyes, he too disappeared too suddenly days after Christmas, long ago. It gets crowded when all these people start turning up, as they do, once a year.

Legend has it that at midnight of Christmas Eve, the animals have briefly the power to speak, but I'd say after spending an hour in the chicken coop once or twice with our little boy waiting to hear what Napoleon the rooster had to say, it's more likely that you'll be visited by the memories of old friends and long gone relatives who turn up for their yearly hour of remembrance. So, like me, I suggest you always make room for them, and keep an open mind, because they'll appear for sure. Then again, this is just what I believe, and you can believe what you want.

But just to be sure, at Christmas when we get together, the immediate family and the extended family, we always have a toast to the health of all of us there and to the memory of all who came before. Sometimes they're actually there with us, too! It can get crowded in that small room.

You can see what I mean about old houses and Christmas memories. You make room for everyone, you set a place for everyone, because it's once a year, and you never know who's going to show up in the kitchen.

WEST ALONG THE RIVER - 2009

Snow Owl Vision *(January)*

Maybe it all started when, as a 12 year old, I had taken to haunting the frozen river bank of the Connecticut along the place we call the Narrows. In those years, it seems the winters were cold, long, and darker than they are now. And for me in those days, the Connecticut River was the gateway to the Arctic. The river always froze solid, a white expanse of snow and ice, jagged chunks of frozen ridge sticking up from time to time, stretching from the Narrows to the French King Bridge and beyond to the north. Already, by then, I loved being out in the winter when I felt like a solitary explorer on the edge of an ice sheet glacier of a river that extended up to Hudson Bay. Never mind that the geography was a bit off, as I found out later. Daily I scrutinized ice, praying for the appearance of a great white bird to come winging out of the north. I needed to see a Snowy Owl, the very spirit of our northern winter. By the end of those winter afternoons spent exploring the Arctic wasteland just off Carlisle Avenue, I had one advantage that Byrd and Peary never did in their quest for the North Pole. I could trudge home through the snow at dark, and settle into a nice comfortable chair in a cozy home, and read until bedtime when my parents turned off the lights. So much for the intrepid Nordic explorer!

Maybe too the quest became all the more acute when on Christmas Eve in '57 my grandparents Abe and Hannah gave me a massive book weighing almost ten pounds, one pound for each of my years at the time! The book was called the "Birds of America" by T. Gilbert Pearson, published in 1917. They had bought the book at Wilson's for the huge sum of $9.95, a dollar a pound by simple calculation, but it sealed my fate as a naturalist, and locked the Snowy Owl and me into mutual destiny. The illustrations were by Louis Agassiz Fuertes, and the 300-page book was filled with narrative and folklore, features that one no longer finds in bird guides, and it linked me with stories of the Snowy Owl going back to the 1870s. T. Gilbert Pearson had collected the folk names of all the birds, names that would have been lost forever but for his recording of them. He wrote that my owl had other names: Great White Owl, Ermine Owl, Arctic Owl, Harfang, and the name given by Native Americans, *Wapacuthu.* He wrote of the Snowy Owl: "the long days in summer where this owl breeds make its habits chiefly diurnal. This fact has been discovered too late by many a Crow engaged with his brethren in the pleasing diversion of mobbing the big white specter sitting on a limb motionless, and presumably blind, because obviously an owl. For let one of the tormentors come near enough and the ghost suddenly launches out on strong silent wings, the great talons strike and close, and there is a Crow who would have been wiser but for the circumstance that he is very dead." Now that's writing you don't see in bird books anymore! All I knew is that I needed to see a Wapacuthu for myself.

I finally got my first chance years later, around 1978, when I discovered the frozen tundra conditions of Salisbury and Plum Island in February. A hardy group of us, a loose-knit band who formed the now-defunct Norman Bird Club, organized a field trip to the coast in search of winter wildlife. The conditions were Arctic-like, with biting penetrating winds, frozen sea ice, seals, gulls and, Snowy Owls! Finally! We just came upon them, three of them, out on the frozen chaos of an ice-clogged estuary, at home and busy catching voles, mice (and I'm thinking maybe lemmings!). The rest of the day went by in a frozen blur, new life birds turned up but how could we tell? Chilled to the bone, fingers blue and numb, our birds appeared as vague images in shaking binoculars through wind-teared eyes, and they just wouldn't hold still what with the trembling we had from the cold.

Back home that night, after thawing out, I was on the phone rounding up members of the coming Snowy Owl expedition. My immediate family took no convincing, all of us eager to see this fabled bird. Back down to the coast within days we went, and sure enough, the Owls were there, and we watched them to our heart's content, from inside the car. At one point, there came a knock on our fogged up window and I heard a voice with a slightly British accent, or perhaps a North Shore patrician accent with British undertones, saying, "I say, have you seen the Ross's Gull?" We allowed as we hadn't and asked what to look for. He stated it was an all-white gull with a slightly rosy hue, and was a very special bird indeed. We responded well have you seen the Snowy Owls, feeling the Owls were every bit as impressive as some gull. He stepped back a bit surprised by the intensity and level of enthusiasm and triumph over our owls find. He shrugged and disappeared into the Salisbury wind and we went back to exalting over owls.

Later that week, Time magazine carried an article about the "Ross's Gull Riot" in Newburyport harbor. It seems that the Ross's Gull was a vagrant from the Bering Straits off Alaska, never before seen in the lower 48, and that every half-mad bird life-lister had come from all over the US to see it. Even the great Roger Tory Peterson had hauled himself out of retirement to join the throng in the Newburyport coal yards where by then had formed a true army, bristling with telescopes and cameras, scrutinizing every tawdry mundane sea gull in search of the elegant Ross's.

Even then, we didn't care. We were feeling pretty superior with our owl.

But I was to have one more Snow Owl adventure just a few years ago. I got a call one dark mid-December afternoon from Betty Waidlich who told me there was a large white owl sitting on the rocky point that juts out into the river at Cabot Camp, where the Millers meets the Connecticut. My totem bird had finally come to me and was waiting just a few minutes downriver. And indeed, there he was, sitting upright on the point. He must have winged his way down from the far north, just as I had always imagined, a white specter floating down, passing under the great bridge, and resting now on the promontory. We approached him slowly; he seemed to pay us no mind. We stayed at least fifty yards away, got our fill of snowy owl impressions and turned slowly away to leave him in peace, when, just then, he toppled off the rock and lay motionless on a ridge above the water. We ran up to him in a flash, he was in a deep swoon, with no strength left. I cradled him in my arms, his fierce yellow eyes opened and looked into mine, his huge black talons gripped my arm briefly, and his white head sagged, giving up the ghost. I was stunned. *Something* had passed between us. From him to me, after a lifetime of waiting. We carried his body reverently back to the car. Later, I called Carolyn Boardman to see what she could tell me. She was the local expert on raptors and the Barton Cove eagles, and a friend. More than likely she said the owl had come down the river, driven south by the lack of food, had probably made it to the confluence, on the point of death by starvation. Nothing more to be said, other than that it was illegal to have this bird in my possession. The ground was by then frozen, and having no alternative, it spent the rest of the winter in the freezer in the kitchen. When spring finally arrived, we buried the owl in the rich earth below the house, along the river, standing up, its great white head facing north.

Old Man Winter's Backside *(February)*

That's what this part of February feels like to some of us. We've reached the mid-point of the month and according to the Old Farmer's Almanac, on the 16th "Winter's back breaks". I'd say not so fast, Abe Weatherwise. I'm not so sure about the back-breaking part, but I know a lot of us would like to plant a boot in winter's backside about now. But we've got to keep up hope, otherwise we couldn't live in this climate. True, the bad weather has held off for a few weeks now, but by the time you're reading this, we could be back in the middle of it. Our customary January Thaw didn't happen until it had to be called a February Thaw, but we'll take it. And it's also true that the sun, hanging around for almost an hour more since early January, has been getting a chance to do its work. Snow banks are becoming sandy eyesores, and our yard is littered with implosions of feathers scattered in small circles, the crime scenes exposed now that some snow has melted. The neighborhood assassin, most likely a sharp-shinned hawk, turned a number of juncos and sparrows into alternative energy to fuel its own hawk's need for winter protein and springtime procreation. We can't really find fault with nature taking its own course, but it'd be better for this household if the hawk made off with some starlings instead our sparrows. Meanwhile, up at the farm on Mineral Mountain, the horses doze in the February sun, their huge flanks turned toward the rays, eyes closed sleeping standing up in late winter bliss.

Nature never stands still for long however, and outside the window, the pine siskins mob the thistle feeder, oblivious to the economic situation in our human world. They could care less about the coming Depression or stimulus packages to avert it. The thistle's their bail-out plan, and they bring in occasionally a redpoll cousin to cheer us up. The world's in a strange state with bank failures and foreclosures, fresh budgetary disasters awaiting school systems and town governments. And as if that wasn't enough, our two months of mud season is still a few weeks away. But just as there's a little optimism in Washington, so too can you find springtime hope in the courtship antics of the squirrels following one another nose to tail, the promise of primal squirrel coupling just a few sniffs away. They play and tussle in slow motion on the rail fence and under the rhododendrons, leaves still limp from the cold. Over on the mountain, the horned owls have already set up house-keeping, after a healthy month of hooting along the river and through the woods, staking out their territory. Of the seven cardinals that show up in the yard at dusk, the majority are bright males, jealous of one another already, trying to chase all other rivals from the few females pecking demurely at seeds and not seeming to pay attention to the displays of late winter machismo.

It's reassuring to find the familiar cycle renewing itself. It's all the more sweet following this winter of discontent. Not unlike the venerable local celebrity author of Jep's Place, I also spent time in the hospital. Like Joe P, I had to make the best of it, and try to keep a sense of humor in that strange place. I spent a week in exile up on the 15th floor of Brigham and Women's in Boston, somewhat against my will, but of course for my own good. A charming young nurse, Saundra, kept a watchful eye on me and kept me focused on my recovery. At least I could look out the window night and day at the cityscape of snowy rooftops and busy streets. It felt particularly unusual for someone like me who is used to looking out the bedroom window at a landscape of flowing river, and birches in the moon shadows. Plus it was like spending a week in Grand Central Station. Whatever happened to the term Hospital Quiet Zone. My ward was a scene of constant 24-hour per day commotion, comings and goings, conversation and confabs in all manner of foreign tongues. I could pick out Persian Farsi, Brazilian Portuguese, several East European languages, and my favorite, Haitian French. Having spent at least half my life speaking French, it was very familiar in that strange place to make small talk with the Haitian nurses, who seemed to be so very natural at care giving. Must be something to do with an island up-bringing.

But it was great to get home and caught up on all the news, especially the news in my little corner of the world. There were robins and waxwings on Avenue A. (And some discussion as to whether they were harbingers of spring or just some robins who decided to tough it out.). A redwing showed up in the yard on Valentine's Day, definitely a spring arrival, almost 10 days ahead of time, and a grackle two days later, also ahead of time. The Red Sox catchers and pitchers were turning up in sunny Florida, while we had the ladybugs here instead, stretching their legs and walking around the sunny kitchen windows. I was eventually able to hobble out into the fresh air, and smell the old snow and the promise of spring on the air. I'd still call this the backside of winter, with all its anatomical connotations, but just now, one of our discreet song sparrows, constant garden companion in summer and winter, has come up to the edge of the deck, looking for stray seeds. And even as he's going about scratching for a February living, his little optimistic song bubbled up in his throat while he worked, whistling like a busy carpenter his cheery tune. Now suddenly, after hearing him tuning up for spring, I feel a whole lot better about this time of year.

Back on Home Ground *(July)*

Morning light filters through the lilac bushes in the bower that serves as my summer office. I was enjoying just sitting at my table, back from 6 weeks away in other lands, enjoying the calm and the prospect of a lazy July morning of loafing. New poems by the Mt. Toby poet, black coffee right where I can get it, and then, I realize I'm not alone. There are six sets of bright black eyes peering at me from the bushes. They belong to a busy-body family flitting around the bush and branches hanging over the table's edge. One of them sings out "teakettle, teakettle". It's a family of southern arrivals, the wrens from Carolina, who have moved in recently to share space with their northern cousins, the Jenny Wrens of New England. Both these families can be sharp-tongued as well as endearing. The one closest to me, of the Carolina persuasion, seems to have set her wings on her stout hips, her tail straight up in the air and since I am the new intruder, she is letting me have it. With a sharp rasping scolding buzz, all of her family, 4 offspring plus her husband, start in on me. "You talking to ME?" I quiz them, hoping no one will notice me talking to a bush. The little wren getting in my face seems to answer, "You better believe it, buster!" Wrens can be bossy in spite of their diminutive size. She bounces from branch to branch, scolding me, and twitching with indignation. Surely she can see I have no intention of devouring her young. Even her husband appears less determined than she about this berating business. He sings his little teakettle song, and watches out of the corner of his eye. She seems to be saying, "Look at you! Just sitting there! Get a move on! There's work to be done this morning!" I protest that I was retired now and can loaf as long as I damn well please. It doesn't impress her. "Ha!" the sassy little trollop says. "Look at us! After a hard winter, all these kids! Cut some wood! Mow the lawn! Write an article! Fix the car! Weed the garden!" And so on. I do ask her when she has seen me last, trying to use human cunning to win the argument with this unreasonable bird who is destroying my morning tranquility. I explain that I am just resting briefly in my human sort of way and innocently enjoying the garden before getting started on the list of chores she has rattled off. Besides,

I say, with a significant look, one eye growing larger that the other, "I've been AWAY." That catches her attention. Even her neighbor the catbird stops his endless "starling-robin-jaybird" imitations and comes closer to listen. I continue. "AWAY means I've been across the pond, speaking strange tongues, up late at night singing with strangers, alone among thousands of people, walking on the edge of a falling sea cliff, talking with seals and birds, standing on the Atlantic shore and in a cathedral almost at the same time. But I'm back now, and happy to see you again." My little inquisitors don't have anything to say to all that. I don't explain to them that in parts of Ireland and Brittany where I had been, poets and other madmen could have conversations like this all the time with all sorts of other birds, badgers, and even fish, but of course in New England it is considered quite unorthodox and not just a little odd, so I'll just be moving off now my little family of wrens, off to get started on my chores. Let's pretend this conversation never took place. I do hope the neighbors haven't seen me waving my arms and arguing with the lilac bush in this fit of mid-summer madness.

I get up and leave my book, notes, and empty coffee cup pretending to get busy on my work list for the morning. But once out of eyesight of the sharp tongued little wench, I take myself for a walk instead. Like our friend Thoreau, I have my self-appointed rounds, but in this season, I count noses and beaks rather than tree rings and the depths of snow banks. I need to see who else is back on home ground and raising families.

A morning's mid-July census starts with a check on the pollywogs' progress in the frog pond. They at least seem happy with the month of rain—their private vernal pond is still brimming with water and they are thriving. Good news in a world where their kith and kin and extended family are disappearing from the planet. A wood turtle munches on a mushroom at the edge of the pond. Check. A few steps beyond the pond and a grouse raises a racket to distract me from the few chicks she has that survived the wet month. She flails around like a demented chicken to draw me away from the little ones. I just back off and let her comedy act play out. Check again. Further along the path, deer have cropped the tops of a swath of touch-me-nots growing in a clearing at the edge of the woods. There'll be no flowers here for the hummingbirds, but there are plenty of other sources of nectar, especially the sea of red bee-balm growing in the yard. Like a teacher taking attendance, I check off families of warblers moving through the lower growth along the river: redstart, black and white, yellowthroat in their dashing black masks, yellow warblers with their light red streaking, all have their young this mid-July. Red-eyed vireos sing tirelessly and the wood thrush is making a late start in his singing after the month of rain. Titmice, chickadees, the three woodpecker families: downy, hairy, red-bellied move noisily through the trees. By now, my breeding bird census has more than 41 species counted within a mile of this house in the little kingdom along the river—down a few from the record of fifty last year. Of course, I only count those species as breeding if I see them on the nest, or if they're feeding fledglings. So some years I miss a few.

At my last checkpoint, standing quietly like the great blue heron, my feet in the water on a quiet stretch of sand, with the Millers rushing by, a cluster of scarlet tanagers streak past and pause in the low branches hanging over the river above my head. Two young are trailing their harried mother, begging for food, and two brilliant males, all scarlet and black, chase each other, stop long enough to sing their buzzing song and move on. Dashing and dandy, the males don't seem inclined to help out with the youngsters. By the end of the morning, I can feel sure that most of our residents are back on traditional summer ground, including me!

Later in the evening, around 9 o'clock, there's one more summer regular to check for. Waiting on pins and needles, scanning the evening sky for our resident bats, the waves of anguish come and go, with the thoughts in mind of horrific news of death in their winter caves, we fear the worst. Yet our bats are back again! Finally they flutter by, overhead in the twilight at 9 o'clock, sweeping the sky over the yard, they angle and dive over the peak of the old house for at least one more season, but for how many more? With that, the house breathes in the cool night air, all windows upstairs and down open in the gathering dark. The whip-poor-will sings his quavering song like a ghost in the distance. We can safely declare summer, one more time. The fireflies add the exclamation point!

September Almanac *(September)*

Oh, it's a long, long while
From May to December,
But the days grow short,
When you reach September.
*(*September Song *by Maxwell Anderson and Kurt Weill)*

These have been the golden days of September when the morning mist lingers long over the banks of the river and then burns off before mid-day to reveal a faultless blue sky. We do deserve these days after the monsoons we tolerated all summer in July and most of August.

September always brings subtle changes to the world outside your window where already the seasonal page has been turned along with the turning of the leaves. Our hummingbirds bid us farewell after a last spin through the fading bank of bee-balm, and the skies have emptied of our swallows. The nighthawks flew down the skies at dusk early in the month, angling through the air, knifing right and left over the river, and were gone too. The "confusing fall warblers" move quietly through the woods, having changed their bright spring feathers for subdued fall traveling clothes. They're off to Belize and Costa Rica, ahead of the crowd.

A walk through the golden wood in the morning is mostly silent except for rustling leaves, until someone sings out *"Bonjour, cousin!"* the response from me is *"Bonjour cousine!"* It's cousin Annabelle from across the Flat walking her spaniel Daisy. We chat for a moment in the language of our *québécois* grandparents, before sharing news of birds and beavers in the woods we patrol. Those beavers have been busy putting up small neat dams across every little bit of flowing water. I call them practice dams, most likely done by youngsters who have been tossed out by their parents to fend for themselves after two years of being tolerated in the family lodge. These early attempts at dam-building will likely be swept away by the rising river the first time it rains hard. I pass by the secret wood thrush nest, empty now since mid-August. The parents reared their two offspring in a nest along the path, a piece of plastic woven into the structure. And in spite of a whole woods filled with predators, squirrels, raccoons, opossums and far-too numerous house cats, the babes fledged and were gone. I get just a little wistful when I pass that empty nest, if you know what I mean.

"Nothing gold can stay," our poet Robert Frost admonishes us, maybe with September and October in mind. And what about the deep green of that big dragonfly hawking insects in the yard? How long has HE got, now that it's late September? Our pale blue wild-growing asters still pull in the bumblebees, our orange and black wooly bears are tucked into a cozy warm curl in the firewood stack, but how many stripes does he have and can he really foretell the severity of the coming winter? Wild fox grapes not yet touched by frost scent the woods, mingling their sweetness with the spice of the yellowing ferns. September has brought out the cricket chorus, indoors and out, but the katydids seem less insistent than in the past, their ratcheting call already slower. The scent of the skunk's nightly visit lingers where he has been busy rooting out ground wasps and grubs from the back lawn. The white-throated sparrows are down from the tall pines of the nearby hills, but despite some of these early signs, summer won't be quite over until the main, last, summer event.

That final rite of summer for many of us is the " 'Bake at the Schuetz"! Tickets are hard to come by, and you need to know where to look, but it's always worth the effort. Sure, all 500 of us get together for the love of the clams and the lobster, but it's also about the end-of-summer ritual, going back generations. This legendary feast brings together people from all parts and from all walks of life, but you're sure to find among those gathered there many of those who keep our community in good working order. The firemen, the policemen, the mail carriers, mechanics, teachers, all those who keep the offices and shops up and running. It's a class reunion of sorts too if you're lucky enough to have grown up here, with old TFHS grads mingling maybe just this once a year. For me it's the yearly chance to chat with Brian San Soucie, or to exchange wise cracks with Dean Letourneau and Benny Rubin, to mingle with the extended family gathered around cousin Tom .Once even Sen. John Olver showed up to glad-hand the crowd during election season. It's always the same familiar scene that brings the summer to a close: billowing pure white steam escaping from the tarps that cover the clams baking on the stones, men and some women quaffing bushels of quahogs as though their lives and reputations depended on it. I stopped Dean Elgosin heading back to the tent with two fistfuls of quahogs. "Dean! You're really into the quahogs!" "Nah," says he, "can't stand 'em. They're for the others back at the table! They can have them!" I go back for more hot dogs. There's an endless supply of clam chowder and dogs before the main event, while the tent and pavilion emit a dull roar of excited devotees of the clambake. Soon three bags of clams, hot melted butter, a lobster, corn, and baked potato are delivered to every person, and you see everyone digging into the closest thing to a feeding frenzy we humans can come up with. All is consumed within an hour and the revelers settle into that glow that comes from a full belly of clams, not just a few bottles of beer, and the warmth of raucous good company. That's about the time the golden sun starts slanting through the pines along the river.

Many in the crowd melt away as the music starts, mindful of Monday morning responsibilities. People like me make the rounds to say good-bye to friends I may not see for another year. I take a last stop at the bar to toss back a toast to the memory of my father, a lifelong member, as was his father, of this Schuetzen Verein Club, but gone from us and this feast now for the past five years. Some of these fall rituals are private.

The day, and in some way the season, close for me with a solitary paddle across Barton's Cove, as the partying still goes on at the clambake. I slip away as the noise of the feast fades over the water. The sun is going down beyond the steeples and I let the kayak drift to my favorite spot near the Bear's Den where I can watch the sunset, sitting in among the cardinal flowers and the cattails. Three bald eagles chatter and flap about their nightly roosting spot on the island. Hundreds of shiners leap out of the water like the twinkling stars in the dusk. The renewed sense of place and belonging, the eagles and heron moving over the water, well that's a fine way to bring the month and the season to a close.

Nature's first green is gold,
Her hardest hue to hold.
Her early leaf's a flower;
But only for an hour.
Then leaf subsides to leaf.
So Eden sank to grief,
So dawn goes down to day.
Nothing gold can stay.

Robert Frost – 1923

WEST ALONG THE RIVER - 2010

Snow Falling on Cedar Waxwings *(February)*

On into February! The calendar has finally turned a page and we are rid of that interminable month of January! Mind you, January can be fine, a month of birthdays, anniversaries, new hopes and, of course, Robbie Burns feasts, but most of us are glad to see it gone, and into a new month. Things have seemed to be a mess out there, what with stories of the leaking nuclear plant just up river, the earthquake in Haiti, the biomass plant proposed to look over our downtown, exploding toilets, undependable weather, and confused voters who forgot to elect a Democrat to fill the seat of the Lion of the Senate. There's even been a survey published that says we Americans are no longer No.1 in optimism, that the Chinese are more optimistic about the future than we are, and from the looks of things, the survey is right. Seems like we can't be No.1 in anything these days.

There is solace somewhere however, and once outdoors away from the media, there is some peace of mind to be found. The days are lengthening and nature is finding its way back to the sun. On mornings before it rises above the valley rim, with temperatures hovering between 0 to 10 degrees, out the door we go for a jolt of that biting New England morning air and black coffee. Porch sitting is still a pastime for a few of us, even in winter; it certainly clears out the left-over cobwebs. As I sit in an Adirondack chair pulled up into a corner of the porch near the wood pile, the hungry creatures arriving, breaking the cold night's fast, pay little attention to me. Waves of juncos pour onto the work table covered with seeds, and the feeders which were stocked while the coffee was brewing. Looking like little turnips, gray-blue above and white below, these slate-colored birds have filled the yard this year and unusually so, with their normally numerous cousins the tree sparrows being almost totally absent. The jay clan arrives en masse also, shoveling down any manner of nut in the mix that they can find, brash and blue and twenty-strong. Some may not care for this bird, but he's a winter favorite and as good as any flock of geese in warning everyone of danger. And danger there is, since the sharp-shinned hawk has been raiding almost daily. Predators have a hard time in this season too, but the open winter has made it easier for them to locate and catch mice and voles who don't have the security of their winter snow tunnels. The sharp-shin and its larger cousin the Cooper's are accipiters, bird hawks, and are perfected hunting machines, capable of navigating through woodlands and trees with laser-guided precision. They knife through the yard hoping for a meal of a hapless junco or sparrow destined to be eliminated from the gene pool. One brazen and hungry hawk stands in the snow at the foot of the brush pile, waiting for a sparrow to panic and flee. At other times he beats the pile with his wings trying to flush out a morsel on the wing. When I step out to break the spell, all birds having instinctively frozen in place at the jays' and chickadees' alarm call, the hawk is dismayed at my intrusion, and flies up to a nearby limb. He lands with jaunty pin-point accuracy from which he can resume his surveillance of the yard, but then gives up and moves on. With peace and security restored, the birds become re-animated, and it's back to the chair on the porch for me. Shortly after, my sassy summertime friend the Carolina wren zips across the porch and perches on the tip of my Sorel boot before heading to the woodpile behind me to investigate the various fascinating crevices needing her daily attention. Jays flood the lilac grove again, hopping in the spread of cracked corn, blue against the patchwork of snow and brown earth. A cottontail ventures out to join them. The rabbit's been long missing from its ecological niche here along the Millers for about 20 years, as in many regions across the State. They seem to be making a comeback; we'll see how welcome they'll be in garden season! Down along the river, black ducks flock to the cracked corn spread out on the ice, and their congregation has attracted an adult bald eagle who swings by regularly to check out the possibility of duck on the menu. The massive bird wings upstream through the vapor rising from the rushing river, the first rays warming the air.

It's been a month of harvesting firewood, the beavers having laid down and limbed a dozen trees for me, mostly maple and American hophornbeam. The cooperative relationship is holding up with them getting what they need from the bark and branches while we are building next year's woodpile. Fox tracks criss-cross the shoreline and into the woods and yard. The tracks of otter bounding and belly-sliding are also clear after last week's snow squall. This morning, the light snow fell on a still sleepy flock of cedar waxwings. From time to time they spend the night in the rhododendron at the edge of the garden, as delicate and discreet as the Tao philosophers engraved in a Robert Francis poem. They know that their sleek tan and pale yellow bodies blend in with the drooping leaves of this shrub. Their crests and black facial markings resemble the flower buds that will open in scarlet in June. Almost thirty have crowded into the bush, and as their breezy call increases, they lift up and blow away in the snowy morning.

By nightfall, the Full Wolf Moon will rise over Dry Hill, helping the hunting foxes with a night so brilliant you could read the Montague Reporter by moonlight, indoors or out. The Farmers' Almanac tells us Candlemas has come, which always brings to mind stories of great-grandmother Lizzie Smith who, true to her childhood days in Scotland, always turned out stacks of wheaten griddle cakes for the occasion in this old house. We'll do the same to bring in this new month.

Out from the frozen marsh, the horned owl's hunting call will boom, telling us the old nest is back in use. Soon there will be eggs and young to feed by early March. The Almanac announces that raccoons are mating, and so there's your proof that hope springs eternal, starting with the raccoons!

High Water Chronicles *(April)*

If you're from these parts, or if you've lived here attuned to the river moods long enough, you know this season is called "high water". Not the poetic "spring freshet" nor the cubic feet-per-second of the hydrologists, just a sparse two-word phrase referring to the essential element here, and its current state. Every spring season the pond, and a visiting muskrat spends time plunging to the bottom of high water has its yearly difference. They still talk about the 500-year flood one fateful March in 1936 that brought torrential rains and disastrous flooding, with ice jams blocking the Connecticut putting deadly pressure on bridges, dams and creating havoc when they finally gave way; such high water never seen before and allegedly not to be seen for another 500 years. But it only took two short years later for another 500-year flood to occur at the time of the 1938 hurricane. Maybe we're good for a thousand years this time around.

This year the water came up early, under warm heavy rains in March, melting snow and quickly raising the level of the water that swirls around the rocky cliff face in our bend of the river. Someone once said of the river, "Well...it runs by here every day". That is its job after all, it carries water away, down river to the sea and most times keeps it away from our door. Some folks down east along the coast didn't have an easy time of it this year. But here, in our old house that sits on the edge of an ancient flood plain, the river, one terrace below us, reclaimed its prehistoric right to spread swirls and new streams of rushing water through the trees and creek paths. In high water season, we hear the roiling rush night and day, through every open window of the house, the constant river sound comes in through the kitchen door and into the upstairs bedrooms at night. The white water flashes through the bare trees beyond the garden. In the evening, the river gleams as silver ribbons running through the woods. In contrast to the rushing noisiness on the other side of the trees, the frog pond is quite still, though brimming full, and on its stillness, trees are perfectly mirrored like an Escher print. One could get lost, staring into the labyrinth of the real trees and the merely reflected trees upside down on the surface. By day, dozens of frogs, the green ones and the bullfrogs, croak and paddle happily in their brief mating and spawning. An elegant wood duck pair dally in pre-nuptial bliss on the edge of to locate succulents, stems and tubers.

The house and the yard, high and dry like Noah's Ark on the flood, edge into spring with the noisy river as a back drop. In these warm days of early April, the morning sun creeps over this corner of the river, over the rushing water sounds. Early reddish buds on the maple give a scarlet haze to the morning air. The birds are resuming their spring calling, over-wintering juncos linger and trill from every limb. Their numbers down now, however, from the 50 or 60 that are here in full winter. White-throats have begun their sweet whistle of "Old Sam Peabody, Peabody, Peabody," sometimes just shortened to "Old Sam" with no Peabody at all, as one of our Amherst poets once remarked. Our phoebe constantly wheezes out his squeeze-toy call while seriously considering the eaves of our summer gazebo in the woods. The morning session we could call "Squirrels Gone Wild" begins as two exuberant bushy tails as zany and deranged as any kittens high on catnip, careen from tree base to tree base, flipping on their backs to tussle or fight with a broken branch on the ground. The two of them do back-flips and somersaults, race furiously to the lilacs to instantly stop and hold position in freeze-tag style before resuming a mad streaking and caroming like a pinball game out of control. Have to check on what they're getting into back there, maybe some strange grass or weed. Or is it just spring fever?

So we have made it through one more winter, and a thankfully mild one at that, compared to past years, and to the rest of the country. Warms days have coaxed out early tender green, and the shadbush billows whitely in the wind, early this year. In the evening, the river pathways through the woods turn to silver again as the sun goes down. More voices rise up in the dusk, an early woodcock has begun its calling and courting in the gleaming birch and stark alders. Hundreds of spring peepers with voices like silver bells rise up in song. Our Tribal friends have recently told us that in their culture, the peepers sing for the elders who have passed away this winter. It is a good way to be reminded of them.

And just now, amid these thoughts, into the fading light wings and lurches our favorite brown bat! She's back, somehow, miraculously. She has not died with the tens of thousands in the winter caves. All alone, for the time being, our bat wings erratically over her familiar territory in the yard, between the peak of the old house and the towering maples. Exactly like last year. The joy of return is mutual, and seems to pass between us like a current .We are thrilled and relieved to see our friend on leather wings, swooping low

over our heads near the campfire before going out over the rushing
river pushing this year's high water to the sea.

Preserving the Land

"The land was ours
Before we were the land's..."

So begins Robert Frost's poem *The Gift Outright*. The words always stuck with me but it seemed like he had gotten it backwards. It always seemed to me that we, the human beings, belonged to the land first, not the other way around. At any rate, before long, we started carving it up and fighting over it like so many fleas arguing about which one of them owns the dog. The land, the Earth, go on forever, but the fleas come and go.

Our little comer of the planet along the Millers River has a history of its own going back hundreds of millions of years. That history got an early jolt here when an earthquake cracked the continent in this place and sent the prehistoric Millers in its westerly flow, angling off radically to the north to meet the Connecticut River near the spot we have named after a French King. Over time, glaciers, mastodons and mammoths came and went. At some point around 10,000 years ago, native peoples arrived, eventually settled, cleared the banks of our river and planted com. It's been said that this river formed the southern limits of the Sokoki, who settled what we now call Northfield (Squakeagh) and who resisted the English colonists as long as they could, well into the 1750s.

The laws of nature have always had their way with our land. That prehistoric earthquake set our modern river on its way. More recently came the floods of 1936 and 1938, which also forever changed the river bottomlands, scouring away the meadows that our great grandfather Judah Smith had acquired in the 1880s.

Judah himself was descended from a long line of river tribal people from the mouth of the Connecticut, displaced by the arrival of the early colonists. Generations of family moved up and down the Connecticut, until by chance and good fortune he arrived here to found our family on the bend in this river with his strong-willed Scottish wife, Elizabeth.

By the fifth generation of us living on those lands along the Millers, the post-flood meadows have become woodlands, home to wild things like the woodcock, wood thrush, wood duck and wood turtle—meadows to woodlands...you get the picture. But the history of a place can weigh heavy on your shoulders when, through accidents of time and destiny, you find your time has come to decide what to do with your small corner of the planet over which you have stewardship.

At some point, like all aging baby-boomers, one begins to actually think about the future! There was no lack of suggestions for the future of our few acres over the years. One of our former selectmen quipped years ago that surely a way could be found to fill in some of the swamps in the floodplain for building condominiums, even maybe putting them on stilts!

A Russian visitor, Nina, upon seeing our land, was thrilled. "Ah, you are the first real American capitalist that I have met!"

Never having considered myself the likes of a capitalist, I asked her for an explanation of the apparent insult. "You own all this land," was her response, private ownership of property being forbidden and impossible in the Soviet Union of those days. She suggested that I at least plant potatoes here.

For many people, the imperative to enter land productivity into the account ledgers in terms of dollars has been the driving factor in determining the value of that land. And yet, how do you put into dollar terms the value of solace, the peace of mind, the peace provided by wild things, the slow flight of the heron over the woods, the glistening perfection of the otter on the green river bank, or the whippoorwill in the early dark?

When the time comes to act, most of us can recognize the moment. This year it was clearly time for me to get in touch with the Franklin Land Trust people. Expert guidance and careful shepherding by two officers of the land trust, Alain Peteroy and Rich Hubbard, had me and my land on a clear preservation trajectory in no time at all.

This land trust had already protected more than 15,000 acres in our region and they knew what to do. So we began the process of placing a Conservation Restriction on our land. The details were not overly complicated: an appraisal of the land value in dollars; a narrative of the conservation value in terms of wildlife habitat; a number of government forms; approval by local and state officials; and within a year, the land we love was preserved and protected in perpetuity. In essence, we retain the property and all the rights to sell it, but forego the option to change or alter it from its existing natural state.

Talk about peace of mind! We, the human occupants of this place, were the only ones able to assure that our few acres would remain wild by signing the proper papers, and we can now take our place along with all the other creatures who have called this land theirs since the beginning of time, and who can now continue to do so.

When you learn to think of history in terms of circular movement and cycles that return upon themselves, it's easier to do what we did. Maybe it was no accident after all that our ancestor Judah came here to what was meadowland cleared by native peoples. Maybe things do happen for a reason. What is clear is that we have come full circle, preserving the land in his name in a way, and securing for ourselves the certainty that all of us who live in this spot will have a place to be ourselves for as long as forever lasts.

(June 2008)

Village Sketchbook

Village Sketchbook

So long, Joe (*November,2005*)

That's the trouble with reading the obits. Sometimes you find names you wish you hadn't. Sometimes the names represent people way too young to be there, other times there may be names of old timers that signal another chapter closed.

Joe lived down the street from us when I was growing up. I guess he was a bachelor then, living with his mother, a sturdy kindly lady with wireframe glasses, who was always walking somewhere or always working in her garden. She herself lived to be quite old, thanks in part, I'm sure, to the durability of people from the old country. Anyway, when I was ten or so, Joe seemed to be quite a character. Always a toothy jack-o'lantern smile and a dry Turners Falls way of talking, all sharp understatement and wise-crack. Joe and I had a few things in common: at 10 years old, I liked to watch ducks on the river, and Joe liked to shoot them, for example. So oftentimes when he headed down the bank to the river with his gun, I'd go along too with my dog who was always ready for a walk, and we'd cover his beat from the Narrows to the Rod and Gun Club. He never shot any ducks, they keeping just out of reach and too far away, but he liked looking at them with me through my father's WWII binoculars. I did have a plan however, just in case, to save my duck friends if ever they came too close within shotgun range: I figured I'd stand up at the last minute or call the dog and wave to somebody I thought I saw back at Red Rocks, but I never had to do anything like that, because the ducks were too smart. "Best eyes in the country," Joe would say about them. So we talked mostly about wildlife and about the creatures that lived along the river and he would tell me things, for example, like which ones were the best to eat. Things like that. So many's the glorious late fall afternoon or early winter evening we'd wander the river bank, him patient with me and my 10-year-old's questions, and me keeping him talking while I kept an eye out to make sure nothing came too close to that shotgun.

Suddenly, I was grown up and it was 45 years later. I don't know too much about what happened to Joe, but he had been living out his life not too far away. Then last summer, in the hospital room in the bed next to my father, I heard that voice behind a curtain. Same voice from back on Carlisle Avenue, and the river bank. There was Joe after all these years, feisty as always .Scheming and anxious to get out of that hospital room. So I introduced myself again and we were pretty surprised to see each other after all that time. He let on enough to show that he sort of knew what I had been up to, and I confessed I knew a few things about him too, even though we hadn't laid eyes on each other all that time. We spent a couple of minutes shooting the breeze, then we both went back to what was on our minds, being in that room.

And now I read that he's passed on. Funny how fate serves up little coincidences to keep you alert. I'm glad we had a chance to say hello again, and then good-bye. Things like that are meant to happen.

So long Joe, see you around.

Joe Banash, 1922-2005

The House on Second and L *(November)*

Saturday morning routine usually takes me down L Street on my way to the river. I always pause at the corner of Second and L to look in the windows of the old house there. By straining my eyes I can see through the ripped curtain and cracked window glass into the old kitchen, down the hall to the next room, light coming in from the farthest window opposite. This is where my grandparents had lived. There were a couple of uncles in there too, back in the 1950s. My imagination has to work hard, because the house really isn't there any more, a wreck of a place torn down a little more than a year ago. But before it was a derelict, it was a home, perched on the corner of a lively neighborhood. Turners Falls-style brick buildings extended down the street to Unity Park, and friends lived in some of them. At the end of the row houses was the wooden house where the family of Frenchie Boivin lived, a boisterous jovial man who called everyone *"cousin"* with a French accent on the second syllable, a québécois wool hat on his head winter and summer, a lumberjack beard and a hearty laugh, and probably never had a bad day in his life. Also on our side of the street was Hermanson's Hall where once Raymie Gray showed us bullet holes in the wall from when things got going one Saturday night back in the 1930s. Or at least that's the legend kids told each other in those days. Williams Garage was the anchor of the neighborhood. Set up in the early part of the century, it was the link between the village blacksmith shop and service stop for the automobile. Everyone dropped by there to chew the fat at some point of the day, to watch cars being fixed, buy gas, get their wheels aligned, and so on. My father toiled there as best he could for over forty years and managed to get things done on time in spite of the interruptions. The wading pool was next to the garage where we all spent countless summer afternoons, trying out goggles and flippers from Pipione's and Rockdale, and once we tired of scaring each other pretending to be the Creature from the Black Lagoon, surging up from the depths of the middle of the pool (all of two feet deep), we'd hot-foot it over the burning tar street to mooch a soda from the machine in the garage (my father was a push-over for giving soda to kids), and we'd stand in the cool of the garage talking about our swimming adventures.

But it's the old house on the corner that looms largest in our memories at Christmas time. There was always a family party there on Christmas Eve. My grandmother Clara,whom we never called Clara or anything else, except Mimi (try as I could I could never pronounce *mémé* in French, so Mimi stuck) and grandfather Joe always hosted the family the night before Christmas. The French tradition was to go to Midnight Mass and then return home for the feast. I don't remember going to the Mass so much. I think we mainly just had the party, until well after midnight. The house had a lot of connected rooms, full of towering furniture and all kinds of hiding places where all of us cousins could romp and play and roll on the floor while the grown-ups laughed and talked. And they were LOUD. French Canadians are boisterous and never dull, especially at parties. There were plenty of other ethnic groups mixed into the family by then of course: uncles and aunts who were Welsh, Polish, Irish, but French hilarity dominated. There were always plenty of *petites galettes* that Mimi made, her famous *tourtière* pork pies, ribbon candy, and all kinds of cake with very flashy frosting. Bright colors were very important to her! Grandpa Joe was in charge of showing the movies. He spent many years as projectionist at the Shea, so before the party was over, the whole family spread out in the living room, and with the old 16 mm clacking away we followed the bouncing ball, and sang Hark the Herald!, Joy to the World!, and Silent Night. When the reel where a pre-WWII Mickey Mouse playing Santa Claus came to an end, the party started breaking up. None too soon for my sister and me, who had spent the last hour with eyes fixed on the kitchen clock, convinced that surely Santa Claus would pass us over since it was well past midnight and we weren't home in our beds yet!

So now that house is gone. But the shell that it became shouldn't be too maligned, since once it was a vibrant home where people had lived out their lives. In its place, a new Habitat for Humanity home will soon go up. New people will move in, a new spirit and life will resume again in the house on the corner of Second and L.

What's Your Moniker? (*February 2006*)

Thank Heavens for Harold Fugere! His notebook was placed in my hands a few weeks ago by Susan Sans Soucie at the Carnegie Public Library.

Many of us knew Harold as the good-natured gym teacher with the whistle around his neck who listened patiently to every excuse in the book for us not wanting to go outdoors in late November to do calisthenics on Sheff Field or for not wanting to jump into the slimy communal shower afterwards. He taught hundreds of TFHS students to drive, always with quiet amusement and a gentle firmness like he was everybody's ideal uncle.

But he did something else before he passed away a few years ago.

Turners Falls is the town of a thousand nicknames, and Harold set out to record as many as he could in his notebook, which he left to the library.

Apparently, his inspiration to do this was sparked after Foggy Bourdeau's funeral in 1993 when Harold realized that a lot of people in town are known solely by their nicknames, with hardly anyone else knowing their real names. For example, Harold's classmate at St. Anne's School, Telesphore Ryan was known as "Tutu" and you can see why.

It would seem that hundreds of Turners Falls natives had the luck, or the curse, of being known by a nickname. Looking over Harold's lists, you're astounded by the variety and lyrical descriptive process at work. I suppose that an anthropologist or ethnologist would have a field day here. We know that Native Americans gave or took names according to exploits or tribal totems, European names came from trades and professions, physical characteristics, ancestry or regions, and so on. But Turners' *noms de guerre* defy categories: you can start out trying names attributed to physical traits like Bung Ears, Schnoz, Shorty, or Wheezer, or ethnic groups like Frenchy or Swede, Staciu or Pitou; you could go with adventures or exploits on or off the sports field like Cannon Novak, Bomber Martin, Bumper, or Machine Gun... But the further in you get, the richness, descriptive quality and imagination is dazzling: there's Buddah Allen, Lace Curtain Ambo, Yabut Berthiume, Hitler and Shadow Bogusz, Buttnut and Peg Leg Desautels, Powderpuff Shea and Bugsy Morin.

Growing up, I didn't ask questions, but now I wonder sometimes: where did Joe Barrel get his name (you can guess), why was my aunt named "Pete" and my uncle "Skunk"? Why was another uncle called "Tootsie" and my best friend's father called "Bow Wow"? My grandfather Alan was called "Abe" and his brother Hair Smith wasn't really called "Hair" (I figured because he was bald) but

"Herr" because he had studied German! Many of us knew the individuals called Chink, Bubbles, Sparks, Soupy Campbell and Jingles, but how did Dynamite Bakula, Pug Aldrich, Rainy Day and Fosdick Dolan get their names? And then there's Babe Fritz, Moon Mullins, Chico Paulin, Peachy T, Joe Dollar, Gizmo, Trip Treml and Murph Togneri. And we're just getting started. On the playground we met up with Krebs Maynard, Hoppy Cassidy, Fenton Yarmac and Coots. There's Buffer, Sprat, Ding Dong, Butts, PeeWee, Stretch, Brush, Popeye, and Pink, as well as Tink. It's fascinating and exhausting. And as Turners Falls natives know this is only a few of the hundreds of illustrious names Harold recorded.

What he didn't record, however, was *why*.

By the way, although his students didn't dare call him that, Harold Fugere's nickname was "Googe"!

The Shamrock on Avenue A *(March)*

If you stand on Avenue A with your back to Norm Emond's storefront where the AV House used to be, and the 5 and 10 Cent store before that, you can see it. Look across the street and up to the peak of the building and you'll see "AOH A.D. 1888" and that's where the shamrocks will be. That building, now named simply the Power Town Apartments, used to be known by everyone as the Hibernian Hall. Built by funds from the Ancient Order of Hibernians, it served the community for close to one hundred years.

The AOH was, and is, a fraternal society founded in Ireland hundreds of years ago. In this country the AOH became a socio-political organization made up of Irish immigrants and their descendants who joined together for social support, mutual advancement, and, in some instances, mutual safety and protection. At the time of the organization's growth in the Northeast, there was extreme prejudice and what would now be considered racial crimes perpetrated against the Irish. You have but to look to the cartoons of Thomas Nast, often credited with giving us the Republican elephant, the Democrat donkey, Uncle Sam and a jovial Santa Claus. He also gave us bigoted and inflammatory caricatures of the Irish whom he despised, often depicted as apes. So, in this climate, belonging to a support group like the Hibernian Order was a necessity. With thousands of Irish immigrants entering Massachusetts, fleeing 400 years of slavery and apartheid conditions in their own land, many reached Turners Falls to help dig the canals, build the railroads, and work in the mills. The AOH arrived with them as well, and the Hibernian Hall came to play an important role in the community. At the turn of the century, dances, political gatherings, and basketball games drew huge crowds there. Boxing matches, town meetings and other extravaganzas were also held at the Hibernian. The entrepreneur behind many events was the famous "Banisher" Shea who also founded and ran the Shea Theater. There are legends around town as to how he got his nickname, but my theory is linguistic: some say he banished something or someone from his sight, but I see a connection between "Banisher" and "*Bainisteoir*"Ba, a Gaelic word meaning "Manager" (and it sounds like Shea was busy managing everything going on in town!). The words are pronounced identically, except that the Gaelic word slips in a flick of the tongue to add the letter *t* in the middle of the word. Who knows? With Gaelic as the native language of most of the immigrant families at the end of the 1800s, this could quite possibly be the origin of the nickname.

During the 50s and 60s, many of us remember the Rag Shag parades on Halloween that ended at the Hibernian Hall with prizes being distributed for various costumes. The High School scheduled basketball games there, adult leagues found a home there, Cub Scouts used it for meetings and yearly events. But the day-to-day role of the Hibernian probably had the most profound effect of all on the community. For a lot of kids in Turners, it was a home away from home. It was a bright and warm place, a place you could go to get away from unpleasant stuff at home, burn off adolescent energy and tension, play basketball until you dropped, and take a warm shower afterward. And if you needed it, you could get support from the man who ran the place, John Skrypek. He was universally respected and admired by everyone who made the long climb up those stairs. He was always stern but smiling, giving no-nonsense advice, fatherly support and a good boot in the behind, if needed. I suppose he was something of a saint, was John Skrypek.

But those memories have faded. With the renewal and renovation that came with Silvio Conte's plan for downtown revitalization, the Hall lost its community role, the building was transformed. For a hundred years however, it provided a gathering place, a safe haven, and a stabilizing presence that could really be helpful in this community nowadays. All that's left are the two Shamrocks high up over the Avenue to remind us of the vibrant days of the old Hibernian.

From Millers Falls to Fenway, 1912 *(April)*

The sun filters through half-drawn shades in the quiet den in the house on Pleasant St. An old man sits primly in the wooden rocker. The left arm that fired the most feared fastball in this part of the state now rests quietly on the arm of the chair, raised once in a while to make a point as the man tells his stories. His two feet in old fashioned lace-up shoes, side-by-side, rarely moving. There's a lingering smell of cigar smoke in the air. The desk and shelves are lined with mementos: various baseballs, a glove, team pictures of rock-jawed men in small baseball caps, family pictures, pictures of dogs long gone. The old man travels back in time to the turn of the century when he and the game of baseball were young. The other man in the room is one of the local reporters who, from time to time, make the trip to Ervingside to chat with a local baseball legend.

The old man in the rocker is Douglas Smith, born in our homestead down here on the Flat in 1893 when this was still a working farm along the Millers River. Doug was born and raised in this house, and lived here along with four brothers (one of whom was my grandfather Abe), his father Judah, and his mother Elizabeth recently emigrated from Aberdeen, Scotland.

Doug discovered early on that he loved baseball and that no one could hit his fastball. He went from playing ball in the pasture and neighborhood ball field to town teams, unbeatable with his brothers making up most of the infield. Abe was his catcher, Clint was his third baseman, Butch played second, and Billy was the manager. By the time he reached Turners Falls High School, he was striking out upwards of twenty batters a game, and rival high schools were trying to lure him to switch schools and pitch for them. It's told in the family that his mother Elizabeth, a stern Calvinist, would allow no breaking of the Sabbath, keeping all family members sitting quietly in the kitchen on a Sunday with nothing but the ticking of the clock to break the silence of a hot summer day. However, she did make one exception: from out behind the barn you could hear a regular *whoosh*! And *thwack*! as Doug pitched hard to his younger brother Abe, that ball burning into the catcher's mitt and resounding as far as the silent Protestant kitchen.

Then at 18 years of age, he found himself on the pitcher's mound in the brand new Fenway Park, having been scouted and hired by the Boston Red Sox, who were into a pennant-winning season, with the World Series in sight. The trouble was that on this particular day, the streaking Sox were being pushed around by the lowly St Louis Browns, a second division team barely holding onto 7th place. Doug's teammates included the likes of Hall-of-Famer Tris Speaker, Duffy Lewis, and Harry Hooper. The Sox manager was Jake Stahl, and he called this young Millers Falls boy Douglas Welden Smith off the bench, fresh from TFHS with a two-hundred dollar contract. Over the next three innings, Doug stopped the Browns' romp and only gave up four hits, one run with one strikeout. The Boston Herald sportswriter R.E. McMillan described Smith's performance this way: "Young Smith did very commendable work while he was on the hill-top. He had fine speed, a sharp breaking curve, and good control. After a year or two of seasoning, he should be heard from." (Hugh Campbell, Franklin Ledger, Oct 1987) Doug seemed to be on the right track, but Boston had a hefty pitching rotation that year: "Smokey" Joe Wood (34-5) Bediant (20-10) and Collins (14-8). Doug sat the bench and was farmed out to the Minors at the end of the season. The Sox went on to win the Pennant and 4 World Series by 1918. Doug Smith's Major League career was destined to have lasted only three innings however. In the Minors, he played in various line-ups along the Eastern seaboard, winding up with the Syracuse Stars in 1916, when he faced the Red Sox in an exhibition game. That day, the Sox manager had a choice: send George Herman (Babe) Ruth out to the mound to duel with Doug Smith, or send in Ernie Shore. He decided on Shore, luckily enough, because the Stars took the Sox 5-2, jumping all over Shore, while Doug held the mighty Sox to six hits. Again, when Doug was called on to pitch for the Stars against the Chicago Cubs and another Hall-of-Famer, Mordacai (Three-Finger) Brown, the game was called on account of rain, with Doug ahead.

During World War I, Doug was drafted and stationed at Camp Upton in New York, where he played ball for the Army team until war's end. He played on through 1922 with various Minor League and semi-pro teams. Those were the rough-and tumble days which he used to regale us with stories about during Sunday dinner. Those were still the days of bare-knuckle baseball when he pitched with a plug of Slippery Elm chewing tobacco in his back pocket for throwing the occasional spit-ball; he used to laugh in telling us how the catcher or the ump would have to wipe off after he laid one of those over the plate! He claimed that most of the players kept a pint of whiskey in the dug-out, and that many's the time they had to fight their way out of Brattleboro or Keene ballparks with their fists, when from time to time they rolled up the score on the local team, showing no mercy. Other memorable games were at the Park Villa Driving Park when Doug finished a game on Saturday night in upstate New York, and caught a train down to Turners Falls for a game there at 3 p.m. on Sunday! ($75 a game was too good to pass up in those days.)

When his pro-ball days were over, Doug went to work for the Millers Falls Paper Company where he worked for forty years. He continued playing baseball locally, but an appendicitis operation slowed down his fastball. One of his last comeback games was against the Colored All-Stars that came to town in 1924. He pitched six innings, then couldn't get out of bed for days.

* * * *

As fate would have it, one day in September 1973, the year he turned eighty, it came time for him to leave his meticulous home on Pleasant St. I was the only one in the family unemployed at the time, so it was up to me and my aunt Pete to drive him to the nursing home. As we wheeled him up the walk to the home, a number of the residents were out on the veranda taking the sun. Wouldn't you know, one of the old timers recognized him and called out, "Well, Doug Smith! What are *you* doing here?" Automatically, Doug's fingers went up to touch the visor of his cap, his face brightened in the old winning smile, much I'm sure, as he the day he walked off the Field of Dreams for the last time.

Within three weeks he was gone, like a wisp of smoke. But these April days, when baseball fever takes over after the long winter months, there are stirrings out in the pasture and behind the barn, the faint sounds of an ancient game of catch and you know who's out there, if you listen carefully.

Remembrance of Two Soldiers *(May)*

The three of us were sitting on the roof of the house on Carlisle Avenue one Sunday morning in late May, many years ago. We were up there supposedly to repair roofing shingles, but we were also enjoying the fine view of the neighborhood and the Connecticut River flowing quietly through the Narrows. One of us was my father, the other was my father's school friend and life-long, next-door neighbor Babe Fritz. And then there was me, fresh from my second year in college and full of my Sophomore self (they don't call us "wise fools" for nothing). I was going on about my coming year in France, sailing on the Queen Mary for Paris in August, and so on. Babe listened. He was the carpenter, and we were sort of his helpers. Mostly we just talked and he worked. He was silent, an enigma. He only spoke in ironic terms, as I recall. Out of the blue he said "Just watch out when you get to Pig Alley." Then he went on hammering and whistling, and that was all he said. I guessed that by "Pig Alley" he meant *Pigalle*, a well-known red-light district in Paris. I had heard it mentioned in a piece of Hollywood fluff called *Irma La Douce* with Jack Lemmon and Shirley McClain, but they didn't teach us about Pigalle in French class.

Later though, my mother recalled an old WWII article that put Babe and Pigalle in perspective. After D Day, Babe's unit found itself fighting door-to-door through the streets of Paris. Right through Pigalle they fought, at the foot of the Basilica of the Sacré-Coeur, just below Montmartre, where Picasso, Renoir and Toulouse-Lautrec used to paint and hang out. It was summer and it was hot in 1944 with the German occupiers stubbornly resisting the allied troops who were taking back Paris, street by street. Babe, our future next-door neighbor, barely a young man of twenty at the time, found himself moving doorway to doorway, stepping out to shoot, ducking back in. At one point in the street fighting, according to the article, he found himself in the doorway of a café, and he heard someone say, "*excusez-moi*!" behind him, and when he turned , he saw a French bartender politely handing him a freshly poured glass of draft beer. Babe never drank, but he gulped down that beer without saying a word, kept stepping out and shooting, and was gone up the street. Somehow it made it into the papers, but I'm sure Babe wouldn't have told it himself.

He made it through the Liberation of Paris, and the Battle of the Bulge, and came home. But I know he paid a price for spending the best years of his youth in the war. Even back then, I could tell that this neighbor of ours spent long restless nights, cigarette after cigarette glowing in the dark until morning when it would be time to go fishing, trying not to think about the enemy coming after him again and again in the dark.

That fall, after the conversation on the roof, freshly arrived in Paris, I went through Pigalle, marveling that just twenty years before our taciturn neighbor had battled through those same streets. Some of the buildings still had holes from the fighting and shelling. Even now, in 2006, when I bring my High School students through that Pigalle neighborhood on the way to Montmartre and the Basilica, I tell them the story of a young guy from our little town who helped liberate Paris more than sixty years ago. Kids need to get a sense of how this history all fits together.

* * * *

There's a quiet suburb in another part of Paris, where we live from time to time when we're not in Millers Falls. Near a park, where well-dressed French children play, scream and romp on the slides and see-saw, there's a plaque on the outside wall of a garden. The street is shady and quiet (except for the screaming kids in the playground), well-kept, sparkling in the morning after the nightly washing crews pass through the streets hosing everything down. The plaque honors a young American from New York, Anthony Vigiliante, who died on this spot in 1944 in the fight to drive the Germans out. And every year, without fail, on May 8 (Victory over Germany) and on November 11, the town holds a simple ceremony on this spot and makes sure there are bouquets of flowers to honor and thank the soldier who died there. Whenever I've walked down this street, whether it was long ago, taking our son to play in that park, or more recently, just out for a quiet walk in the evening, I always stop to think about this young man honored by the plaque, who in a lot of ways made it possible for me to be there, and who never got to be as old as I am now.

The wars come and go, call them Korea, Viet Nam or Iraq, the nation unites or divides, the wars are just or unjust. But it's mostly the small towns it seems, that provide the common people who pay the price. Sometimes they don't come back, oftentimes they do, to resume their lives as best they can. Simple stories of soldiers like these two could be repeated tenfold or a hundredfold in our town. It's just important to remember and reflect, each in our own way, on Memorial Day.

A Wedding in the Country *(July)*

It was to be a wedding under the full moon of July, and the planning had been going on for months. The relationship between the betrothed had already withstood the test of time, and so this event was finally going to happen!

Indeed, family and friends knew that our Jesse was a goner years ago when the winsome Sarah first set her sights on him! With the dwindling number of bachelors in our aging clan, we all watched the process with keen interest, for in our opinion, the groom was quite a catch. A brilliant and diligent scholar, a graduate of the best Massachusetts schools and a doctoral candidate at Cornell, our young man was destined for a rich and rewarding career in the field of ecology. And Sarah herself was bringing a promising artistic career to this union, so the future certainly looked bright.

My main job in all of this, as uncle to the bridegroom and father of the Best Man, was to make sure that said Best Man, Kevin, got to the chapel on time. No small planning chore, since the night before the beginning of the rehearsal and ceremonies, we were thousands of miles away deep in the limestone moonscape of the Burren, County Clare. We had spent hours sitting in the middle of an Iron Age ring fort, contemplating the ironies of Irish history! Nevertheless, through the very familiar workings of a series of modem transportation connections, within hours, deep in culture shock and weary with time traveling, we were in the chapel, the night before the wedding.

The wedding itself was a celebration of rural village life as one rarely sees nowadays. For the young groom was truly a product of the hamlet of West Whately, his parents, my sister Sue and her husband Bob Bellemare, having left their native town of Turners Falls and headed for the rural hills in the '70's. The inhabitants of this neighborhood have a deep sense of place: it's a spot tucked away in the hills between lake and forest, farmland and country garden. Dogs and children have always roamed freely between the scattered houses and as often as not, the families here have played an important role in raising each generation of young ones—dogs and children alike!

So it was with great pride that July afternoon in the 1896 chapel that neighbors and extended family participated in the wedding. To see our Wild Boys, one the groom and one the Best Man, dressed to the nines with the radiant bride between them, brought back memories of the two boys when they weren't acting so civilized. They have been as close as brothers, these two first cousins, and had traipsed every inch of wood, field, shore and swamp, near and far - from Whately and Barton's Cove to Cape Cod, Florida, Brazil, Ireland, and Brittany. There was many a tear in the eye of those gathered there as the memories of the boys now grown to strong young men washed over family and neighbors alike.

As for ceremony, it was mercifully brief. The heat was baking those of us in suits and ties, even though the windows were wide open and the late afternoon sun was going slowly down. The air fluttered with fans placed at every row and provided some respite. The bride's uncle did the honors as pastor, vows and rings were exchanged while we fanned away in the late afternoon heat of the chapel.

Then it was time to party! A huge tent had been set up in the field opposite the chapel, the cows kept at bay behind new fencing. Again this was a communal effort: the wedding party had worked the whole evening before, as well as much of the morning, under the direction of the bride-to-be, who had worked out every detail herself. Neighbors Dickenson had donated the use of the field, the Mahars and the Newland-De Tullios provided the electricity and tech support, best friend Jamie provided the wedding march, and so on. French Gypsy jazz accompanied the cocktail hour, the champagne flowed and the revelry began. The Bellemares, Brules, and Aherns had traveled up from Turners Falls, Millers Falls and Greenfield, as well as from Florida, to represent the bride and groom's immediate family, while friends came in from Maine, New York, New Jersey, all from far and near for this joyous event. For hours, the 150 guests mingled, chatted, feasted and partied until dark.

As dusk drew near, many of the elder guests drifted off, but the rest of us were just getting started. And then there were the bats. The nightly spectacle of the bats began in the fading light as hundreds of the creatures began queuing up and pouring out of the chapel roof in the dusk. The bat spectacle had been worked into the wedding plan, just before the sparklers and skyrockets were scheduled, the natural and human events blending into the age-old cycle. The dancing went on late into the night, children running through the dark field, sparklers trailing, mixing in with flickering lightning bugs in the distance. And above it all the full moon of July shone down, keeping a watchful eye on the revelers, as they drifted home, off into the darkness.

Sarah Ahern and Jesse Bellemare were married on July 8, 2006.

The Eleventh Hour *(November)*

The Eleventh hour of the eleventh day of the eleventh month. They had a sense of the dramatic in those days. The Great War, the War To End All Wars was over on Nov 11, 1918. The cannons finally fell silent, the slaughter of the flower of European youth ended. The towns around here joined the war belatedly, like the rest of the country, and the impact didn't seem that great. In fact you have to look pretty hard, up in Highland Cemetery to find graves that indicate WWI service. I can't say that the war affected this house down on the Flat very much either. Doug Smith, drafted by the Red Sox in 1912, did get drafted by the Army in 1917, but he spent the war drilling, marching, and playing baseball for Camp Upton in New York. One great-grandfather, James Heffernan, recently emigrated from Killorglin in Ireland, joined the Army by lying about his age (he was actually older than he claimed), but it did provide a steady job and square meals, for what they were worth.

Many of his countrymen, however, were not so lucky. In Ireland, and throughout the working class British Isles, tens of thousands of young men joined the British Army for the same reasons, figuring it would be easy money and a walk in the park. Many of them became part of what was known as the "Great Falling of 1916", 90 years ago this past July. At the Battle of the Somme more than 60,000 young men died on the Allied side alone, most of them in one day of futile fighting. Officers sent these men over the top in wave after wave to be mowed down by German machine guns, and gained hardly a few yards when the day was over.

Years ago, I had the chance to talk with two men who were there on that day now more than ninety years in the past. It happened that one day, after my English class in the Berber village where I was teaching, one of my students came to tell me his father wanted to meet me. I actually did have the time to walk out to his village, and knowing it would be an insult to Moroccan hospitality to turn down the invitation, we started out along the dusty road through the Middle Atlas foothills. After an hour and a half of steady walking, we reached the village made up of earthen houses the color of the hills, set in the draw of a dry stream.

The house of my student's father was below ground, strangely enough, but it was definitely cooler down there than the baking temperatures above. Down the ladder we went to a dark room where an elderly man sat cross-legged on a thick rug decorated with the designs typically found in this region. He spoke clearly and carefully in French, tossing in Arabic from time to time, and once we had completed the required litany of inquiries about the health of all the members of the family, thanking Allah for the good health of each, we talked politics and history.

On the wall hung a framed photograph of a man in a WWI French Army uniform. The sweeping black moustache and turban tipped me off that the young man in the portrait, and the old man pouring my tea were the same. The mint tea arched from the silver teapot into glasses set on the low table. The pot was held high over the glasses and was poured Arab style, precisely and noisily. His moustache was now white, as was his beard, but his eyes burned the same as those in the portrait. As a young man growing up in the French Protectorate of Morocco, he was drafted in 1914. He had fought at the Somme and at Verdun, and had survived to be pouring me tea in this lost corner of North Africa. He described what it was like to survive during those times, but coming from a harsh existence on the edge of the Sahara, he had an easier time than most, except for the cold. When we had finished our tea and conversation, I indicated I needed to start back, climbed up the ladder and headed out along the dark road, lit only by the stars. Some of his words were burned into my mind as I thought about what I had heard, on the long walk back.

"We Moroccans fought hard in those battles, we are famous warriors and strike terror in the hearts of our enemies. When the Germans knew they were fighting against us, they would flee before us. They knew we fight well with our knives, and we never,never took any prisoners..."

Another glimpse into that long ago war came on a quiet Sunday afternoon in a calm suburb of Paris. We were sitting in the kitchen after Sunday dinner listening to Georges Bourgeois recount in bits of phrases and halting sentences what it was like to have been there. He was a young man in Paris when the war broke out in August of 1914. His father made him join the army right away, assuming he would move up the ranks before the war got too nasty. His father was right. During a long initial period which the French called *la drôle de guerre (*the strange war) both sides entrenched themselves and there was very little fighting. This was the time of the war when Germans, French, and English took time out from sniping at each other on Christmas Eve to sing carols and play a game of soccer in the No Man's Land between them. *Silent Night, Stille Nacht, Sainte Nuit,* all blended briefly on the battlefield. It is a well-known fact that the foot soldiers on both sides had more in common with each other than they did with their own officers. The old social system was about to be swept away after this war, this was the last gasp of the old aristocracy. Officers on all sides, often drawn from families of the nobility, had few qualms about sending the peasantry and working class conscripts over the top as cannon fodder.

Young Georges did rise up through the ranks, although at one point, one of his responsibilities was as a running courier, going from trench to trench with messages for the officers. He did live to tell us about Verdun and the Somme and what he saw there. Breton, Normand, Touraine peasants and farmers surviving in calf-deep freezing water in the trenches, the gas attacks, the rats, being sent wave after wave over the top to slaughter, and about a man called the *nettoyeur des tranchées*, "the cleaner of the trenches", oftentimes a butcher in civilian life, who was one of the last through the trenches after a battle to finish off his French comrades who were mortally wounded and suffering. This man delivered the *coup de grâce* with the knife of his trade.

The Great Falling it was, with millions of British, Germans and French dying in what was a stalemate. The peace that ensued was just something of a parenthesis in a long war, for it started up all over again within a generation.

It is said in these parts that the Irish-American poet Joyce Kilmer , author of the poem that begins "*I think that I shall never see, a poem as lovely as a tree...*", wrote about the old maple growing at the Farren Hospital. The legend has it that in 1917, as a guest of the Farren family who were old friends of his, he was recuperating there from wounds received in France. After his sojourn at the Farren, he went back to the war and was killed in the trenches, another one of that Lost Generation. The old maple came down just a few years ago, a metaphor for the last survivors of that war. There are now fewer than a dozen veterans (members of that Last Man Club of the WWI battalions) left from all sides out of the countless millions who were caught up in the entangling politics of 1914. On November 11, as we remember the fallen, we also need to remember that if we don't learn the lessons of history, we are doomed to repeat history again and again and again.

Hidden Landscape : A Film Preview Event *(February 2007)*

February First. The night of the full Snow Moon. People gathering in the hall of the old mill on the banks of the Great Falls. Tribal peoples from the Wampanoag, Mohawk, and Narragansett are here, scattered throughout the seventy-five or so people quietly waiting. Abenaki, Pocumtuck, and Sokoki are also present in spirit. Native peoples and the rest of us, allies, or potential allies are waiting, most of us on the verge of a voyage of discovery this evening. (We are gathered in the Discovery Center after all!) What most of us don't know, but are about to find out, is that the Hidden Landscape portrayed by Theodore Timreck in his film is all around us in our valley and hills, and we are about to learn how to see into it.

"This film is not offered as politics, not as science. It is offered as art." And with that, Timreck begins the premier presentation of his film, a work still in progress. The filmmaker is a research associate with the Arctic Studies Center of the Smithsonian's National Museum of Natural History.

The film opens with some historical perspective, giving us a context in the linear European way, in which to peer into and learn about the cyclical, four dimensional native-people time. Timreck introduces us to generations of antiquarians who investigated the ancient stone formations and mounds in our national landscape and who oftentimes applied faulty scientific techniques with enthusiasm, determination, and visionary imagination. These antiquarians kept the mystery of sacred places alive through the colonial and modern eras of this country by wondering, exploring and questioning until finally in this century non-native people have begun listening and perhaps moving to action to protect these sites. The film envelops us and takes us far afield, through landscapes far and near, from Vermont and New Hampshire to Labrador, the Dingle Peninsula in the west of Ireland, to Stonehenge, to Carnac in the west of Brittany. Although this historical and geographical perspective also includes visits to sites in Ohio, Virginia, and Kentucky, a good part of Timreck's film focuses more on some recently discovered stone ruins in our own region. Hills, forests, ledges and outcroppings, glacial erratics materialize in familiar shapes. This is *our* landscape, *our* hills and rivers. We are reminded that 450 generations of native people (12,000 linear years) have kept the world in a state of harmony and balance, and that they have left signs of their time spent here. We are reminded that there are places still around us, sacred places revered by generations of tribal peoples, but that these places, many of them kept secret up to now, are in increasing danger.

When the lights come on, after 90 minutes of intriguing film, Doug Harris, Tribal Historic Preservation Officer for the Narragansetts, steps to the front of the hall, and takes us to the next level of understanding. His message is carefully woven using calm and inclusive language, circular open gestures to illustrate his meaning. He evokes the Pocumtuck, the native peoples of this exact spot, who had lived here for 12,000 years and who were present among us in spirit. He evokes the Great Falls, next to which we are assembled, which have always been a place of truce, peace and harmony. "Is this not true," he asks, "that we are in need of peace, balance and harmony now, more than ever?" The native peoples who lived here before knew, as do their descendants, the sites in this landscape that were honored for thousands of years, places where the physical world and the spiritual world met together in balance. The tribal peoples now need the help of allies. "There are not enough of us to go around," says Harris. His message becomes clear. On the local level, we need to enter a pact with one another, towns and tribes, to protect these sacred sites. The United South and Eastern Tribes Association has been working on a way to reach out to non-native people so that all may assume stewardship of these sites in the Hidden Landscape. This has been the point of the film, true in the film-maker's desire to produce art: the scenes are breath-taking, the mysteries evoked prod our curiosity, open our awareness,and Doug Harris steps up to provide the political inspiration. Towns and tribes. Tribes and towns. The assembly in the long hall draws to a close, with small groups lingering, getting acquainted and re-acquainted.

Outside, the full moon with a wide snow ring shines down through the frosty air. Geese sleep on the rocking dark waters of the Connecticut not two hundred yards from us, the eagles shift on their perch near the nest towering over the cove. Each of us leaves with our own thoughts about what to do with this new inspiration, what path next to take.

The Cottage on Commercial Street *(March)*

The crowd builds Saturday night at the Shea Theater , Avenue A. Roger Salloom is doing a benefit for the theater, and all sorts of people are showing up: some hard-core Salloom-heads, others vaguely familiar with his free concert reputation at the Pines, and others who are looking to break up a late winter Saturday night. Me, I'm headed for a reunion with my old friend. The evening is to feature an award-winning documentary on Roger's life, *So Glad I Made It*, followed by a bit of Q+A with the filmmaker Chris Sautter, then a set by Roger himself. They don't mention the 'prelude' on the program. That's because it's a private showing: It's playing inside my head. It features a couple of young guys ready to revolt in the summer of '65. Maybe this prelude could be called *Roger and Me*. That was the year our paths crossed, before either of us was famous. I'm still not famous, not by a long shot, not even working on it, and Roger's making something of a living out of being the least famous Best Songwriter in America.

The prelude starts (this private showing) when I got my ticket out of Turners for that summer long ago, finally escaping years of working on tobacco by landing a dish-washing job in a home-style restaurant on Commercial St. in Provincetown that was run by a Millers Falls family—Wes Felton, his wife Mildred and son Richard. Roger was working on getting out of Worcester that same summer, and our paths were about to intersect. He actually wrote a song called *"Gotta Get Out of Worcester"* that dallied with becoming famous, but didn't quite make it. The Feltons ran one of the three top restaurants in P-town at the time, The Cottage, and it was wildly popular with waiting lines out the door and down Commercial Street.

Provincetown in those days was an eclectic mix of artists, writers, Portuguese fishing families, folk musicians, and a small but growing gay community. You could catch Nina Simone at the Atlantic House, the Jim Kweshkin Jug Band at the Blues Bag, maybe even Mississippi John Hurt. If you were lucky you could see a drunk and pugnacious Norman Mailer get tossed out of a bar on his arrogant arse. My best friend Rod Bergiel and I, imagining bohemian adventures like those of Jack Kerouac and Neal Cassady, had to be there, to make that P-town scene. So I took the job washing dishes at Felton's. I could see the harbor out my window through the steam of my dishwasher. It sure beat picking tobacco in Whately. It was *clean.*

This is when Roger showed up. He managed to get a job as busboy at The Cottage, so right away he outranked me. Usually it seemed like I was just getting ahead of my dirty dishes pile when Roger would show up with another mountain of dishes and silverware to do. As testimony to his deep humanity and understanding of this repetitive indignity (his words, not mine) that he was committing, he'd dump the new mess of breakfast or dinner plates full of table scraps, maple syrup and cigarette butts in my corner and gently apologize. It truly concerned him to have to be doing this, but we both needed the money. That was the beginning of a wonderful friendship. We hit it off right away, even though Roger was one station above me in the kitchen caste system.

A group of us managed to rent a place not far from the restaurant, a converted barber shop, and settled in. We were on the verge of starting the musical bohemian summer of our lives. Already at that time, Roger had a crowd of musician friends and a lot of them were in Provincetown, drawn by the folk scene and the lifestyle in this village set between the dunes and the sea. Every evening after work, a jam session got going, with Roger in the middle of it plus anybody else with a blues harp or guitar who happened to be in town at the time. Roger would wham away on his guitar, and he *belted* out his music, lots of Leadbelly, blues, and lilting ballads he wrote himself. Musically, I was way out of my league, having left my piano accordion back in Turners. Besides, the only tunes it would accept to play were polkas and marches. Definitely not cool in the age of Bob Dylan, Joan Baez and John Hammond.

It was a wonderful summer to be alive, footloose and a year out of high school, keeping the harsh realities of the Vietnam War and politics at arm's length for a while longer. Roger was just starting out, wondering about which road he would take, just beginning to try to find some answers, taking some newly-discovered truths around to show the rest of us through his songs.

The reel playing in my mind flickers out in black and white, and in the blink of an eye, I'm sitting in Turners again, the applause growing as the real movie at the Shea begins.

It does blend with the rerun in my head, that mental flashback over, and it's tracing the young Roger through his formative years, skipping the P-town part. As the film evolves, the portrait of an original artist emerges. On many levels, it's a fascinating and entertaining film about making music and it's all about Roger, his endearing quirks, non sequiturs, obtuse musings where he finds humor and irony that the rest of us miss—lots of vintage Roger and his music, the personality melding with the talent that so many in the valley have loved. What also emerges is the portrait of a somewhat reluctant pursuit of elusive fame and recognition. The path to success in the music business was going to take a fearsome toll and the movie leads us to wonder if this is what Roger really wants. The filmmaker captures the questioning part of Roger's psyche and the paradox of his musical life thus far: does the songwriter, composer-poet, dreamer and seer sacrifice health, self-esteem and family to do what the pursuit of fame requires? The film poses the question of what happens to an artist who won't sell out. It's really about an existential struggle between the artist and life's contradictions: choices about self-preservation, integrity, family, and his two sons.

The film eventually brings us full circle by ending with a wiser, whimsical and still crazy Roger, back to flirting with fame, ever the reluctant suitor, still the poet savoring the lyrical quality of his life, day by day—philosophical about the price he paid, musing about the ride so far. In hisown words, "So glad I made it."

Working on Tobacco *(June)*

We couldn't wait to get started! Most of the gang had turned 14 over the winter and spring, and so it was time for us to go to work, get a summer job. Ed Bourdeau and Bill Connelly, our teachers at TFHS signed us up in the spring, and before long we had our social security numbers that, little did we realize, would keep track of us for life.

Maybe if we had thought a little bit more about it, we would have put off joining the work force for just one more summer, maybe spending one more season playing baseball, hanging out at Thomas' pool, mowing lawns or loafing. But no, we were of age, our fathers and mothers, uncles and aunts had jobs at the paper mill or tool shop, brothers and sisters were on tobacco, so that's what we were supposed to do too. Join the labor force, for the next fifty years of our lives!

Working on tobacco meant getting up and catching the blue Consolidated Cigar Corporation bus at 5:45 to head down to the fields in Hatfield or Whately. My bus was driven by my math teacher, Eddie Bourdeau. He was a big burly guy (in my 14-year-old eyes) possessed with great authority, and a voice that could cut through fog, a crowded room, a tobacco field, or from the sidelines through a roaring crowd at high school football games. He always wore an impeccable blue workshirt, a jungle -style pith helmet, and white gloves, because he was allergic to tobacco leaves! Down the Valley we'd go in the quiet bus, most of us still half asleep, in our oversize work clothes and lunch pails.

Then began our introduction to the art and science of cultivating tobacco. First task early in the summer was to do the suckering. That meant we had to tie burlap bags to our behind through an ingenious method of twines and string, then sit down and drag our can for miles a day breaking off useless leaves between the stalk and good leaves of each plant. Thing is, when you break off a sucker like that, it squirts a sticky juice out onto your hands and forearms. That was our introduction to nicotine juice, and it convinced a lot of us to not even think of putting that tar into our lungs. It usually took several days for a crew of thirty of us to finish the suckering. At day's end, our fingers, clothes, even way up into our nostrils, were coated with a thick crust of nicotine juice and dirt. Not to mention having a sore butt from sliding it through miles of rows of tobacco plants in the summer heat for eight hours!

Next came the twisting. To help the plants grow up straight, they were guided by strings that were attached to each individual plant and to guide wires overhead. Before they grew up too high we needed to walk the rows and wrap strings between the leaves and up the stalks. That part was easy, and almost fun, except for the string burns and painful raw grooves you wore into the index finger. We could walk through the rows, twisting the strings, talking and singing without having to drag ourselves along on our behinds for hours.

Eventually, we began picking. First Pick, Second Pick, Third Pick. Starting at the bottom, First Pick meant taking the first three leaves and making a neat stack between plants before humping yourself forward on knuckles and burlap-covered backsides to the next two plants on your right and left. A hauler would drag a canvas basket down the rows between pickers and place the leaves in the basket, gently! If ever anyone of us bruised the leaves by careless picking, or a random thumb print on the delicate green surface, we got chewed out fiercely by one of the Polish overseers. Sometimes it was hard to tell why we were getting chewed out because their English was very approximate. But we knew he was mad. Since our leaves were going to wind up as highly prized outer wrappers for cigars like William Penn or White Owls, we usually had enough respect to keep the bruising down. After sitting down and picking for weeks, by Third and Fourth Pick we were kneeling! For miles! Just when your behind was healing, the pain and blisters transferred to your knees. Same routine: shuffle forward on your knees for miles, picking, stacking, and hauling.

But the word was out: pretty soon we'd be going on piece work, which meant that the speedsters, the older and experienced pickers among us, could start making real money. By then, we could pick standing up and move through the rows faster, each row picked being worth about 25 cents, so that by the end of the week you could make 60 or 70 dollars. For guys saving for college or a car, that was good money. This is where Mr. Bourdeau's math came in: he stood at the end of each row as pickers and haulers came out to move to the next rows. He tabulated each man or team's total accumulative number of rows picked, but of course he never got too close to the plants, because of the allergy I mentioned.

People like Dougie Reil, Don and Bobby Brown were the speedsters, racking up good scores day after day. One of the sweetest sounds was Mr. Bourdeau bellowing, "Waiting time!", because the pickers were too far ahead of the haulers or the tractors or the sewers in the barn, so we had to take a break while the system caught up with itself. The speeding pickers chafed at the wait, they figured they were losing money, but the rest of us crawled into the shade created by the water wagon to rest and catch our breath. By then it was full summer and the heat under the netting was extreme, not to mention the dust and orange insecticide floating in that enclosed air from the crop dusters that regularly coated the fields and netting. More than one of us passed out from the heat, but we all revived and survived.

There were a variety of characters that we came into contact with, some of them were our bosses, some were more or less fellow workers. In addition to Eddie Bourdeau, there was Bill Connelly, our English teacher. A profoundly decent man, he was a bantam rooster of an Irishman, as witty and gentle as the day was long, but possessed of a fiery temper. You never wanted to get on his bad side. He oftentimes impressed us by speaking Spanish with the migrant workers up from Puerto Rico, because Bill taught us Spanish in the high school too. None of us had ever met any kind of Spanish speaker before, so we were very intrigued. Then there were the Jamaicans. Fascinating, friendly, exotic and always joking, they spoke a wonderfully lilting British English from the islands that we all tried to imitate unsuccessfully. They usually worked on the tractors, picking up baskets of leaves and driving them away to the barns. They were immensely popular with the high schoolers because of their infectious good humor, elegant accents and that foreign exoticism. Not to mention the fact that, being from Turners Falls, none of us had ever met a black person face-to-face! We were enthralled, and to this day, we can't talk about men with nick names like "Bronch" and "Born to Lose" without smiling.

Sometimes, some of us worked for a day in the tobacco barns, where our female classmates spent the summer sewing the leaves onto laths to be hung up to dry. When from time to time we volunteered for a job in the barn, we were considered slackers, since it wasn't very hard or very dirty. But it was a good break and a change of scenery. The girls more often that not wore oversized work clothes and babushka-style kerchiefs while they worked, a far cry from their usual prim attire during the school year. So much for the change of scenery. In the barns, once the leaves were sewn to the laths, the Jamaicans took them and passed them up to other black men in the rafters, way up to the top of the high ceiling of the barn. Swaying leaves, laughter and chatter drifted down from the green leafy maze twenty feet up as the barns filled one by one.

We had our share of Polish overseers too, each with a different temperament. There was Staciu, Edjiu, and Joe, among others. Joe was a gentle man, as wide as he was tall, he smoked a corn cob pipe which he carried upside down in his mouth when it was raining. He often reclined at the end of the rows as we worked our way to him. On the other hand, Edjiu was a mean-acting sort, stern and always threatening in broken English, "Don' you no bruisa dem leave!" He did crack a smile at the end of the season however when the picking was all done, and we good-naturedly gave three cheers for each of our field bosses. Another hero of ours was Dave Yez, a TFHS grad who went off to college, but came back in the summer working as a field boss. He too would inspect the picking and hauling, but most often we'd get him to tell us what it was like to go to college, was it hard, how to get in, did it cost as much as they say? We all figured that sooner or later we'd do like Dave Yez and apply and maybe be accepted. But we weren't too sure about how it all worked.

Then there were the days when Eddie Bourdeau telephoned at 5:30 to say there would be no work that day because of the rain. Those were good days because we could stay in bed longer. There had been times when we worked after an early morning rain, and that was miserable. The orange dust from the crop dusters, the sticky nicotine juice and the drenched leaves soaked us through to the skin and made for a miserable day, all day long.

One time, the call came through canceling work for the day. But by 10AM the rain had stopped and a flat calm gray and warm day presented itself. Before long, Dean Letourneau had called and said he could get us a couple of canoes from the boat house at the end of Ferry Road and that meant we could spend the day on the river. Out onto the flat gray Connecticut we went: Dean, Billy Beaubien, Ron

Tuminski, John Pond, and me. Out over to Barton's Cove, we had the place to ourselves. Swimming, laughing, splashing, tipping the canoes over, and best of all, a day off! Not worrying about the future, it was summer and we were free for the time being. There was no one to tell us, and who was to know, which one of us would have a happy life, who would move far away, which ones of us would battle disease or addictions, whose children would be successful or not, which one of us would die in a jungle in Viet Nam? These are not things young boys who are wild yet, with a day on the river ever wondered about. That day, we were far from the future, far from the tobacco fields and that's all that mattered.

When you're fourteen, life starts piling on the lessons and sometimes the apprenticeship is hard. Tobacco field work was hard and dirty and didn't pay much. Eddie Bourdeau's words stuck with us for a lifetime; he always reminded us: "Take a good look at this job! If you don't want to do this for the rest of your life, stay in school! Get an education!"

All of us who could, took his advice, and after a summer or two, never set foot in a tobacco field again.

To Honor the Fiddler *(September)*

It was one of those Saturday mornings, unlike this brilliant September Thursday. It was wet. A drenching rain which we had needed since early August was pelting the trees in the overgrown pasture, causing the din of a rain-forest cascading waterfall through the leaves still holding on to their green. Doubtful about the forecast, we headed for Greenfield around 10:00, not unlike some residents of our villages who go over the hill for various reasons of a Saturday morning. But we were going to the Green River Cemetery, the one recently made infamous because some of its tombs were sliding into the Green River.

In this cemetery, wet, cool, and grey, the distant sound of spirituals and hymns drifted up from among the worn gravestones. Eighty or so of us were gathered to celebrate the placing of a tombstone, and to honor the memory of John Putnam. He was a man of many identities, but until today had no stone to identify his grave. He was a celebrated musician who traveled far and wide throughout Franklin County in the 1870s through the 1890s to play his left-handed fiddle and to call the contradances in town halls and grange halls for miles around. The contradance, for those who don't know, is a dance form existent in New England since colonial times and still thriving today in most of our hill towns and our river valley towns.

But John was more than a fiddler. He was a renowned barber, and as has come to be known, he played a key role in the Underground Railroad in helping slaves from the South, following the North Star constellation "The Drinking Gourd", to freedom in Northern New England and Canada. You see, John Putnam, the fiddler and the barber, was also a black man. And clearly he took risks to help his people move from slavery to freedom on the way north. So deep was his family's concern about vengeful slave owners finding and desecrating John's remains even after the Civil War was over, that a headstone was never placed over John and Julia Putnam's grave until Saturday. That's why we were there—family, extended family in every sense, blood relatives, as well as community activists, historians, musicians and dancers. Juanita Harris, his great great granddaughter, herself a celebrated vocalist who attended the New England Conservatory of Music, lifted her voice in her ancestor's honor. Later, she and her daughter Christine Lacey joined in with the Amandla Chorus, lending their rich textured voices to the ethereal light quality of the others .Then in the mist of a Saturday morning, Susan Conger of Montague Center and Randy Miller of New Hampshire tuned their instruments and played a few dance tunes, fiddlers invited to honor the fiddler.

Afterwards, family and friends visited, drifted in and out of the various gravesites of many of Putnam's relations, many well-known in Greenfield's musical and athletic history: the Barnes, the Harrises, the Peters, and now at long last the Putnams. The celebration then moved on to the Energy Park downtown. Now, as an aside, for some of you who may be curious, the fiddle is something of a mystical instrument. The mystery all starts in the making of a fiddle, or a violin, since there's no difference, except perhaps in the way it's played. A good maker carefully chooses the maple for the body and the spruce for the top. The great violin makers can thump or strike a tree high up in the hills and know that that tree of all the others can make the sound long sought after. Then oftentimes that tree's wood might spend ten or more years in a violin shop before being transformed. The voice comes from the skill of the maker, the careful whittling of the body, even the secret formula of each maker's varnish! And when the right musician comes along, and if the maker knew his trade, that violin can sing, wail, hum, whisper, cause grown men to weep and dancers to soar to the heavens. Then there are those of us, too, who make the strings sound like shrieking cats, and make dogs howl, holding their ears as they try to harmonize or to drown out the pain or just simply, beg you to stop. So you can imagine the endless possibilities when fifty or so fiddlers gather to make music together.

My own connection to all of this? Other than pursuing the elusive art of fiddling over the past years, the connection may be written in the tombstones. One, up in the Green River Cemetery, and one in the Highland Cemetery in Millers Falls. The one in Millers belongs to my great-grandfather Judah W. Smith. He himself was a fiddler of sorts, also a contemporary of the honored John Putnam, although Putnam was an old man in the 1880s when Judah and he lived on the same street (Wells Street) for a few years. I'd like to think they knew each other, and that maybe John showed him a few things on the fiddle. My great-grandfather was young at the time, about to be married and to move to Millers Falls, where he founded our family on the Flat in the house along the Millers where we live today. So beyond the remembrance and the festivity of communal music, I was looking for something far more intangible, trying to conjure up some feel in the air for my own ancestor.

The Energy Park scene became a happening. Musicians gathered in impromptu groups to jam, dance and swap tunes. The clouds had rolled away, and although many fiddlers puffed on fingers to keep them nimble, the music rose up from all corners. Members of John Putnam's extended family gathered in a sort of family reunion, to retell tales, visit and welcome newcomers to the circle of extended family. Musicians and the curious drifted in and out. I welcomed a chance to renew contact with Susan Conger. Susan has been residing in Montague Center for years, teaching fiddle to young people as well as adults in her home there. She edited and published a collection of dance tunes composed by contradance musicians from the Connecticut River Valley, fittingly called *Along the River*. Susan had been invited to play at the gravesite to honor John Putnam and for most of us, to evoke for a short time there the sound of that distant fiddle and to give tangible sense to the image in peoples' minds of the jubilation of dancers, balancing and swinging, ephemeral couples set to *dos à dos* and promenade in the brightening morning air. Susan said that as a fiddler, she was deeply pleased to be able to honor another fiddler in this way. She said it was visible, tangible proof that this centuries-old New England tradition, that Putnam helped to keep alive, is still thriving today. Susan feels that this idea of a "session in the park" where people get out and play is quite unique: "As musicians, we're used to playing in homes, pubs, and dance halls. But to get out into the park to play, to help people realize that many, many people of all ages do play, for them to get out and see live, non-commercial music happening...well, it's moments like these when it feels lucky to be a musician."

And so, if you're at all tuned in to that bright stream of music flowing through our villages along the river, you'll get out and listen, learn to play or dance if your mind takes a fancy to it, and you'll be there too, come next September.

What's In a Name? Or, Pardon My French! *(December)*

There's a mosaic of family names from all over the world represented in our villages. You can trace our evolving demographics over the past 200 years by scanning town histories, town reports, and street lists. As for me, I've always been fascinated by the French Canadian family names, partly because I've carried around a Quebec name all my life, but also because we Canucks have such descriptive surnames! Granted that our Anglo-Saxon, German, Polish, Irish, Italian, or Hispanic neighbors have family names they're proud of, but they can't hold a candle to the boisterous French *Canadiens* for sheer originality, vigor, even poetry of our family names.

Immigrants came down to our town from Quebec over a period of hundreds of years. They came to work on the building of the power canals, dams and factories. Then they came to work *in* those factories. Some came down the Connecticut with the log drives, many came to town looking for work during the Depression. Strangely enough, it's been noted that they didn't really leave behind any lasting vestiges wherever they went and settled, rather seeking, like a lot of immigrants, to blend into the American stereotype. And now, with the fading of St. Anne's church, and earlier, the French School, there'll not be much left in our landscape to remind us of the role the *Québécois* played here, although the Rendezvous, Couture Brothers, and Aubuchon Hardware still evoke a French past. Yet, the names of those early French-speaking families do remain.

Historians tell us that family names came into usage well before the first explorers reached Canada in the 1550s and the first settlers in the 1600s. In fact, by the year 1000 AD, family names became more and more common. As the population grew in France and the rest of Europe, it was no longer easy to identify people as the "son of so-and so" as the Scandinavians still do (Carlson: son of Carl) or even some Irish names like Fitzgerald (son of Gerald, which is really French: *fils de Gerald*!). And so on. French family names became very descriptive, and their origins came from basically four sources:

1. Names based on trades and occupations ,e.g. *Chartier* (wagon maker or driver), *Cloutier* (maker of nails).

2. Names derived from locations, villages, or where the family lived ,e.g. *Dubreuil* (one who lives near a clearing in the forest), *Bellemare* (one who lives near a beautiful pond).

3. Names based on physical or moral characteristics e.g. *Lemieux* (the best), *Tetreault* (a headstrong person).

4. Names based on nicknames or memorable exploits e.g. *Boivin* (drinker of wine).

My own family name could also serve as an example: *Brûlé* is based on the French word for "burnt" (As in *crème brûlée*!) The name possibly derived from ancestors dwelling near a burned-off place at a time when slash-and-burn agriculture was common practice, or perhaps an ancestor was literally burned in an accident, or at the stake?

Below, I've gathered just a few Montaigu/Montague names to serve as examples to illustrate the point. But first, a note on French pronunciation. I'm sure that some of our elder citizens of French descent still use correct pronunciation, as do some of us who have studied French, but for the rest of you, there are a few basic rules in dealing with the problematic French accent.

One main rule involves intonation. That is where the emphasis falls in a word with several syllables. I'll use for example, a familiar French family name from our town: Letourneau. Anglo pronunciation has this name as LeTOURneau. Whereas a French speaker would say: LetourNEAU. The French speaker always emphasizes the *last* syllable, while English speakers tend to emphasize the next to the last syllable (which leads to the infamous American accent in French, and vice-versa). By the way, with further apologies to my friend Dean, there should also be an apostrophe after the "L" (L'etourneau.); the "*étourneau*" is a familiar bird, the starling , but it also means "a silly fellow".

The second basic rule of pronunciation is that the last consonant in a word (if it's the last letter) is never pronounced, and the letter "n" is rather special: it's a nasal. You can't pronounce it, but rather you have to send it up your nose, where it remains. For example the name *Beaubien* or *Paulin* would be pronounced with the emphasis on the last syllable, and you couldn't pronounce the "n"; the tongue isn't involved at all! Try getting someone who has some French to say the expression *un bon vin blanc* (a good white wine) to get the feel for the four nasals, then have a glass for yourself! The wine helps you to speak the best French, and a good head cold or at least a sinus problem also helps to get those nasal sounds out!

Here's a list of some local French names:

Beaulieu: beautiful, good place

Bergeron: shepherd, guardian

Bordeaux, Bourdeau: variation on the city of Bordeaux, river's edge.

Boulanger: baker

Boucher: butcher

Chapdelaine: woolen cap, hood

Chevalier: horseman, knight

Croteau: one who dwells near a small grotto or cave

Cournoyer: one who lives near a hazelnut or walnut tree

Couture: one who dwells on a small parcel of land (a *couture*)

Delisle: someone from the island

Desautels: from a place called Les Autels (the altars)

Desrosiers: of the roses

Ducharme: one who lives near a beech grove, a charming person

Duguay: one who lives near a ford of a river

Fugere: variation on *fougère*, a fern, or from the city of Fougères

Gagné: farm laborer, based on old French *gaainier*

Gagnon: nickname designating a ferocious person

LaPierre: a rock, stone

La Pointe: one who carves stone or wood

Leveille: he who is clever, alert

Martineau: diminutive of Martin

Nadeau: variant of Nadal, meaning Noël in Occitan from Provence

Paradis: one who lives on excellent land, as opposed to one from the same village living on poor land (Enfer)

Pelletier: one who sells furs

Poirier: one who owns pear trees

Prunier: one who owns plum trees

Routhier: a highwayman, mercenary soldier

Saulnier: one who harvests or sells salt

St. Germain: celebrated French saint, and one who lives near a holy site of the saint

Tessier: weaver

So, I think you will agree that there is, indeed, poetry in our old family names!

The Bridge over the Millers *(January 2008)*

The post card, mailed from upstreet in Millers on August 12, 1916 arrived here the next day. It was addressed to Lizzie Smith, my great-grandmother, and it was sent from a friend in the village center. The message was just a simple hello. More than likely the two women hadn't seen each other for awhile, even though they didn't live far from one another. The post card made its way into a drawer upstairs with other souvenirs for ninety years or so, until I took it out the other winter day, remembering having seen it long ago. And the way things work out at this time of year, with a few hours to spend outdoors, the rest of the time can be for indoor chores, a good book, or in this case, a visit to the family souvenirs tucked away in various drawers, nooks and crannies. That's how it tends to be when you live in an old family homestead; the walls have memory, but beyond that, here and there are letters, postcards and pictures with legends on the back. Now, because of that post card, plus the current state of affairs of the bridge over the Millers, and the way this day lends itself to some musing, slowly various mental pictures, bits of conversation and village lore begin rising to the surface. Before long, that picture postcard from 1916 has brought to mind a loosely connected story involving the bridge, a legendary parish priest known as Father Mac, plus another preacher from the Congregational Church, a wedge of chocolate cake, and my own grandfather, Abe.

Now, as a few long-time residents will testify, Abe was quite a colorful local character who lived out his entire life in Millers Falls. He was instantly recognizable by the way he wore his wool cap (he was never without it, indoors or out) which was always cocked at a rakish angle, his corncob pipe jutting out and set firmly between his teeth so that when he spoke, it was out of the corner of his mouth. He often had a shrewd look in his eye, especially when he squinted at you while telling you a bold lie, or even a little fib, just to see if you believed him. For example, he swore he had pet alligators in the pasture along the Millers, and they liked peanut butter sandwiches and could sing the *Beer Barrel Polka*. And so on. You just never knew with Abe. So when he explained that he wasn't the one who hit the preacher in the forehead with a wedge of chocolate cake at the Congregationalist picnic in 1906, I didn't know whether to believe him or not. All this came back to him when, in his seventies, we were looking at the 1954 Montague Bicentennial book. I flipped the pages to the section on Millers Falls to see what he remembered from the historical pictures in the book. When I turned to the page with the pictures of the pastors of the First Congregational Church in Millers, the picture of Rev. Charles Clark got Abe started, still protesting his innocence almost seventy years later. To hear him tell it, he was framed! He claimed that he, an innocent Abe of 10-years old, indeed was at the Church picnic in 1906, and indeed maybe he was among some of the boys who were doing what most 10-year old boys do, which is to get rowdy and unruly. And just maybe, he was one of the three boys who were winding up baseball style to throw pieces of chocolate cake at each other, *EACH OTHER*, not the preacher, when he, the truly innocent one, ducked as the first piece of cake left the hand of one of the boys and smacked that preacher on his venerable, substantial forehead.

Now, you didn't mess with men of the cloth in those days, and the Congregationalists didn't shrink away from corporal punishment, so my innocent bystander grandfather got caught by the nearest available appendage which was his good-sized left ear, and got a good thrashing on the spot. So down came Abe to the farm here on River Street to tell his parents how he was so unjustly punished. Back up the street went Abe's father Judah, not one to spare the rod and spoil the child, but wanting to get the story straight first. (I wonder did Abe have that foxy gleam in his eye, or was he thinking he'd get walloped again once Judah talked with the pastor?) Now Judah himself was an impressive man, well over six feet, a teamster for the Millers Falls Tool Company, a stalwart member of the volunteer fire department (Franklin Engine No.2), and probably a close equal to the preacher in the eyes of some in the village. Judah had a few stern words with the Reverend Clark, and when father and son got back home, Abe was told that he no longer had to go either to Church or Sunday School ever again! But to hear him tell it, he never got that flying cake accusation out of his system.

So how does this story get back around to the bridge? It turns out that the bucolic scene pictured on the post card of a 15-foot-wide plank deck called the White Bridge was replaced in 1954 by "a forty-foot roadway with seven-foot sidewalks, a deck of reinforced concrete with bituminous concrete on top for a wearing surface," according to historical accounts. This is where Father Mac comes in. He spent years in Millers Falls as the pastor of St. John's Church before being sent to another post in the early fifties. He was an old-fashioned no-nonsense rough-hewn Irish priest with a hearty sense of humor, a contagious laugh, and a deep sense of enjoyment of the social life in the village. So, of course, he and my grandfather hit it off right away, two very hearty gents, full of life and mischief, both of whom filled the room when they entered. Considering that my grandfather was, shall we say, an outcast from the Protestant Church, when my Catholic Irish grandmother married Abe, Father MacCormick became a fixture in family life here, spending time in the warm kitchen of this old house when he got the chance. I do remember him myself.

Well, to tie this disconnected story together, it was Father Mac who was invited back to Millers Falls in 1954 to dedicate the new Vets Memorial Bridge, which is now taking so long to replace, by the way. He was the keynote speaker on that day in 1954, and according to the Montague Historical Review "he opened his talk by noting: It's great to be home." Apparently, a First Congregational Church pastor was present also, a Reverend Lawrence, and he gave the Benediction. I'm sure that both Abe and Father Mac gave each other a roguish wink at one point in the ceremony, and luckily, there was no chocolate cake within reach.

The Multiple Perspectives of 1704 *(March)*

Pocumtuck...Old Deerfield...

If you happened to be a child growing up in the valley at some point in the last fifty years, you became familiar with the story of the Deerfield attack recounted in *A Boy Captive of Old Deerfield* by Mary Wells Smith. You might even remember the distinctive voice of John Haigis Sr. reading from the book on WHAI. For most of us, that version of the incident set the images and events permanently in our minds—the savages against the Christians, the evil French and Indians against the honest hard-working English farmers seeking a new start in a New World. That simplistic view has been shaken to the core by volumes of recent research that re-defines Deerfield, and by the way, has significant implications for Turners Falls.

Saturday morning, March 1, the snow lay deep, and still swirled thickly in the Deerfield air as we gathered outside the Tavern for a walking tour of the town from a different perspective, that of the Native American.

The day before had been bright and sunny, with light streaming through the windows of the First Church of Deerfield for the commemorative service that drew from three perspectives: the settlers in New England, the officers from New France, and the native peoples who had been in this spot for the last 12,000 years. (And who are still among us, as has become apparent.)

The Executive Director of the Pocumtuck Valley Memorial Association, Timothy Neumann, in his address to the group, evoked a phrase which had particular resonance,that of *multiple perspectives*, on what happened that day in Deerfield, February 29, 1704. That phrase has taken on considerable importance in interpreting and understanding Connecticut Valley culture and history. While that phrasing still echoed in my mind, Margaret Bruchac shared two Abenaki songs of remembrance and thanks for all those who preceded us, who define who we are because of their lives and efforts over the years and generations. The Abenaki words filled the church. This time, I said to myself, the visit to Deerfield will be different.

So when the surprisingly snowy Saturday morning arrived, we set out, a hardy small band trying to keep up with the long strides of our guide Marge. She was impressive in a knee-length coat of royal blue with dashes of dark red, cut in the early colonial style that had been copied by the Native Americans of this region. She had carefully researched the style and material and made her coat to be as authentic as possible to what her Abenaki ancestors might have worn in the 1700s. While walking we were reminded that to envision a new perspective on this place, you need to suspend bias, shed ethnocentric modes of thought and be willing to time travel. Doing so, you begin to see this place, Pocumtuck (Deerfield), as it had been: both a way station and camp settlement for tribal people for at least 10,000 years before the first white settlers arrived. This was a pivotal place in tribal histories. There had been constant fluid movement through tribal sites in what is now known as Massachusetts, New York, and Quebec. The Abenaki and associated Algonquian tribes were deeply attached to the Connecticut River Valley, and Deerfield was central to that sense of place and homeland. In fact, in spite of the arrival of whites and subsequent conflicts, even after the 1704 attack, native people continued to appear at Deerfield for visits to their ancestral homelands even 150 years later. Our guide mentioned that during the visit of tribal people in 1837, the most moving sight for them was the famous "Indian Door" which their ancestors had unsuccessfully attempted to hack through to get into the Sheldon House in 1704. They were heard to say that it symbolized for them how hard their ancestors had fought to get this land back. How's that for perspective?

That hints at what motivated the tribes to instigate the attack in 1704. Scholars Evan Haefeli and Kevin Sweeney, who have authored numerous groundbreaking works on the 1704 attacks and aftermath, state, "diverse motives—a mixture of personal, familial, spiritual, strategic, and possibly commercial considerations" probably inspired the attack. We could also add revenge to that list.

This is where Peskeompskut (Turners Falls) comes in. In the history of the conflict in the Valley, the so-called "Falls Fight of 1676" stands out as a singularly vicious and genocidal massacre of elderly men, women and their children by Capt. Turner's forces. It was, in military terms, a devastatingly effective event. It was a massacre that left the Pocumtucks, the Norwottocks, the Sokoki of our region demoralized and terrorized. Many survivors fled to Canada and sought refuge in villages and missions near Trois Rivières, Montréal, and upper Québec three hundred miles away. (It should be noted that many of us of French Canadian descent are also of Abenaki /Native American descent, and some of us are right back here in Peskeompskut!) Another perspective to keep in mind: These refugees sought support from the French for the attack on Deerfield, and in 1704 they exacted revenge for the Falls' massacre only six miles away and twenty-eight years later.

Back on the streets of modern Old Deerfield, Marge Bruchac continues her tour, citing history, folklore and oral histories, and the names of individual sachems and tribal leaders that you can't find in Sheldon's History of Deerfield. Luckily our guide, armed with her PhD research and immense knowledge of the native presence in the Valley, has authored numerous works, including a small self-guided walking tour entitled "Pocumtuck: A Native Homeland" that can be found in the shops of Old Deerfield. You could do this walk and see for yourself!

Before leaving, we reflected over a cup of coffee. I needed to talk about the Falls Massacre of 1676. What importance, if any, did it have for our modern Turners Falls? That seems so long ago, and hasn't everyone forgotten? Marge suggested that the events of May 19, 1676 are not "someone else's history" but ours. Maybe it's time we deal with the massacre. Native people feel that the onus of what happened there lingers in the spiritual life of the town. I thought of the controversial *medicine stones* on the edge of the Montague Plains, standing in the way of a new airport runway. The tribal people tell us those stones are keeping that area in balance, and should be respected as per a new agreement signed by the town and tribal representatives, as one step in reconciliation, in 2004. If those stones are assuring and preserving the equilibrium of that place, maybe it's time we take more steps in the reconciliation process to heal the spiritual wounds that linger at the Falls; it just might help us re-establish the balance that's within our grasp, in our little town on the river.

Montague Garagemen *(May)*

It seemed like a simple plan that day, coordinated to fit into a busy schedule after school between 3 and 5 PM. The plan involved two stops at different garages in town plus a trip to the dentist in Greenfield. The garage work was to be done in town because of a long-standing relationship that has developed between Benny Rubin, Mark Johnson, and my cars. The dentist was another story. I was going all the way to Greenfield for the drilling because my late lamented dentist, Dr. Arthur Charron, told me to, years ago, when he retired. My career as a dental patient had started out in Millers Falls when Doctor Charron was launching his practice out of a small second-story office above Ward's Clothing Store on the corner of Bridge and Main Streets. He was a member of large family of medical professionals, his own father being remembered for his heroic efforts treating patients during the Spanish Flu epidemic of 1918. His brother Rosario delivered me into this world at the Farren. Small town loyalties run deep and are built on hard-earned respect. When Dr. Charron moved to 58 Fourth Street, we of course followed him there. The old office is now converted into our Montague Reporter newspaper office. I have to admit, even now I find it eerie to go down those steps, still half expecting to see nurse "Sis" Charron peering at me over her wireframes, telling me Doctor (she always called her brother that) would be with me in a minute. Ghosts in the newspaper office. Or maybe it's just the glowing radiation in the walls from all those x-rays. When my lifelong dentist, who performed painless works of art on my post-adolescent teeth, finally retired, he told me I should go to a certain dentist over the hill in Greenfield, so I went.

On this particular day of the Simple Plan just last week, before making my way to the dentist—who by the way is less concerned about the pain to the patient both in the tooth and in the wallet than our good Dr. Charron—I planned to get the car inspected. I always look forward to going to Benny Rubin's. It's always enjoyable to drop in for a good-natured healthy session of cussing and swearing while your car is being worked on. It's part of the oral tradition around here, completely devoid of animosity and aggression, and healthy cussing is sometimes good for the soul, especially after a day in the classroom. Besides, Rubin's garage is a time capsule. It's got all the atmosphere that you want in a garage: postcards from all over, quite a few babes in bikinis in Florida, some water skiers, a picture of a donkey in a hat, plenty of testimonials to Benny and his father Meyer, and the usual inventory of slogans that make up the working-man's Americana. "You don't have to be crazy to work here...but it helps!" Or, "I feel like a mushroom— everybody keeps me in the dark and feeds me xx##!!"

Then for me, there's the link between Benny's and Williams' Garage, my father's former place of work. I spent a lot of time in Williams' Garage in the 50s, where my father toiled six days a week for Dickie, and apparently never really lost his sanity in spite of it. Whenever we visited my father at work, he always treated us to sodas and candy bars. Looking back, maybe my father and Dr. Charron were in cahoots in the dental cavity scheme of things, but on opposite ends of the business. Dickie's office in those days was a place of wonderment for twelve-year old boys. The clanging of the cash resister, the ringing of the pressurized air line sounding out over the noise of the garage, indicating a customer had pulled up for gas, and most of all the pin-up calendars high up on the walls, just far enough to make it hard to see. That's where we all got our first glimpse of a buxom and appealing Marilyn Monroe smiling coyly without a stitch on her. Those were the days of innocence. We would cast a glance up there every once in a while, but we shouldn't be caught staring by the grown-ups.

Benny's office reminds me of those days, minus the naked ladies. Benny himself makes the visit worthwhile: unlit cigar, dapper moustache, infectious good humor. He knows everyone in town and beyond, he's helped everyone in town, and I'm pretty sure everyone owes him a favor. Luckily for us he's not intent on calling in all those favors. He's a part of the oral history and legends in town, his near-visit to the White House Inaugural Ball that almost happened, being one of the best. So Benny was the enjoyable part of the plan. My inspection was flawless, Greg Williams whisking me and my car in and out, courteous and efficient. So, feeling pretty good, inspected and found worthy of approval, off we went to a more challenging visit in Greenfield. No cussing or swearing there—too difficult with a mouthful of gauze and all sorts of drains and such. Even if you wanted to, you couldn't. Forty-five minutes later, just before five, out I came, somewhat numbed in the tooth and much lighter in the wallet.

Approaching the car, I should have known: She wouldn't start, and I really needed to get to the next part of the plan which involved getting this car back over to Montague to Mark's Auto before closing. Looking under the hood as if I knew what to look for, plus some mean-tempered cursing this time, didn't work either. Back into the office. Of course I wasn't carrying a cell phone. I had to call the only one who could save my schedule now, Ralph Rau Jr. Silence at the other end of the line as I told him of my plight way over here in Greenfield. Ralph patiently explained it was close to closing, there weren't many people to look after things if he went out on the road, and told me to try another thing or two, and then call him back. Outside in the lot nothing worked, so it's back to Ralph who says he'll be right there. Sure enough the Rau wrecker appeared as though it knew a shortcut over the hill. Ralph squeezed his big frame behind the steering wheel of the diminutive Toyota, tried a few things, and pronounced the battery dead as a doornail. So it's a jumpstart, and a drive back over to Montague Center, and within minutes a new battery is in and the car is humming contentedly. Ralph's speedy service got me almost back on schedule. A smooth operation, a few words from the big quiet man, and a bill that was reasonable, and couldn't touch the cost of forty-five minutes spent in the dentist's chair.

The final part of the Simple Plan involves a scheduled drop-off at Mark's Auto, about three minutes from Ralph's as the crow flies, when that crow is flying straight, but if you've noticed, that's not often the case. Into the modern office I step (the fourth one in the space of two hours). It could almost be the dentist's office with comfortable chairs and a week's worth of current magazines for you to read while you wait. Big Terry Prentice is ensconced at the command center behind the desk, all calm, pleasant, and oftentimes sympathetic to customers the likes of me. He takes the keys, and will shortly hand them off to Mark Johnson, proprietor of Mark's, and as honest as the day is long. The car will stay overnight for some transmission work first thing in the morning. This car's been around the block a bit, especially today. I've relied on Mark for years and a neighbor has remarked that I probably hold a share in the new addition that Mark built a number of years ago, given the amount of work he has had in keeping my old cars running. Mark knows how to keep a customer satisfied and coming back.

So for me, the Day of the Simple Plan, ended up on a positive note despite the complication. Always one to look on the bright side, I had after all contributed to the local economy, provided business for some important people who keep the engines of our town in working order, and in the end, they had hardly cost me any more than the forty minutes in the dentist's chair!

You're a good man, John Roach! (July)

If you were a church-goer at St. Mary's in the 1960s, you would have been part of Father John Roach's flock. He came to Turners Falls and St. Mary's fresh from the seminary, intense and full of fervor, just as he was just last Sunday when he retired from St. Joseph's in Shelburne Falls.

The young curate appeared on our horizon early in his vocation and before long began making his mark on our parish. One of his early projects was to convince and recruit a good number of our Hill Gang of unruly and free-roaming eleven-year olds to become Altar Boys. Many of us, myself among them, took a lot of convincing, but like any adolescent, once the band wagon starts rolling somehow you want to be on it too. Besides, as all of us familiar with Father Roach know, he drives a hard bargain, and is especially hard to resist. He employed all sorts of psychology, calling upon the sacred and the divine, as well our primitive sense of societal and parochial duty. So the trajectory of our lives and his converged and we all became Altar Boys. Our training was as intense as our curate's passion for his new parish. There was a lot to learn: timing in serving the Mass was everything—exact timing in getting just right all the genuflecting, bowing, incense burning, bell-ringing and Latin, for which we Roman Catholics were known. Training a bunch of foolish boys such as we were took time and infinite patience on the part of our mentor. As we practiced and practiced, I can still picture our Pastor, Father Paul O'Day, rolling his eyes heaven-ward, not only at our growing incompetence but also I'm sure, at the intensity applied by his young curate in taming and training us.

Father O'Day had long before established his role in our congregation. An elderly priest, although he was only getting into his sixties (which doesn't seem that old *now*), he had an athlete's physique. The word was out that he had been a boxer in a former life before the priesthood, which gave him tremendous stature in the eyes of the eleven-year olds that we were. We kept on his good side for sure. He had a sly smile and crinkled laugh lines in the corner of his eyes, and spoke out of the side of his mouth like any street-wise kid brought up in a tough neighborhood. He could have played any of Cagney's roles or been a Boston Irish politician if he had wanted. He loved his big black car and his vacations in Florida. We heard that he loved to play the horses among other things, and we imagined that he had all kinds of fun down there when he had his yearly holiday from running our parish.

So the day came when two of us served our first Mass. Was it Francis Dobosz or Jimmy Higgins and me? I'm not sure. Francis and I were great friends with a tendency for foolishness, so Father probably put Jimmy and me on for our first go at it. Big mistake as you shall see. We had been assigned the 7AM Mass for the first three days of the week. So down the hill we walked in the early light of an October morning. You may recall walking? We all walked everywhere; if we wanted to go somewhere, we walked. From home to the skating rink, from home to the Robustelli pizza parlor in Riverside, to school and back. Soccer moms hadn't been invented yet, and the one car you had got your father to work, so you walked. So Jimmy and I arrived in the sacristy at 6:30 AM, where we had to begin laying out the vestments just so, coiling carefully the rope-like belt just as Father Roach had drilled into us. Father arrived, checked out our preparations with the hawk-like scrutiny that is his trademark. Father O'Day came by too, probably to reassure us, and I'm sure rolling his eyes when he turned away. So far so good. As soon as we stepped into the Sanctuary and faced the altar, things went down hill. I hesitate to say all hell broke loose, given the circumstance, but it seemed to us something akin. Luckily there were only a few devotees of the 7 AM Mass in attendance. Succumbing to stage fright and butterflies, Jimmy and I were off to the races, serving a sort of Mass that was different from the one Father Roach was doing. Kneeling on either side of the priest, we began our Latin "Ad Deum Qui Laetificat, juventutem meum." As in mayhem. Our heads were bobbing towards Father as we knelt but at different times, and we were bowing and genuflecting totally out of sync, first him, then me instead of doing it as a well-rehearsed pair. We flew through our memorized Latin as though we were running the hurdles, eager to get to the end of it and move on to the next part up ahead. At some point I was the one who was supposed to go to the side of the altar and strike the chimes, solemnly, musically, and at the right time during the service. Having no musical ability, and the little bit that I remembered from the hours of practice, I was hitting the chimes a bit too hard with the mallet and coming up with something resembling *Three Blind Mice*. Jimmy got one of those early-adolescent giggling fits, the kind where if you're not careful, something could shoot out of your nose. At that moment our good Father Roach fired a glance at us that could have turned us both into pillars of salt. We were pretty sure priests could do that if the situation called for it. Somehow it all got a little better after the point in the Mass where we all took a break and sat on the side of the altar in the special chairs, one of us on each side of Father. It gave us all a chance to collect ourselves: Father Roach got back to thinking about the business of the Transubstantiation, while Jimmy and I reflected on our next Altar Boy moves. We needed to redeem ourselves in the eyes of Father Roach, who we feared would surely get an earful from Father O'Day after our awful performance. But by the grace of God, we got through the rest of the service without too many more mistakes, and soon we were out the door and up to school, feeling a little bit holier and mature than when we had started out that morning. (We were given tardy excuses because we were serving Mass, and besides, our 8th grade teacher, Rita Kersavage, was good friends with the Church. It helps to have contacts.)

We got through the rest of the week, and the timing of our moves and our Latin got better and better. By the time our careers as Altar Boys had ended, years later when we got to be Seniors at TFHS, Fr. Roach had helped us master all sorts of ceremonies from weddings and funerals, High Mass, First Communions and Confirmations, Holy Thursdays, Good Fridays, Easter Sundays, and everything in between.. Father had become a part of our lives by then. In those days in Turners Falls, the Church, the School, and the Scouts formed a triangulation that kept you in line. Your teachers, priest, parents, and neighbors turned up in all three of the triumvirate groups, and every adult kept the others informed as to what you were up to. If you did something wrong, the news got home before you did. So it was with Father Roach. When we were kids, he organized picnics, outings to Look Park, and counseled us, in the Confessional and out. When we were getting ready for college, he took us to visit a variety of Catholic colleges (of course) including his alma mater Holy Cross. He convinced me that Fairfield was the choice for me, although others went to Boston College, Creighton, St Louis U, Providence, and all. None of us made it to Holy Cross, though.

Eventually Father Roach moved on, and we had to share him with Greenfield, Pittsfield, Amherst, and finally, Shelburne Falls. He has been an activist all the while, involved in issues arising from the Vietnam War through the AIDS epidemic, bringing the same intensity and fervor to every activity and goal in his life We kept up a correspondence through all my time in the Peace Corps, and we met up from time to time in Amherst, when he was pastor at St. Brigid's. He came back to town for weddings and funerals, helping send off the souls of many of his former parishioners, including my father, just four years ago.

So when, last Sunday, it came time for him to retire from his final parish, hundreds of people turned out. I took my place in line, not far from Ron Dobosz (another ex-Altar Boy from St. Mary's), knowing my role to be a footnote in a small part of parish history, someone from his first parish from long ago, waiting to shake his hand and congratulate him as he left his last parish. His handshake and embrace were as strong as ever, as strong as they were fifty years ago. Firm jaw and piercing eyes, he's already got the next ten years of projects and service planned out. More power to you, Father John Roach!

Closing Up The Old Camp *(September)*

One of those first September mornings right after Labor Day, the broad Connecticut was calm, maybe like the first days after creation, mist rising in wreaths from the flat surface. I put in at the Deep Hole, intending to paddle upstream along the stretch the old timers used to call the Horse Race, up to the old camp on the river. Putting the boat in the water, I was greeted by a wildly enthusiastic four-month old Chesapeake retriever, quivering and soaking wet from his early swim, he angled and wiggled around my legs all delighted with the feel of the water and wanting to share his joy of being alive and a puppy on this morning. His owner came up the bank behind him, a retired gent who liked this part of the river as much as I. We talked about the river, the ducks, and his new pup of a dog while he lit a cigarette.

"Won't hunt him this year. Too young." I, too, figured it would be a good idea to wait: I couldn't picture this dog holding still for very long in any boat. The dog wiggled with delight, full of adoration for his owner. Good friendly chat, a little soaking from the dog, and I was off across the water, skimming the flat surface like a water-beetle Volga boatman.

I made good time going up river, the summer weekenders with their boats the size of Coup de Ville Cadillacs and the yahoos on jet skis all gone to their homes and jobs elsewhere, far from my river, maybe gone for the season, and even better, for the rest of the year. Labor Day marks a turning point in the river year, and soon it will be the haunt of a few lone fishermen, a couple of hunters now and then, the water fowl and then the ice.

Up the river a ways, the shore gliding by, and the old camp came into sight. It had belonged to my grandfather, old Joe Brule, who had sought out a place to get away from it all back in the thirties. His family, a house-full of kids born in different cities all up and down the East Coast from New York City to Maine, followed him from job to job during the Depression. When they finally entered Turners Falls at the height of the 1936 flood with all the bridges washed out except one left to lead in and out of town, my grandmother, Mimi, was famously heard to tell Joe, "Don't unpack the bags, we're not staying!" That was over seventy years ago and guess what? We're still here! For a French Canadian, with a big joyful family and a wife who thrived on life, laughter and family gatherings, Joe was odd. He was quiet, something of a grouch, didn't really like kids, and was a loner. I guess that's why he bought this camp. To get away from it all. His neighborhood on L Street was friendly enough as I recall, populated by families with names like Prunier, Reipold, Brunelle, Galvis, Sokoloski, but as soon as he could, Joe would light out for the camp with his dog. And although he complained that nobody went to the camp with him (if he could help it), when we did show up, he fussed all around us and didn't want us kids to touch anything, didn't want us to use the scary dank latrine. It was easier to slip off into the woods than to deal with his complaining anyway, or to wait until we got home! In spite of his crankiness, most of his family and grandchildren spent time up there once or twice a year.

For me and my cousins, it was an adventure: no running water, no electricity, kerosene lamps, breakfast and supper cooked on the old woodstove or outside over the campfire. In spite of all, we spent enjoyable long summer days, sometimes playing 78 rpm records of WW II vintage on the hand cranked Victrola, songs by Arthur Godfrey, Gene Autry or the Andrews Sisters. Sometimes we scaled the 78s over the bank, sometimes used them for target practice with the .22. Birds whose names I learned later, the phoebe and wood pewee, called in plaintive tones all day long. The bare wood walls inside were decorated with typical north woods camp scenes: fishing and hunting calendars from Freddy Macker's package store on L Street, artists' renditions of bears intruding on hunters' camps, an Indian and his frightened maiden girlfriend facing down a grizzly bear with a drawn knife. Other walls had pictures of movie stars like Charles Bickford and Vivian Leigh. (Joe was a projectionist from the early days, having had jobs at the old Howard in Scollay Square in Boston and later at the Shea Theater in the fifties.) Faded black and white snapshots of the family at Revere Beach or Hampton Beach, others of the frozen river in front of the camp and the uncles, Butch and Toots, holding the family dog Sandy. That dog by the way, some sort of Spitz, was just as cranky and ornery as her owner: she would just as soon snap at you and snarl as let herself be petted.

Old Joe lived almost to be a hundred years old, but by his late eighties, he stopped going up to the camp. It came down through the family to my father, then me. And a few years ago we had to make the decision to close it down, and sell it. It was a relic of the family history, but had finally lost its relation to our family life. So over a period of months, I began the solitary task of removing its insides.

The door creaked and slammed shut in its familiar way with each armful or bagful of valuable junk that I hauled out and up the steep hill. Bit by bit the years peeled away, as the stuff picked up at tag sales and auctions was removed. Some of you well know that when you do that kind of job, emptying a house after an elderly relative has left, your mind gets to working and you remember all sorts of things. Things crowded in on me like the creak and yaw of the swinging couch on the screened in front porch, the thwack of snapping forefinger on the screens that sent the gypsy moth caterpillars whipping out into the woods, the voice of Curt Gowdy on the old transistor, rowing back in the dark from a late evening of half-hearted fishing and seeing the pale light of the camp kerosene lamp up there in the kitchen, the smell of crackling bacon and eggs in the skillet on the top of the pot-bellied stove, the full moon shining down on the water.

Old Joe, ever the recluse, was over in his widower's house on Second Street by then, and past caring about who was going through his stuff, while we were closing up the old camp that September years ago.

But now this September, just a few days ago, after my chat with the Chesapeake and his old gent of an owner, the trip up the river brought me within shouting distance of the camp. I called out, "Hallo up there!" But no one answered. Even so, there was a nice new roof on the place, new stairs leading up the steep hill, some 30 feet having eroded from the bank where the horseshoes used to ring out as we passed the time in a friendly game years ago. The old camp once closed, is open again, with a new lease on life. And even though old Joe's grumpy ghost is probably lurking around somewhere, the new people will probably never notice. Unless of course, somebody tells them the story!

The Village in a Snow Globe *(January 2009)*

The time between Christmas and New Year's Day is always the occasion for visits, parties, winter walks, and especially a chance to pause and reflect on the past year. For many of us, our lives are still regulated by a rural, agricultural calendar that designates the twelve days or so between Christmas Eve, New Year's Day, and Old Christmas on the sixth of January, as different from the rest of the year—as time set aside. Schools, with their winter theme cutouts still decorating the windows, await the returning pupils. Most of the seasonal farm chores up in Gill or over in Montague Center are done, although the daily chores keep farmers busy from dawn to dusk and beyond, as always. Teachers take a break, the postman gets relief in the season between Christmas cards and seed catalogues. The garagemen up at Benny Rubin's or over at Mark's seem more convivial than ever, the Shady Glen is warm and welcoming, the Rendezvous is packed with regulars every night throughout this season!

And the world outside is beautiful enough that it would even give brief pangs of wistful homesickness to our smug exiles and ex-patriots in Florida, Texas or California, or at least, I hope so! This December has been one of the old-fashioned kinds, with snow swirling in the air daily and nightly, the white blanket obliterating the severe bareness of November. A drive up Taylor Hill Road in Montague is like an excursion through the Russian countryside, a trip to see Ron Croteau in his new job at the Lake Pleasant Post Office like a winter scene worthy of Norman Rockwell.

The Connecticut River from the dam to the French King was earlier covered in a sheet of ice, although a break in the weather has opened it up from time to time. The ice fishermen have been out on Barton Cove since early December, the guys up at the Schuetzen Verein, their season of clambakes over, have hunkered down at the Clubhouse for the winter to cheer on the Patriots, curse the Jets, and generally, to winter over 'til spring. The kids are out sliding at Unity Park, and others still try the trails on part of the Sandbank at the end of Crocker Avenue. Hardy souls are skiing the new bike path; counters are counting birds along the Canal below the Patch. We have a real New England winter on our hands. This could get interesting!

By December 27 this year a curious familiar change starts taking place again. As we all recover from the frenzy of wrapping paper, those endless carols boring into our eardrums, the over-indulging in food and drink, out of doors the brief thaw causes the snowfields and sidewalks to become icy. The wild creatures are a bit more desperate in their search for food. But luckily, the Solstice celebrations, both pagan and religious, have once again managed to encourage the sun to come back, and the darkest nights of the year are already giving way to more light, one minute at a time. Some townspeople, like our own George Bush, are planning their annual migration to the sunny South, leaving the rest of us hardy souls to face the frigid temperatures of January.

At this year's end, we've have a respite for two days. Warming temperatures permit reviewing our early winter situation, thawing has loosened the icy grip on driveways and gutters, it has melted ice dams on the roof, and given us a chance to restock the wood pile near the back door. Those of us who feed the birds are blessed with throngs of bluejays, brash, loud and full of confidence in the snowscape. Their muffled cries reach inside the kitchen into the circle of morning lamp light on open book and coffee cup. Give us this day our daily jays and a flash of cardinal for spice and accent. Up at the Waidlich Farm above the French King Gorge at the mouth of the Millers, horses gallop, wheel and play in the new snow and icy air. So this is how we keep the days and nights of the winter season, with life in the villages and surrounding countryside, on winter schedule. In the fading light, the Library reading rooms are bright, warm, and calm. The re-dedicated Veterans' Monument stands sentinel in the dark at the edge of town, the newly-burnished names of the town's sons and daughters who served engraved for all the ages to come. Snow plows on their familiar rounds thunder down roads and streets, their flashing lights briefly brightening up the ceilings in the darkening villages. The snow swirls again to end the year and welcome in the new.

" *Bold Christmas is past,*
Twelfth night is the last,
We bid you adieu,
And great joy to the new"

The Crack of the Bat. *(April)*

I t might be the chill wind of early April, or the teasing faint green of the grass coming from the bare ground, but there's that old ephemeral springtime feeling that comes over some of us. The saying goes something like: "Ah! Springtime! When a young man's fancy turns to …baseball!" It happens to many of us, the young and not so young and it is a wonderful feeling indeed, however brief. This bit of reminiscence intertwines a wistful poem, memories of a ballfield here on the Flat, the Housing Project, and a baseball stalwart from the village of Millers Falls.

As a youngish University student far from home in Paris, invariably the fever would come over me when, as a sure sign of spring, the International Herald Tribune would publish a poem by sports writer Dick Rorabuck, his tribute to baseball. He probably wrote it to send an attack of homesickness through the American ex-patriot community in Paris. And it always worked. It began:

> " *Away on this side of the ocean,*
> *When the chestnuts are hinting of green,*
> *And the first of the café commandos*
> *Are moving outside for a 'fine'*
> *And the sound of spring beats a bolero*
> *As Paris sheds her coat and her hat,*
> *The sound that is missed more than any,*
> *Is the sound of the crack of the bat.*
>
> *There's an animal kind of a feeling*
> *That's a-stirring down at the Vincennes Zoo*
> *And the kid down the hall's getting restless*
> *Taking stairs like a young kangaroo*
> *Now the dandy is walking his poodle*
> *And the concierge is sunning her cat*
> *But the heart's with the Sox and the Tigers*
> *And the sound of the crack of the bat... "*

Then the memories would always come back of Turners Falls, when as even younger boys still, the gang would all meet up for a pick-up game at the Housing Project on the Hill. We never called it sandlot baseball, but that handy term probably best describes it. It was a wonderful way to play ball when you were somewhere between nine and thirteen! The Project and the nearby neighborhood were full of classmates and friends. There was Thomas and Ducharme, Couture, Cadran and Dobosz, all kinds of Curries, Tuminski, Higgins and I. Whether or not we lived in the Project, we all showed up for a game after school or during those glorious summers before working on tobacco, when we were still free. Those were days of wonderful kid-directed games. Hardball for sure, a piece of cardboard for a base, or just an x on the ground. No adults to organize us, we made out just fine in the field in the center of the buildings. We played with Mantle, Musial, Schneider or Williams in mind, and we played hard. When we weren't playing, we practiced throwing a tennis ball at a wall to work on fielding skills, playing catch with your Old Man, or if you had no choice, with your sister! Later, as we reached Little League age, the pick-up game at the Housing Project faded. Baseball got more serious, adults were in charge, uniforms, standings and play-offs were important, and I do still miss the feel of the crack of the bat from those days.

" No, a Yank can't describe to a Frenchman
The rasp of an umpire's call
The continuing charms of statistics
Changing history with each strike and ball
Not the self-conscious jog of a the slugger
Rounding third with a tip of his hat
Not the rhubarb at home plate
Nor the half smothered grace of a hook slide
Nor the sound of the crack of the bat."

Now as an ex-pat no more, and safely ensconced back in the family homestead in Millers Falls, or Ervingside if you prefer, the April baseball mood continues to tug at memory. Well after I settled back here, the stories of baseball in this family began to surface. Long Sunday dinners spent with my grandfather Abe Smith and his brother Doug brought out baseball tales about which I've written in other articles in other Aprils. Abe always liked to repeat stories of the team he and his brothers had formed with himself as catcher, his brother Perry at second, brother Clint at third and brother Doug on the mound. To hear him tell it, the Smith brothers were unstoppable in those days. And although Clint was reputedly "quick as a cat" at third, it was undoubtedly the burning fast ball of Doug Smith that crushed opponents game after game. Both Abe and our uncle Rusty Smith caught for Doug on occasion, and had the twisted, even broken fingers as reminders of that fast ball. While a star at TFHS Doug drew crowds in the thousands to his games and he often fanned upwards of twenty batters in an outing on the mound. As some of you may well know, he was recruited by the Red Sox in 1912 and pitched that year in Fenway Park. (There is a book on that 1912 Red Sox championship team currently being researched and written, and should be published in time for the 1912 centennial).

Then just the other day, once again giving in to April pangs of springtime fever, something drew me to the family collection of old newspaper clippings and a photo taken in 1935 of a team with many of the legends in the Millers Falls Hall of Fame. In the middle of the picture, not far from my grand-uncle Doug, sat Red Yez, born and raised on the Flat, just a few doors up the street. In no time at all, after a quick phone call and short drive from Ervingside to Erving Center, I made my way up to a snug home on Flag Hill, to where Red, 93, now lives with his daughter Judy, a classmate of mine, and Judy's husband Craig Moore. Red had a gentle smile and a good chuckle as we looked over the old photo of that 1935 team, at the kitchen table. The names of his old teammates came back to him and to all of us because of the local legends and contemporary connections with the descendants of the players in the photo. Red recognized Shorty Marvel, a tall lanky 6 foot 2 inches in spite of his nickname, who played first base with the Smith brothers team. There was Kibby Cole who still lives up on Old State Road, cousin Ken Smith, a curly-headed Joe Cafarella, and Red himself, among many others. He played shortstop on the team and laughed when asked if he could get a hit off Doug and his fastball.

"Was more likely to get beaned," said Red. Doug not only had a the fast ball and a mean spit ball, juiced up with a chaw of old Slippery Elm, but also he was known to " dust off" a batter or two just to loosen him up!

Conversation in the Moore kitchen led to reminiscing about the old days on the Flat and past games on that sandy ball field across from the house where Red was born ninety-three years ago. The talk came round to all of us sadly admitting how baseball has gone from the neighborhood nowadays.

The ball field on the edge of the Millers Falls Tool company land where Doug and his brothers got their start, and where generations of neighborhood kids played, is now the backyard of the Lane house up the street. The Smith family barn were Doug was allowed to practice even of a Calvinist Sabbath Sunday has vanished. And a quick tour of local parks has no neighborhood pick-up game going on, just a few kids shooting baskets, or skateboarding. To be sure, there's the Sox on TV and soon there will be Little League, and Softball. But although my own baseball career ended when I was twelve, the yearning for those spring sounds comes achingly back again, when early April comes around. Though it's great fun to watch the games at Fenway, and there are plenty of other choices at that,

"But the thing that's not HERE
At this time of year,
Is the sound of the crack of a bat."

One Day in July – 1937 *(July)*

Downstairs in the kitchen, Ma was up first, as always, getting breakfast together for the children who were still sleeping upstairs. Soon they'd come pouring down those stairs, but for the moment it was quiet up there. It had been hard to fall asleep the night before with the excitement that the next day would bring. There was the promise of fun and something different to do on that summer Saturday morning of the Millers Falls Tool Company picnic. The kids all up and down the street on the Flat had been talking excitedly about it for days. Depression or no Depression, the Tool Company was still going to take the whole lot of them—all the employees and their wives, husbands and a neighborhood full of kids up to Packard Heights in Athol for the summer outing.

The birds had been up for hours. The catbird had started his repertoire of noisy imitations at first light, chattering endlessly from the center of the bridal veil bush in the backyard, but the children were used to the racket and had slept on. The rooster had been announcing daybreak since four AM, trying to outdo his tireless catbird rival in the backyard tangle of shrubs. Crowing and flapping his wings, he was cajoling his hens to get up and at 'em. In fact they *had* been busy and had produced a clutch of eggs that Pa gathered up for breakfast. The two cows had spent the night out in the pasture along the river after the evening milking, grazing, listening to the hooting owl and the whippoorwill while the river flowed swiftly past the fields in the moonlight, but they had come back up to the gate below the barn for the morning ritual. Brothers and sisters upstairs began stirring in their beds as the daylight worked its way into first the south-facing bedroom where the girls slept, then slowly brightened the north bedroom where the brothers were.

School had been out for weeks. The Depression was deep and getting deeper. The danger of war in Europe was growing and FDR had been on the radio the night before, but today was the picnic! The workingmen could look forward to something different other than the usual one day off from the Shop, usually spent smoking, drinking beer upstreet in Equi's, or at any one of the other bars in town. Kids usually played as much as they could between chores—maybe baseball over in the ballfield at the edge of the Tool Shop barns, or roller-skating up and down the sidewalks, shaded by towering maples that formed a leafy arch the whole length of the street.

Today the men could look forward to bottled beer and shooting the breeze up at the picnic. They would be meeting up with all the others they worked with day in and day out, plus there'd be men from the other shifts. The conversation would likely never stray from the talk of work, fishing, the Depression, and baseball. The wives of course would get a small break too—for once not having to scrape a meal together, cook and wash dishes. They would enjoy a bottle of beer maybe, and converse with other women about what everyone talked about in those days, how to get by. For the kids it was going to be great fun, soda pop, all the hot dogs they could eat, games and fire works by the lake. Plus, the getting there—the ride on the bus!

After breakfast, the families started heading up the street to the Tool Shop where the buses were parked and waiting to take everyone to Athol, a great trip in itself for families that had no car and had to walk or hitchhike to Turners. The families there on the Flat were almost all employees at Millers Falls Tool, the street lined with the cottages where the workers lived. Out and up the street went the Dodge clan, the Williams, Sokoloskis, Yezes, Cherwas, and our family of Smiths.

Later in the day, after the picnic and before the evening fireworks, a photographer captured the moment. There they all were in black and white, frozen in time, all those people, that community of factory workers caught in the middle of the Depression and just before the years of WWII, gathered for a small break from worry and cares on that day in July…

The sunlight poured through the same south-facing bedroom window this July just a few days ago, the first sun after a month of rain in June. The catbird sang endlessly from the lilacs, the bridal veil bush of long ago having disappeared. The cow barn and pasture are gone from here, too. The Tool Shop closed in the sixties a few years after Abe retired, having made its hundred years' run. But today, it was just the right time to write the story of that photograph of the picnic more than seventy years ago. In the quiet living room on Carlisle Avenue, my mother and I went over the names of those in the picture, names that I had heard vaguely while growing up, others that are as familiar as family members. She worked through the photo putting names to faces. There she was in the front, Shirley Smith, and her sister June, then came many, many others: Eleanor Cherwa; Mary, Sis, Hazel, Ellen and Jake Dodge; their grandmother Sarah Jeffers; Guyla Rockwell; Rose and Tony Silva; Charley and Etta Deprete; Anna Goly; Anna Yez; Barbara Borthwick; Laura Williams; the Glazeski twins; the Ray Bartletts; Laura Podelenski; Sophie Goly; Clara Dziema; Pearly Jemison; and of course our own Abe and Hannah Smith, all in a crowd of faces. There they were, perched on the edge of hard times, with the Depression, the years of the war to come, the devastating Hurricane of '38 in the near future, boys who would go off to war, some never to return. Marriages would come and go, families would thrive or fade. There would be happiness somewhere in there, punctuated with heartache as well.

Old photographs can have a strange effect on a person: shadows frozen in time, names and faces from long ago, they look out at us from the past. Some of us know how the stories of their lives played out, but rather than telling, oftentimes it's better to see them as they were on that day in July of '37, and let it go at that.

146

Class Reunion *(August)*

There are few events woven into the cultural and social fabric of our town that carry the same import as your class reunion. Sure, there are yearly town-wide veterans' memorial days when you pause to reflect on those from our town who have fought, fallen, or passed on. There are parades for various reasons, such as significant victories or championships in our sports life, there are family benchmarks like Christmas and Thanksgiving. But there are few gatherings that pull together such a diverse and far-flung community, now oftentimes a cyber-community, where social lines, career trajectories, and forty years of a lifetime intersect. There are few events that evoke the old days, revive old anxieties, and generate so much pleasure as when we take the risk and meet up with classmates from long ago, after life has had several decades to play out and do its work on us. Think of it: some of us who are native to this town spent most of our formative years, our painful and vulnerable adolescence, as well as early adult years with a specific group of friends, many of whom we met for the first time in Kindergarten. So it's no wonder that some of our classmates choose to opt out for those very reasons, and why others can't wait for a class reunion to come around again.

So when Montague Reporter Friend Nancy Currie Holmes came to the office and said we should cover the 40th reunion of TFHS Class of '69, how could we refuse? With my own 45th coming up (TFHS Class of '64) I figured this would be a chance to practice up and play the eavesdropper/fly on the wall thing. I'd go to the '69 reunion and see how those opposite poles of joy and anxiety scenarios play out. The class motto proclaims, "Life should not be a journey to the grave with the intentions of arriving safely in an attractive and well preserved body, but rather to skid in sideways, chocolate in one hand, wine in the other, body thoroughly used up, totally worn out and screaming 'WOO HOO What a Ride!'" I figured it'd be worth a visit to see if they had all lived up to their motto, and if they could still party with the best.

I got in the mood by looking at yearbooks, a collection of which can often form a small section in any family library. When I got to the class of '69, I checked the Administration and Faculty and found that by then, some familiar faces were missing, that there were new faces, and some of the same going back years. Missing by then were the traditional pictures of Superintendent Arthur Burke, an imposing figure in a double-breasted suit, and of George Wrightson the archetypical New England school teacher and headmaster who had guided TFHS for decades as Principal. In their places were the first of a series of revolving door administrators that has become typical of modern public education. The yearbook of the class of '69 was addressed to Robert F. Kennedy, assassinated in the summer of '68. My own class of '64 had dedicated our yearbook to his brother John F. Kennedy assassinated in our senior year, five years before in 1963. These were reminders of the years of turbulence we all experienced through the mid-sixties that would last until the mid 70s.

Others pages brought forth familiar teachers: venerable and durable Fred Oakes had served once again as yearbook advisor. Durable indeed, he had lasted well into his 90s and only this year passed away. The list continued: John Zywna, Bill Connelly, Eddie Bourdeau, Bob Avery, Jack Bassett. There was vintage Charlie Galvin in his bow tie and hair parted down the middle, George Bush at his post teaching European history to generations of novice historians, Mery O'Brien who patiently taught Art appreciation to the same budding intellectuals, and my personal favorite the amiable Harold Fugere doing the best he could to keep us physically fit and safe on the road!

I dwell on the teachers because they form the common strand that links the disparate classes and years of young scholars who passed through our high school. The teachers are the ones who link us and connect us over the years and create a common history.

And of course, for the class of '69, there was the victory in the fabled Turkey Day game. They took that game over much-despised Greenfield High 26-12. Co-captains Robert Cadran, Mark Galvis, and Mike Lewandowski, along with all the others of that class earned bragging rights in town for a lifetime!

It had been decided that the ice-breaker for this 40th would be a pub crawl from establishment to establishment in downtown Turners. They started out at Ristorante DiPaulo where they were treated to a before-hours wine and cheese happy hour. Many remarked on the quality and class of the restaurant. No such dining opportunities existed when this class was passing through in the 60s. Suitably impressed with the setting and reception at DiPaulo's, they headed off for other venues: Jakes' Tavern, Between the Uprights, and for those still upright by then, off to the Rendezvous for a night cap.

They all seemed none the worse for wear when I caught up with them the next evening at the Schuetzen Verein for the main event. Catered by Bub's Barbecue, the feast began after hearing from the local oldies duo "Ruby's Complaint". This class even had its own pastors among its graduates: Father Stan Aksamet of Our Lady of Peace and Reverend Gary Bourbeau of Gill offered up prayers and blessings for classmates both present and absent. Providing the dinner music was river poet/songwriter John Currie (Class of '78) and David Shea ('78 too) migrating through from the Canary Islands and sojourning among the Shea clan in Turners Falls. A life-sized photo of Barack Obama smiled confidently from a front corner of the pavilion. What else could you expect from a class that had featured a nativity scene with a black Jesus and that had staged sit down protests in the school cafeteria? Equal to their early sense of political engagement, placing a photo of Barack seemed a fitting symbol for their 40th, although some were heard to query, "What is HE doing here?"

The socializing continued long into the night with the groups of old friends finding themselves together again, as some of the old cliques re-formed after forty years, but now in a more ephemeral sense, and just for a few hours. Old boyfriends and old girlfriends exchanged brief conversations, sensing the unwritten rules that go unsaid yet well understood: that was then, this is now, and tonight no one crosses the line. Some people danced, mostly the girls, happy to be seventeen again. Then, like all reunions, there came a time when slowly people turned and disappeared from the circle of light under the pavilion, and headed out to the darkened parking lot.

That's how it is with these reunions: you take the step, you take the trip, back to your hometown, apprehensive, hesitant and excited. Once you've made the pilgrimage, oftentimes you're ready to return to your real life and familiar surroundings, yet still wistful. Your friends were there, however briefly, and for better or for worse you could relive those years and laugh. As far as the class of '69 is concerned, one of the classmates later quipped in a parting shot, "When I looked in the mirror on Sunday morning, I expected to see that yearbook face that was on my nametag last night—even though I hated the photo back then—oh, to be eighteen again! But WOO-HOO! What a ride!"

Wind in Wings, Prayers in Stone *(September)*

The grassy expanse of the Turners Falls airport shimmered in the summer heat. It would have been the summer of 1956 or '57 when a couple of boys rode their bikes over to the airfield on the edge of the Plains. We had those old Schwinns or Raleighs, clunkers really, and a pair of heavy WWII vintage binoculars between us. We were both at that age, fascinated by wingèd things. Our interest was sparked by our 5th grade teacher, Mrs. Keough, and her colleague Mrs. Pearl Care, who came to our class every month to talk to us about nature. After that, we often peddled out to the airport to look for horned larks and sparrow hawks. The heat rose in waves from the tarmac runway and the killdeer on the far edge seemed to dance and wave like a mirage on the desert. From time to time, a noisy Piper Cub took off, startling the bird into flying and calling its shrill alarm. I watched the bird, but my boyhood pal Fran Dobosz watched the plane. He knew he wanted to do that. He knew he wanted to fly. As for me, I was definitely going to keep my two feet on the ground, watching the birds. Who was in that Piper Cub? Maybe it was Freddy Macker, Lenny Doton or Henry Waidlich heading down to Plum Island or somewhere up the Maine coast. Whoever it was, Fran wanted to be up there too, with wind under his wings, pulling away from earth's gravity.

Fran did learn to fly, spent a lifetime in the air, and he started out at the Turners airport, like many had before him, inspired by the proximity of the planes and the possibility of flight. From this local airstrip he went on to the Air Force, then three years in the Phillippines and Vietnam, before piloting commercial 727s as a Captain. As for me, I did keep my feet on *terra firma*. As was true for my friend, the small country airstrip made up of a couple of hangars and a humble windsock, was a field of dreams for many a young man, and some not so young.

I suppose it all started with the Wright Brothers at Kitty Hawk in 1903. The joy of flight that affects some of us began spreading across the country. By 1927, the White Coal Farm, an experimental agricultural development that lasted maybe 10 years, allowed private flying on its property on the edge of the Montague Plains. By 1930, the Turners Falls Airport, Inc was founded by Charles Mosher. The corporation purchased the White Coal Farm, and other properties, extending the airport-owned land to 116 acres. Later during the Depression in 1936, a W.P.A. project (read Economic Stimulus Package!) enabled the town to develop the site as a public airport and increase the land holding to 185 acres. By 1942, a certain Dr. Joseph Levy leased the facility and brought in seventeen planes. During his association with the airport over a thousand pilots were trained here. These trainees put in three months at the airport and then transferred to a college for further training. Among them was one Ted Williams who not only trained at the airport, but spent time fly-fishing for trout in the then-pristine Millers River. By 1945, the first Airport Commission was appointed by the Montague Selectmen. Arthur Davis, Ed Pleasant, Henry Waidlich, Frank Kuzmeskus and Dr. Levy were the first to serve in that capacity. Problems arose fairly quickly, with the lack of funding being the primary concern. Local businessmen founded a corporation to give a boost to the airport. Among them were many names familiar to long-time residents: Peter Mackin, Ron Zschau, Sam Blassberg, Sam Couture, Freddie Macker, Walter Garbiel, Henry Wasileski and John Broslick. Again, in spite of the support provided by the local business community, various commercial operators at the airport failed to make it a profitable concern. It was written in the *Turners Falls Observer* of 1960, that "only two members of the board of directors had faith in the future of the airport, Fred Macker and Sam Couture. These two purchased the remaining shares of the corporation in 1953," and by the way, kept the dream alive. Finally by 1960, a paved 3,700 foot runway was completed and dedicated. More than 5000 people were in attendance for this gala that included stunt flying and parachute jumping. Later, in 1970, Pioneer Aviation set up business on the airfield, providing fuel, repairs and maintenance for pilots choosing to locate or drop in at the airport. This business, founded by Charles Bohonowicz, provided the link between those historic early efforts and contemporary times by drawing business to the field. Without the Bohonowicz family, Charlie and son Bruce, the airfield may well have disappeared.

But before the daring men in their flying machines ever arrived on the scene, the rolling hills on the edge of the Plains already had a long history. We have to turn back the calendar about 14,000 years or so for a few minutes here. Imagine you are motoring along the Millers Falls Road, but back in those days, you would be moving under thirty or forty feet of water. A post-glacial lake called Lake Hitchcock lay over the Plains from 17,000 to 13,000 B.P. (Before Present). At the bottom of the lake along which we are traveling, deposits formed that make up the soils we find today in our own back yards. Move the time machine up a few thousand years to when the lake had drained completely, when the lake sands had dried out, and pushed by the winds, formed dunes that we can still see today. If we had been there then, as we moved along the road to Millers Falls, we would be dodging mammoths and mastodons, moving out of the drying delta of the Plains on their way to the Connecticut River to drink and feed. Not really a Jurassic Park, but more like a late Pleistocene Park! Eventually, around 10,500 BP small bands of Paleo-Indians moved into the region to hunt the mastodons, caribou and elk that thrived here. They were the first Tribal people to arrive on the scene, to camp and hunt. Later populations followed over thousands of years, and by 1000-450 BP the Late Woodland Tribes were settled in large complex villages throughout our region. It is estimated that the population along the Connecticut River in Central/Western Massachusetts and southern Vermont was in the vicinity of 75,000 inhabitants! Ten thousand years of tribal history and habitation with their accompanying artifacts mean that our region is highly sensitive in archeological and cultural terms. Many State and Federal laws now protect such artifacts and sites. Federal law specifically states that projects receiving federal money must be surveyed in order to locate and identify any archeological resources that might be affected by the proposed undertaking.

The Turners Falls airport is now under reconstruction and therefore archeological "clearing" of sites is currently being undertaken. Representatives of the only federally-recognized and sovereign tribes in our region, the Narragansetts, the Wampanoag (Mashpee) and the Wampanoag of Gay Head (Aquinnah) have been on site daily for the last two months, and intermittently over the past five years working to identify and protect sensitive cultural areas of the earlier tribal populations. Cairn sites have been located, most likely spiritual locations to which stones were carried by individuals over thousands of years, perhaps as a memorial, an offering, or a prayer. Another example is the Ceremonial Hill on the Plains now under the protection of the Tribes and the National Register of Historical Places, as are other sites nearby such as the Riverside Historical District.

The convergence of aviation interests and Tribal mandates provide challenges for the current and future development of the airport. A third overlay is the jurisdiction of the Massachusetts Natural Heritage and Endangered Species Program which designates the airport lands as Priority Habitat for several threatened species. This agency identified one rare bird species that depends on the disappearing grasslands environment like that of the airport, and an additional eleven rare species that occur on or near the property. For the record, they have identified the following:

1.Wild Lupine Habitat which hosts the rare species Frosted Elfin

2.New Jersey Tea Habitat necessary for the endangered New Jersey Tea Inchworm

3.Heath/Blueberry Habitat vital for 3 moth species of special concern.

4.Pitch Pine Habitat which harbors moth species of special concern

5.Grasslands/ Mown Areas where the threatened Grasshopper Sparrow breeds.

We are fortunate to have within our town lines a gem of a country airport, much appreciated by pilots and passing visitors alike. But with it come responsibilities to protect the 11,000 years of Tribal history on the site as well as the unique habitat afforded creatures in danger of disappearing from the planet. These multiple perspectives on this unique patch of land we have were not evident to me or my boyhood pal of long ago. With time, comes knowledge. And nowadays, if you time it just right, you can still see young and old watching the planes, and the birds too, but now they may also be thinking of their own Native American roots or imagining mastodons in the distance, moving slowly across the tundra, heading for the river.

Talking at the Deep Hole with Buddha *(January 2010)*

It was one of those dark afternoons when the old year was winding down. Standing on the frozen shore near the spot on the Connecticut called the Deep Hole, I watched dark waves lap the edge of the ice, small diving ducks busy as the pale sun went down beyond town. Standing there, I scrutinized the marsh for the snowy owl, that elusive totem bird. I had been told the day earlier that the enigmatic arctic owl was hunting near here. Lost in thought, I wasn't expecting Buddha. He seemed to step out of a swirling snow squall, striding towards me. He was a tall man, trim and fit, a broad smile and creased eyes as he looked out over the river.

"You're Bud...Buddha, Right?" I stammered, instantly recognizing him although we had never exchanged words all these years.

"Yep. Buddha Allen." I knew that. We shook hands.

I told him my name, and added, "I'm Art Brule's son," to help establish links with old times fast. Around here, it helps to explain who your people are and what you're doing here to begin with. Of course, he knew my father, and even my grandfather Joe. Both have been gone, five and ten years respectively, but it was natural of him to mention. Both of us being good talkers, especially concerning the townsfolk and their times past and gone, we got right into it. We talked about Joe's camp up the river a short way from where we stood. He remembered always stopping there for water pouring out of a pipe where my grandfather had a spring on the shore. His in-laws the Welcomes had a camp just up from ours. "We moved that camp higher up the bank quite a few years ago," he mused. "And you know, the door finally shut better when we moved the whole thing the hell out of there!" Knowing I was in the presence of someone who loved local history, and was interested in talking about it, I asked if he knew where the term "Deep Hole" came from, because I had never found the underwater hole in years of paddling over the spot. Buddha didn't know either. "They used to hay this spot before, maybe there was something there then." It's true that the dam had been raised in the 30s, putting fields under water and creating Barton's Cove, maybe that's what happened here too. I shared that there had been an experimental farming effort up where the airport is now, called the White Coal Farm back in the twenties. It was intended to use local hydropower, sometimes called white coal, to irrigate crops on the land where the Plains reached the high riverbank. We agreed that maybe the local name had something to do with that.

The conversation drifted to the days of harvesting ice on the river, Buddha being one of the few who still fondly remembers those days. "Skipped school to work for 25 cents an hour cutting ice. I remember cars driving right up the river here. You could walk or skate right up the river, but you had to watch it at the Narrows 'cause ice jammed up and it was hard to get through." I mentioned I had grown up on the Narrows in the fifties and had a rowboat tied up there in the days before summer work on tobacco. We reminisced about the beauty of the Deep Hole in those days: a wonderful lagoon surrounded by a wall of cattails, the bank lined with thick-trunked ancient weeping willows. "You'd paddle a canoe in there and be lost to the world—think you were in Wild Kingdom like Marlin Perkins!" We both laughed at the reference.

I knew he had been friends with Eddie Pleasant, a neighbor of ours on Carlisle Avenue. "A real gentleman, Eddie Pleasant", Buddha said as he recounted anecdotes about their trips ice-fishing up to Lake Champlain forty years before. He even knew my maternal grandfather Abe Smith from Millers Falls. And wasn't it my aunt he asked, who went off the Hairpin Turn on the Trail one day in the forties when she was skipping school? I chuckled, having read the newspaper account found up in the homestead closet. So much for skipping school, if you wind up in the newspaper!

By then I had totally forgotten about the snowy owl I was looking for. I mentioned that Mark Fairbrother had tipped me off about the bird.

"Don't know Mark, but I sure know his father, Gordon." And I remembered the elder Fairbrother too, when he was Scout master of the Turners Troop for years. We could have gone on, but it was getting dark.

"Well," said Buddha, "I'm going in for a beer! Nice talking with you." He spun around and strode off into the clubhouse. I watched the dark waters for a little while longer as a swan moved slowly across the open channel of water between snowy banks, and faded away down river in the dusk.

Kimon Gregory's Time Machine *(June)*

It's not every day you get to take the road down to Boston with the Father of The Country in the car, along with John Field, 18th century tavern keeper, plus Kim Gregory, Town Crier. The old Jeep could have been getting crowded that day with all of us in the front seat! Luckily for me, the Tavern Wench had stayed home nursing a sore back. But we did miss her salty tongue and fine skill at cursing. As it was, the Tavern-keeper was keeping us all entertained, and fortunately the Jeep had no sunroof, otherwise GW would have stood up all the way through Athol, Fitchburg and Concord, much as he had done in that boat on the Delaware. He did keep us amused with stories of his youth, and by the way, confirmed that the business with the cherry tree and wooden false teeth was just a lot of hooey and hogwash. Never happened.

When things quieted down a bit, the trip became a little more manageable as GW's current incarnation, Kim Gregory of the multiple personalities, filled me in on his mission this time. As we motored down Route 2 towards Logan Airport, Kim shed the various identities he assumes as an historical actor, to be just himself today, or at least to be Kim Gregory, the 18th century Town Crier. And today, his tri-cornered hat was safely stowed away in the luggage and replaced by a jaunty driving cap. So there we were on the road to Boston in early June. Kim was on a mission for sure. He had been chosen, one of four, to represent the US at the International Town Crier Competition in Chester, England. This would be a sentimental journey of sorts for Kim, since he had spent a good part of his younger days in Europe as a Marine in the Army Intelligence Corps, and later as a news correspondent. But more about that in a bit, that's the time machine part.

This current chapter started out when Kim, as official greeter for Historic Deerfield, Inc., knee britches, colonial tri-corner and all, entered a town crier competition as a member of the Town Criers' Guild. An original essay (a piece of cake for a former news reporter), and a few recommendations, and there he was, a finalist. Once the spot to represent the US was secured, he needed a sponsorship, which he got from Historic Deerfield's President, Philip Zay. As he explained during the drive to Logan Airport, Chester, England was hosting the event which included criers from Canada, Australia, France and Germany—thirty in all—including a woman from New Zealand. The event was funded by the participating businesses in Chester. The competing criers were to compose four cries: one mentioning the sponsor numerous times; another (in Kim's case) an upper echelon chain store featuring high-end women's apparel; and two of personal choosing. Kim wrote an original cry touting Old

Deerfield, and his *pièce de résistance* was to be a cry reminding Boston residents (of the 1700s) *not* to have a Merry Christmas, because in Puritan New England, Christmas was banned. His eyes twinkled as he told of the mischievous way he would turn his phrases, and how he had talked the Santa Claus at Yankee Candle out of a bag of snow (artificial that is) to be used as his *coup de théâtre*. He would doff his tri-cornered hat at the end of his warning about Christmas and taking a bow he planned on waving his hat with its brimful of Yankee snow! This, said Kim, was going to be fun.

My job in all of this was to make sure George Washington, the tavern keeper, and Kim Gregory all got to the airport on time. As I mentioned, unfortunately the Tavern Wench was home nursing a sore back, so Carol Gregory herself was not making the trip.

As the Jeep ate up the miles, Kim regaled us all with tales about his WWII adventures and later capers as correspondent for CBS after the war. Good talk shortens the road, and good talkers are never lacking in stories. Kim took us back 66 years when just after D-Day he landed in France, working in military intelligence (a wise-cracking friend would call that an oxymoron). He was with the 97th Infantry, 3rd Army and was headed through the Ruhr towards Czechoslovakia. Kim's job was to move along with General Patton's army, just behind the front lines, so close they could hear the bullets ripping through the air, and liberate and clear sensitive sites such as government offices or officers' headquarters used by the Germans. Documents needed to be secured before they were damaged or removed by soldiers clearing the town, and looking for souvenirs. Kim's unit had to hold documents before valuable evidence could be lost. Some of this evidence eventually would help convict and hang German war criminals at Nuremburg.

Other adventures were on the humorous side; one that he could tell, and we could print, involved the priest of the unit who ran out of wine for the mass one time in Normandy. Kim and a few others volunteered to go out looking for some *vin rouge*. The mayor of Fécamp in Normandy opened his wine cellar to them, gave them what they needed, and then some! Kim chuckled in telling how his group of buddies turned over most of the wine to the priest, but kept a few bottles for personal use. They also managed to liberate a few bottles of Benedictine brandy. "We had excellent breakfasts for days," commented Kim, "that brandy sure went well with our powdered egg rations!"

Shortly after the war, Kim was taken on by CBS to work in various European news desks. London, Paris, Rome, and Bonn were part of his beat. Fond memories flooded back while on this road to Boston. He remembered having accumulated ten weeks of paid vacation, and you can believe he cashed in on that debt owed to him by CBS. He spent every last day of it visiting Europe and CBS news desks, and included a visit to his parents' homeland in Greece.

Before we knew it, we were standing on the curb at Terminal E at Logan, with half our stories finished. Out came the luggage from the back of the Jeep, Kim adjusted his sporty cap, and stepped into the terminal, off to challenge the world for the Town Crier's cup.

A few week's later, Kim provided the postscript to his visit to Mother England. The competition was strong, commented Kim. Some of the costumes and wardrobes were even extravagant. Kim had opted for a conservative set of clothes, feeling that was more keeping with his identity as a New England Puritan. He had worn his home-made cloak with pride, elegant and simple as it was, and stitched by his wench, er, wife! Carol. But clearly many of the competitors had invested hundreds and hundreds of dollars in their outfits. Kim counted on the inspired originality of his cries, touting the businesses supporting him, Historic Deerfield, and reminded everyone of the ban on having any sort of fun at Christmas. In the end, the first and second places were taken by the English Criers (are you surprised?) but the 3rd place went to a member of the Abenaki tribe from Quebec, whom Kim allowed, was outstanding. Many spectators felt Kim deserved a place in the top three, but that was not to be. Back in his home in Erving, Kim was satisfied with his trip and his effort. Besides he said, with a sly look in his eye, there was a tavern in his hotel in Chester, and there they make a most excellent ale!

Travel Sketchbooks

Postcards from France

Four Rivers - (May *2005)*

'You can't stand in the same river twice,' or so says the old adage. But this April, I turned the saying around by standing in many different rivers, just once. Traveling far from the modest Millers, I found myself on the banks of the muddy Rhône in southern France. That Saturday morning, free from my study group with the whole day stretched out ahead of me, I faced the Rhône, turned on my heels and headed through the village of St. Peray with the intention of hiking up to the pinnacle fortress that has looked out over the village and the river for at least the past two millennia.

Up the gravely path I hike, and then head to the Crussol, the name of the ruined fortress, its old walls bleached the color of the limestone cliffs where it has perched since Gallo-Roman times. From the ruined walls, hundreds of feet above the river, the view is strangely familiar, like that of our own valley viewed from the Summit House. The Rhône is broad just here, and it winds its way through the valley, moving south through tree-lined banks and vineyards, Côtes du Rhône, of course. Local legend has it that Napoleon, as a young artillery student living in the city of Valence, just across the river, scaled the sheer cliff up to the ruins on a dare and a promise from a young woman he fancied. Apparently he managed the climb without a problem, and she had to give in to his advances, Napoleon not being one to take *"non"* for an answer...

To the far side of the valley lies the Vercors, rugged snow-covered plateau and site of some of the fiercest guerrilla attacks on the Nazi forces by the French Resistance, and the scene of unspeakable massacre in retaliation by the German occupiers. On the opposite side of the valley, behind me is the Ardèche, more deserted and savage yet, where rocky terrain and lack of water have made life difficult for goat and sheep herders since the first people arrived here in prehistoric times.

But all the harshness of those times seems far away on a day like this; a cool up-draft is bringing the first cheery swallows kiting their way along the ridge stretching out to the south, cherry and apricot trees bloom far below, blending with the pale haze of the first leaf buds of the willows on the shore.

A week later, my feet find their way to the shores of the Loire, which winds its way through the region known as the garden of France. My group is spending a night here in Amboise, exploring the history of several of the chateaux built along the Loire river by kings and nobles wishing to escape the smell, intrigues, and routine of 17th century Paris. For me, a solitary walk in the evening is a pleasant enough escape, and fits nicely into my habit of evening walks back home. Standing on an arched bridge over the water, I watch swarms of swifts and swallows moving upriver, headed north like all spring migrants in April. They swirl excitedly over and under the bridge, reappearing behind me, moving steadily over the relentless spring flood. The Loire is probably the last wild river left in France, broad and sweeping in many places, freely flowing and meandering in its floodplain, making sand bars here and sweeping them away in other places. With no dams, and scarcely any industry from source to mouth, the Loire runs free, and in this season like all rivers, it runs high, past banks of trees budding pale green, flowering cherry trees, and past stately rows of the famous Vouvray vineyards.

From the fort high above the river, the early Gauls watched as Julius Caesar moved up the current, calculating how he could best assure the conquest of these unruly Celtic tribes. Later, the site emerged as an ideal spot for a fortress, with its ramparts assuring a broad sweep of the valley, making Amboise one of the most formidable domains of the French Middle Ages. By the 1500s, Charles the VIII, Queen Anne of Brittany, and François I turned the castle from functional feudal to light-filled and airy Renaissance, launching the Italian style that would dominate Europe for a century or more. Jean Jacques Audubon himself spent formative years on the banks of this lovely river, exploring the Loire estuary near Nantes, and probably dreaming of the birdlife and wildlife waiting to be discovered in the New World.

Farther north flows another river, quietly and sullenly beneath the bridges of Paris. The Seine makes its way, channeled and constricted, through miles of stunning architecture, cultural treasures, and some of the most coveted living space on the face of the planet. Yet this urban river adds its romance to the heart of the city, assuring wide sweeps of sky with dramatic sunset and cloud effects.

On a quiet and rainy afternoon, I made my way to the Carnavalet Museum and in this museum dedicated to the history of Paris, I came upon a diorama of the Seine in its primitive state when only the tribe called the Parisii lived here. By peeling away the centuries you can see the marshes and floodplains, the tributaries, the pirogue boats that were used for fishing and hunting where there are now cathedrals and museums, expressways and palaces. The contradictions are almost overwhelming: longing to climb into the diorama to escape for a quiet afternoon on the river, in spite of being in the heart of the most beautiful and exciting city in the world. Here on an island in this river, the massive Cathedral of Notre Dame was built, universities sprang up, kingdoms, revolutions, republics, invasions came and went, while the river was tamed and channeled. It now squeezes itself through the city, winding past the Louvre Museum, the Orsay full of Impressionists (who loved to paint the effects of light on water), Napoleon's tomb, the Chamber of Representatives, the Eiffel Tower, and so on. Eventually, it gets free of the concrete channeling and resumes its meandering through more natural settings on the way to the English Channel. In fact, on the way out from Paris to our school near Versailles, our train crosses the Seine four times as it meanders towards Normandy and the sea!

Weeks later, I step off the back porch into the dusk gathering along the river. Here on the Millers, we are almost a month behind the seasons in France. The sounds of this spring's freshet fill the woods mixing with the occasional nasal "peent!" of the woodcock and the soft evening warble of the robins. The river flows among the trees, turning little hills into islands perfect for wood ducks to paddle and preen. Now and then a hint of greening grass spikes. There's a reddish hew around the maples, a green cloud that hovers over the birch branches, and the white flowers of the shadbush glow like the ghosts of recently past snowfalls hanging in dark branches.

Provence - *(May, 2007)*

Les Deux France

April 22: It's election Sunday in the village. By ten o'clock the café on the square is filling up, small groups at tables here and there, morning cigarettes, *café crème,* the Sunday newspapers. Sun bakes the square even at this early hour. Everyone is remarking on how early and hot the spring is, and will there be enough rain soon to get through the dry summer months? Lilacs, wisteria, roses in bloom, odd-shaped sycamores, branches truncated, massive and blunt, will create dense shade when they leaf out. For now, just the pale to brilliant blue of a Provence sky overhead, as clouds of screaming swifts streak ten feet above, whipping and maneuvering in the sheer delight of spring. They've made the migration up from Africa, and are swirling around the familiar tile rooftops of their summer homes. Clusters of sleek and gaudy cyclists, in their bright team colors breeze by, chatting loudly and pleased with themselves, the prospect of Sunday morning on the road, physical exertion and challenge ahead, the week's work behind them. The first *pastis* of the morning are having an effect by 10:30 and the talk about the elections is heating up.

The first round in the presidential elections is today the 22nd of April, with 12 candidates on the ballot, ranging from the extreme left (Trotskyist, Communist, the anti-globalist candidates, the Green Party and on through the Socialist, the Center, the Gaullist, and onto the far right wing represented by the *Front National.*) Everyone knows it'll come down to the first serious woman candidate for the presidency in French history, Ségolène Royal of the Socialist Party versus Nicolas Sarkozy of the center-right Gaullist party. The big question is will the huge field of candidates prevent either main candidate from garnering enough of a percentage to ensure victory in the second round in two weeks. Typically, this first round must produce two top candidates for the final round on May 6. Anything can happen. Will Ségolène pull enough votes from the Left and Center to assure herself a place on the ballot for the run-off? Will Sarkozy pull enough votes from the fascist Right to dominate the Center and the Right? Will the mild-mannered former school teacher, Minister of Education and Center candidate François Bayroux fool all and knock one of the other two serious contenders off the ballot for the final round? Speculation abounds as to whether the French voters will vote their conscience in the first round, as is typical, and cast votes for a radical candidate as a form of protest. (For example, one would vote for the ecologist or fascist, knowing full well they could not ever be on the final ballot for the presidency, but to protest, to vote in an angry and radical way, to rock the boat, and send a signal.) In the second round the French want their votes to be more 'useful.' For example, in the last presidential elections, the first round went to the fascist candidate, to protest the continued social unrest, immigration, unemployment, and lack of security on the streets. This protest vote so shocked the country, that in the second round, the Gaullist candidate, Jacques Chirac, easily defeated Jean-Marie Le Pen of the far Right. But the protest vote totally eliminated the Socialist Party, something which Ségolène Royal is fighting to avoid. We will know by tonight, but for now, it's Sunday in the south of France, and *Garçon! Un autre pastis, s'il vous plaît!*

May 6: Climbing high above the Rhône valley as the sun bakes into the hillside of the vineyards of *Tain,* we hike up a zigzag path to the top of a hill, with the visit to a small chapel there, as our first objective for the morning. Rows and rows of two-foot high stocky grapevines march up and down the hills in each direction, each vine supported by a sturdy four-foot high stake. These grapes will produce the world's entire production of a wine called *Crozes-Hermitage* and will sell for around $27 a bottle back in the US. On the other side of the hill, a different sort of wine, *Tain-Hermitage*, will be produced, and given the soil composition, the different amounts of sun exposure and rainfall, a quite different bottle of wine will result. Looking at the soil, you wonder how the vines draw any nourishment at all from this hillside. It seems a pebbly mix of broken down limestone, sand, something vaguely resembling dirt. But, for the sake of consumer research and quality control, we will make our way shortly to the wine cooperative at the foot of this hill, to sample as much of this wine as possible, just to be sure that indeed the quality of the wine is acceptable! Far below, the Rhône flows sullen and dark under the bright sun along tree-lined banks, bordered by flowering apricot trees, cherry, and almond. Up here, we reach the chapel, bemused at the thought that so many of the vineyards of France began as sources for wine to be used by priests and monks to celebrate mass. French religious orders oftentimes developed the best wines, and eventually champagnes, brandy, and other liquors. To some in the US that may seem to be a fundamental contradiction between religious message and actual practice, although France has made an art of savoring contradiction and paradox!

The French electorate has remained true to form in the first round on April 22, by choosing two fundamentally different and contradictory figures to oppose one another in the second round, and thus represent *Les Deux France*. Today, May 6, is the showdown between two different concepts for the future of France. The Socialist Ségolène Royal is facing the controversial and fiery Nicolas Sarkozy in the final round, and they have brought two decidedly different programs to address the concerns of the French electorate: what to do about internal stability and secure neighborhoods, the marginalization and alienation of the immigrant populations (North African Arabs for the most part), unemployment and a stagnant economy, relationship with the US and the European Community. Two weeks ago in the first round, the beautiful weather brought out more than 80% of the electorate that gave Sarkozy a 5 point lead over Royal, but that lead seemed to be shrinking with the "Anything-But-Sarkozy" movement that was growing rapidly.

The elections are always held on Sundays in France, and by 6 PM, back from our hike to the hillside vineyards, we gathered in the living room in front of the television to await the results. Presidential elections are different here: Sunday voting, direct suffrage (no

Electoral College), no opinion polls published within 48 hours of the vote date, no exit polls, the new President will take over immediately in two weeks. At precisely 8 PM, after a dramatic 10-second countdown, the image of Sarkozy was flashed on the screen with approximately 53% of the vote going to the Gaullist and 47% going to the Socialist. And it was over. Shock and dismay in our household, jubilation next door.

This election had divided the French, and the final vote confirmed the split. In the end, a slender majority had chosen the hard-liner: Sarkozy had succeeded in drawing in the Far Right to support him, while holding the Center with his promises of aggressively pursuing policing of the troubled neighborhoods, creating new jobs through Bush-like economic tactics, and creating a new Ministry of National Identity and Immigration which smacked of early fascist Germany for some. Ségolène, on the other hand, had espoused a more humanist, inclusive and integrated approach to solving the nation's woes, more in tune with the trends of many current European governments and their populations. However valiant her campaign was, she had to deal with a divided Socialist Party that was none too sure they wanted her as a candidate at the outset, and a classic leftist formula that may be becoming obsolete in the increasingly disarticulated social landscape and growing global economy. The Socialists will have to confront the new realities and make serious decisions about the evolution of their party's platforms and very existence. The French voted for a strong authoritarian leader who promised a strong France, a leader who has promised to undo the culture and the gains of the May 1968 revolution which for so many of us represented , albeit briefly, social change and political hope. Strangely enough, this leading European nation, which could never understand how America could have chosen George Bush, may well have elected a neo-conservative who admires the Bush/Cheney style of governance! France has always been a sister Republic to America, and now also finds itself at a crossroads.

Things are moving fast however. Already by May 19, the new President Sarkozy has been sworn in, and has named a cabinet composed of eight women and nine men. A notable appointment was the Minister of Justice, a woman of modest background, a daughter of Algerian immigrants, who will be France's main magistrate! Are such appointments a sincere effort to open a new era in French politics, after the years of the tired government of Jacques Chirac? Or are we witnessing the beginning of a relentless though brilliant liquidation of the aging Left? For many of us, France has always been a bastion of individual liberty, the land where national health care, social security and paid vacations for the working class were invented, where artists, intellectuals, and the oppressed seeking asylum and opportunity were welcomed. We must now wait to see what will be lost and what will be gained, and which France will emerge from this divisive election.

Postcard from Breizh

Dark November (*ar miz Du*) - 2008

The train that brought us to the center of Brittany streaked across the countryside from Paris, heading west. Fresh plowed autumn fields already had spikes of green new growth piercing the furrows, the winter grass starting a new cycle. The sky was low and grey.

Bare trees lined the hedgerows, their limbs hung with mistletoe, which grows wild in these parts. The ancient Druids collected the perfect spheres of holy mistletoe in early winter. To them, it represented the roundness of the sun, and staying green even as the darkness of the season deepened.

We traveled in comfort as the super-fast train - the *TGV* - rocketed along at close to 200 m.p.h. The train from Paris to St. Brieuc follows the same route Jack Kerouac describes in *Sartori in Paris*. He was on a mission from Lowell to Brittany to trace his Breton routes. In the 50s, his trip took seven hours. Our modem trip took only three.

Our destination was the little family farm way out into the country. St. Brieuc station was the end of the line for us; the rest of the trip was by car, in a miniscule Peugeot.

In this part of France, Breton is the native language. Breton is a Celtic language, a close cousin to Gaelic and Welsh. Many still speak the language or are learning it, but French, imposed by the central government in Paris, became the *lingua franca* centuries ago. November, in the Breton language is *ar miz Du*, the Dark Month. The first of November coincides with Samhain, the beginning of the Celtic winter. December, by the way, is *ar miz Kerzu* - the Really Dark Month!

Out here, in the farthest western reaches of Europe, where the continent ends, the Dark Month begins with the Day of the Dead: *La Toussaint*. All Saints Day and All Souls' Day is the time for remembering departed family members. At this time of year, the skies are traditionally dark, with swirling clouds driven across the landscape by the damp northwest wind - the *Gwalarne* -blowing in from the North Atlantic and the Irish Sea.

This western tip of Europe, Brittany, is a place of legend and myth, where, according to the lore of the earliest peoples, the wandering souls of the dead drifted westward across the continent toward this region where the sun sets. Megalithic tombs dating back to 5000 BC dot our landscape; standing stones called *menhirs* rise up from fields and edges of woods, placed here by a vanished people that even predate the Celts. This is a place where the realm of the Dead and the Living are separated only by a thin border, where marshes and springs are passageways between the worlds.

November the First is the time when Bretons, and indeed most of France, return to the home village and churchyard cemetery to honor the ancestors. This homecoming is not unlike our migrations at Thanksgiving, bringing those who live far away back to the family's roots.

Central to the ritual is the family tomb in the churchyard. So into the churchyard we went on the blustery morning of November 1, arms laden with a riot of colorful flowers to brighten the tombs of the Breton branch of the family.

No grass grows here, but neat rows of granite and marble slabs lie flat on the earth, much like the burial stones of the ancient peoples here before Christianity. These tombs are already crowded with chrysanthemums - the brilliant fall flower that has the task of brightening these dark stones. Yellows to represent the sun dominate, but also pale to forceful blues, subdued autumnal russets, others white and rose. But it's the sunny yellow lions' heads that throw their sunburst of color in defiance of dark November and the finality of this place.

Families like ours thread along the neat gravel paths among the tombs, children learning and re-learning the names of their forebears, of family lore, the exploits and chagrins of each. Names of old neighbors and old heroes of the wars are read again and again, their memories evoked once more.

A visit later in the day, near dusk, with the sun far in the west on the edge of the horizon sending its last rays to flare up the colors of the flowers on each and every grave, reveals not a one has been overlooked or forgotten, from that of the early pastor from the 1800s to that of the humble gravedigger himself, whom we met one day in the family kitchen. He himself is finally entombed after putting so many others down with the crumbling bones of their ancestors. Dark thoughts maybe, but part of the circular movement of seasons, the wheel of life that turns and figures in so many vestiges of this place: in the megalithic circle of stones, the legends and poems, with roots going back thousands of years.

Our familial chores done, we end the day sitting around the fireplace, roasting chestnuts gathered down the lane, growing wild for the taking, untouched by the blight that wiped out our New England trees. An evening of roasted chestnuts, homemade cider fermented in its bottles, amber and bubbly like fine champagne, with stories of the old folks who inhabited this house, their tales of hard times we hope will come no more.

November 11th, 1918 - 2008

The next benchmark of the month is that of the Armistice of 1918. Whether or not the cannons really fell silent on the 11th hour of the 11th day of the 11th month is a matter for historians and legend. The grandfather of this farmhouse left his fields and family when the bell (*le tocsin*) tolled on that fateful early harvest day in August of

1914. He left his wooden sabots behind, was issued ill-fitting leather boots; a gun was placed in his hands and off he went to the slaughter of a war that lasted four years and took ten million lives. The bells in the village regulated the day in the countryside: the *matines*, the *angelus* three times a day, vespers on Sunday, the *tocsin* for emergencies, the *glas,* for death.

Almost miraculously, grandfather Honoré survived the four years of war, whereas others in the Breton peasant army died by the tens of thousands. He survived Verdun, where 600,000 on both sides fell. He was to be cannon fodder like the other Bretons, many of whom didn't speak French, but knew how to follow orders and protect their home-land. And after the Armistice of 1918, he came home to the farm, having managed to stay alive and keep the troops of Kaiser Bill away from the village.

These parts were not so lucky in the Second World War, when the Nazi blitzkrieg drove deep into Brittany and brought a new Reign of Terror, an Occupation that lasted four years. In the sinister house near the village square, the screams of the tortured villagers who died for resisting the invader, still echo in the minds of those here. Bodies were hung in the trees on the square as a warning to the townspeople. Hostages were taken to the killing field by the nearby forest to be mutilated and executed. Here, by day, sons and husbands hid in the fields and woods from the German patrols; by night they came from the darkness to ambush, to attack the invaders, to blow up trains and tracks. Innocent hostages were taken by the invader for revenge. They paid with their agony, while the Underground resisted the overwhelming force by night.

When D-Day came, Patton's march through this region drew out the population that had resisted and endured. Every household still has a story of the Liberation, and the gratitude for the arrival of the Americans. Every village square has its Monument to the Dead: a million and a half lost in the Great War of 1914-1918, close to that lost in the Second World War, just a little over 20 years later. These are the thoughts that come to mind when the cycle of the year brings November back around to Brittany.

But of course, there is a way to lighten the spirit, and brighten the dark month. The way the Bretons reaffirm their resistance to dark thoughts and the waning year is the Dance. They dance to drive away the dark, dance to show they have endured in spite of all. Arms linked, dancers side by side in long lines of thirty or more celebrants, the ancient intricate steps stamp down hard on the earth. The endless linking of the call and response of the musicians propel the dancers to another world; the line snakes around the farm courtyard, the village square or the assembly hall.

The *fest noz* this November night is in full swing and will last 'til dawn. The piercing medieval sound of the *bombarde*, a wind instrument and ancestor of the *clarinette*, the *biniou*, (Breton bagpipes) drive the dance. All over Brittany this month, people are dancing, linking arms, two steps forward, one back, three to the side, the *An Dro* (circle dance) snakes around the room amid shouts and whoops, rhythmic stamping.

"We're still here!" they seem to shout. After 8000 years of untold adversity, invasion, war and destruction, we still go on, we're still here, we're still here! The steps stamp out an. irresistible rhythm. Like the circle of megalithic standing stones on the hilltop outside the village, the people have endured. And that is how, in these parts, we bring back the sun, we bring back the light to brighten the Dark Month of November.

Postcard from Paris

Rambling in the City of Light – *(May 2009)*

There are days here when the light is just right, and the mood coincides with the light, when it's just enough to be in Paris, to take a hike around town.

Rambling in a city like Paris doesn't have any rules, that's the good part, much like just ambling, whereas, if you'd like to saunter like Thoreau in Concord, you'd actually have to pay attention, take notes, measure things, or find deep philosophical meaning in the light upon Walden Pond, or the Seine. So no splitting hairs today, it's a ramble for sure.

On go the walking shoes and a backpack—you never know what you may pick up along the way, and need to carry. You're set for the open road, or rather, the open street. There's certainly no need to pack a lunch, and when your thirst overcomes you, there's a cafe on every comer, and a glass of wine will do you just fine. And there are plenty of chances to fight off starvation; pastry shops were invented just for that!

The train from the outskirts brings me to St. Lazare station, and I find myself following my feet, angling up the winding streets to Montmartre. Easy enough to keep oriented, with the white Basilica of *Sacré-Coeur* high up on the hill overlooking the city, seeming quite Byzantine and out of place as though it should be in Constantinople rather than Paris.

When I walk, my mind rambles like my feet and being fascinated by history, I can't help thinking about the curious events that put the basilica up there. It seems that the Emperor Napoleon III, having gotten France into a war with Prussia in 1870, managed to get himself captured on the battlefield in northern France, which put a quick end to the Franco-Prussian War as you can imagine. The Prussians showed up in Paris, bringing their word *bistrot* with them, when ordering in cafes, so that eventually cafes also became known as Bistrots, which means "quick," *"tout de suite"* in their language.

Taking advantage of the power vacuum, the working classes of Montmartre and surrounding quarters rose up and proclaimed a workers' republic in 1871, which was shortly thereafter put down by a new French government, after executing thousands of Parisians. Talk about class warfare! At any rate, it was decided to put a basilica on top of the rebellious neighborhoods to symbolize the redemption of the Marx-inspired atheists who had revolted. You don't find that in many history books, but I have it from reliable sources and apparently, it's true.

So as I said, when you're rambling you have license to do whatever you please, and to think about whatever you want, since on a day like this there are no rules, no agenda. When you're out walking you see things you'd miss if you were in the underground Metro or even on a bus.

Most Parisians, like New Yorkers, seem to be in a rush to get somewhere else. But there are plenty of others with little to do but pass time on the streets. There are Edith Piaf-like street singers, violinists or even entire quartets playing Mozart or Bach. There are flute-players from the Andes, and gypsies from Central Europe playing mad, intricate jazz variations.

Parisians are prone to open displays of affection in public—it is, after all, the City of Love as well as the City of Light—so you get used to all the necking in public. Most people pay little attention as they rush by entwined lovers, oblivious to all around them. Then there are the little children out walking with their teachers in file, two-by-two, giggling at the kissing couple, singing and speaking impeccable French, for six year olds!

Parisians seem to have a lot of time on their hands, what with lunches that last an hour and a half and although the American concept of the 20-minute sandwich in between job tasks is unfortunately catching on, the cafés and parks are usually full during the noon hours. Kids still have time to sail their little sailboats in the reflecting pools in the Luxembourg Gardens, in front of the Senate, and you can sit as long as you like on a bench in the sun if you can wrestle one away from the couples in deep embrace. In the past, you had to pay twenty *centimes* to a war widow who had the privilege and the duty to collect the charge from you and give you a ticket good for a seat for as long as you wanted it—a kind of welfare system with dignity that lasted for decades after the last war. But little old ladies don't collect anymore.

After a respite in the park, and a self-satisfied doze in the sun, the desire for espresso becomes overwhelming. Any café will do: you don't have to spend the equivalent of $5 for a cup at the *Deux Magots* when you can have a pure drop of that essence of coffee, standing up at any cafe counter down a side street, for $1.50! Although you don't get the atmosphere and the enjoyment of watching the spectacle of the promenade on the Boulevard St. Germain, you can eavesdrop more easily at the counter,

The politicians, of course, get raked over the coals: Sarkozy gets points for stealing issues from both the Left and the Right, and the Socialists are fighting among themselves, frustrated by their inability to develop a new political formula, infuriated by the bobbing and weaving of President Sarko. Meanwhile, everyone has an opinion about the various strikes: university professors and students are on strike, hospital workers are on strike, a few wildcat strikers working for the government-controlled gas company shut off gas for a number of neighborhoods over the weekend to protest the economic slowdown, office workers have taken to *le boss-napping* (keeping the executives locked in their offices overnight), And so on.

Outdoors at the sidewalk tables, clouds of cigarette smoke rise up during the debates. The French are far from giving up their cigarettes. No smoking indoors, but outside it's just fine; as a matter of fact, it is a right, almost recommended. Takes some getting used to, all over again.

Moved by the caffeine-fueled inspiration, and the growing dark clouds indicating the arrival of the daily downpour, the Impressionist Museum seems just the right thing. The Orsay museum is crowded, full of foreign tourists. It's certainly hard to imagine there's a global economic crisis going on, judging by the number of people who have the time and means to spend a weekend in Paris!

I head to the upper floors, where the crowds are thinner and where some of the more beautiful canvases are located, up near the top floor skylights, where the natural light can bring out the feel of the paintings as the artists intended. These painters made a reputation for themselves by breaking the Classic rules: they painted outdoors, depicting ordinary people doing ordinary things, and capturing the fleeting moment on canvas.

This drew the wrath of the painting establishment in the 1860s, so that the rare few who bought these paintings were the Japanese, and ... the Americans. A great many Renoirs and Monets have wound up in our local museums back in the States.

The subjects of the paintings are held there, caught in time, in evocative light, while the world outside—our world—keeps changing. After coming here yearly to visit some of these works that have now evolved into old acquaintances, one develops a rapport with a Pissarro, a Sisley, a Monet or a Van Gogh; it's like visiting old friends who never age. They've remained the same, captured in time: it's the viewer, the visitor who is forced to recognize the toll of the passing years. But before I can fall into wistfulness and sentiment, two little girls in pig tails and matching red-framed glasses take a picture of a Renoir with their digital camera, say something silly, and pirouette off to another painting to continue their own growing up.

The rainstorm outside having passed, the late afternoon sun shines on the bright wet pavement, and it's high time to be getting back to the quiet suburbs. One last spot down the street brings me to a plaque on the wall next to the playground where the neighborhood children play on swings and see-saws. This being May 8th, celebrated in France as the day the War ended in 1945, the plaque is decorated with a bouquet of flowers for an American soldier who died here on this spot in 1944 in the effort to push the Germans out of Paris. It's always the last stop on my rambles, and I make it a point to thank the young man who ran down this street so many years ago, and was stopped by a bullet, just here.

It's important that the French have not forgotten, and that I be the one to brush over his name with my fingertip, after such a fine day in May.

Postcard from Brittany

Two Churches – *(May 2009)*

Jour de Fete à St. Maurice:
Preparations had been underway since Friday, as everything had to be ready for the feast day of St. Maurice on Sunday, May 24. The church, a rather small country chapel, had been built under the Reign of Jean IV, Duke of Brittany in the 15th century. It's situated just a short walk from our house, and is closed almost all year round, except for this feast day. To get there, we walk along a small tree-lined path, next to a hand-dug channel of water called the *Rigole d'Hilvern*. An

engineering marvel, about six feet wide and five feet deep, it was calculated to drop just enough over the distance to allow for a natural flow to the main canal, 30 miles away. Stone walls, now covered with flowers, form the banks, a clay bottom was placed down to prevent leaks. Developed in the early 19th century to provide a source of water for the Nantes to Brest canal, the *Rigole* is lined with columns of stately ash and chestnut trees, their branches echoing with the songs of cheeky little robins, mistle thrushes and chaffinches. The banks overflow with the bright yellows of buttercups, the deep blues of hundreds of *clochettes*. We reach the ancient chapel by leaving the stream and following a dark path between fields, a tunnel created by overarching trees, to step out into the sunny space around the humble church.

The day before the feast day, I visited the site. A cavernous tent was set up in the field, as well as a rectangular bar next to the church, ready to serve wines and cider to the celebrants. The area behind the chapel was groomed for the competition of *boules* (the French version of *bocce*) guaranteed to draw neighborhood specialists and artists of the sport. For now the grounds were quiet, but by early next morning, churchgoers and celebrants of all inclinations will begin showing up, and both the sacred and the profane will naturally find themselves side by side for this typical Breton *pardon* in memory of a martyred Roman saint from the distant 5th century.

Sunday, of course, began with a mass. About 150 of us gathered for the short procession around the outside of the church and then we filed into the ancient building. Over the door, cherubs from the 15th century were chiseled into the granite, looking strangely like naive Celtic mischief-makers with a wry medieval smile. Inside, statues of obscure Breton saints looked down upon us. Parts of the fieldstone walls were covered with ancient plaster, streaked with water stains from centuries of rain; other walls were bare, their ancient stones needing no cover. Every seat in the chapel was filled. From the back of the church where I stood, a sea of gray-haired faithful watched the mass; others, younger, followed the ceremony too with curiosity. I was standing in the back, both out of duty since I towered over most of the shorter, older congregation and partly because old habits are hard to break! So whether I wound up standing near the doors of St. Mary's back home, or in the back of humble St. Maurice, there I was among the guys who liked to be in the back. Easier to sneak away from time to time, I suppose. In fact, we did slip away after the sermon, to check out the other less religious preparations. At one point one of the faithful attending the mass appeared at the back door of the chapel, asking the five or six drinkers at the bar tent a few feet away to lower their idle chatter and laughter, since it was disturbing the services!

After mass, we headed for the tent where the food would be served. 15 tables, seating 36 people each had been set up, while the grilling of sausages and pork cutlets had begun. As the meal progressed, a number of acquaintances filed by, visiting, exchanging jokes and news with the older members of our family. Many hadn't seen each other in ages, or at least since last year's feast day. Stories of the St. Maurice feast from before the war circulated again, some remembering exploits of men and boys in road races, greased pole climbing, vaulting over the canal, and famous games of *boules*. Old neighborhood stories of course, and considering this has been celebrated every year since the 1490s, there's a lot to remember!

After the meal and the talk, we headed back home, five minutes away. The 80 year- olds in the family had had enough partying for one day, so back home we found ourselves, enjoying coffee in the sunny late afternoon, listening to the birds and the sounds of the revelers that went on long into the evening, just a few fields away.

Return to St. Sulpice: May 30. The massive form of the church of St. Sulpice rises above the hustle and bustle of the busy square down a side street in an ancient neighborhood in Paris. The city noise of cars, buses and jackhammer fall away as you penetrate the silence of the church. The interior is awesome, and quiet. Occasionally a chair scrapes the stone floor, and echoes in the cavernous, muffled silence. Light streams through the towering stained glass windows. Visitors shuffle counter-clockwise around the outer aisle, hundreds of cane-woven chairs fill the center facing the main altar. Like all huge baroque churches, this one is also laid out in the form of a cross.

One unusual feature of this church is a bronze double line across the floor, running east to west. This is the infamous "*gnomon median*" laid down in the 1700s with the permission of Rome, as a scientific experiment intended to establish a permanent way of measuring the earth's seasonal movement in relation to the sun. It has however become infamous because it's featured in the Da Vinci Code as one more clue in the novel of the clandestine secret brotherhood that protects the mysteries of the Holy Grail. The Church of course insists the material in the book is pure fiction. There are numerous disclaimers to this effect on the wall near the obelisk where the bronze line ends, and where the sun, entering from a distant window in the opposite wall, makes its seasonal climb up and down the column.

Respectful visitors file past the various altars around the church, but many are looking for the median. As for me, I stop at one of the side altars: all the church-upbringing in my past makes me pause in front of the sanctuary of St. Anne, patron saint of Brittany and Quebec. I light a candle for the ancestors. For indeed, recent research into the genealogy of our family, has placed one of our early forebears in this very spot in the 1600s. Working painstakingly through long hours of research from her home on Crocker Avenue, Barbara Ripingill, as historian of our extended family, was able to pinpoint the ancestral parish of my 7th-great grandfather as this very same St.Sulpice! His name was Michel Aubert, and he was born in this parish in 1610, and later married his wife Jeanne here in 1635. Their daughter Elizabeth, also born here, immigrated to Quebec where she married in 1670 and began a new life and family in New France. In their day, this place was a simple parish church in the fields and woods surrounding Paris. Of course, the city grew up around the parish, and as the congregation grew, the need for a bigger place of worship grew with it until the earlier more humble building was replaced in the 1650s by the massive edifice standing here now, five times bigger than the original. I feel like somehow, once again, life has come full circle. A branch of the family came from this very parish more than 400 years ago. I've frequented this neighborhood, and passed by this church off and on for the past forty years without realizing my ancient connections to this place. And now I wonder, with this revelation of the ancestral ties to this parish putting some perspective to the story, could it explain in some strange way how some of us with a certain amount of imagination, are attracted to certain places, and that some of us sense we've been there before?

Postcard from Paris

Back to the Future Perfect – 1609 (*November 2009*)

It's not often you can catch up with a 400-year old ancestor. It can happen, though, if you've got some imagination and a fondness for historical speculation.

As fascinated as we Americans are with genealogy and ancestral origins, it's startling when you pick up the trail of a forebear in a faraway place. That happened for me just the other day on a Paris street called the Rue St. Honoré.

Family history can be very instructive. It helps explain who we are by telling us where we've been, and sometimes even tells us where we're going. The search is something of a mystery novel, and the trail this time led to No. 129 Rue St. Honoré.

The ancestor in question lived on that street, just outside the walls of the Louvre, which is now the famous museum. But in Louis Hébert's day, it was royal palace, and a place of dark and deadly intrigue.

Louis was born at No. 129 in 1575, or at least that's what the plaque affixed to the outside of the building stated. The house in those days was called the Mortier d'Or and Louis lived there with his father Nicolas, his mother Jacqueline, and various brothers and sisters. Louis was an adventurous sort, luckily for thousands of us who count him as our progenitor and ancestor, because he brought our DNA from Paris to New France in the New World in 1607.

We descendents of Louis Hébert can point to that year with pride. We're a bit tired of the Anglo-Saxon bragging of those ancestors who came over on the Mayflower in 1620. We French -

Canadians beat the Pilgrims by 13 years, crossing the Atlantic with Samuel de Champlain.

By 1617, we had already started a small settlement called Kébec, where Louis and his wife and children were surviving as best they could in a new land, ravaged by fiercely long winters. Take that, Miles Standish, Priscilla Mullins, and John Alden!

Back in Paris though, there were years of bloody goings-on outside Louis' doorstep on that busy street in the late 1500s, and it's little wonder that men like him were more than ready to head out to the New World to make a fresh start. His childhood was spent in unsettled times, and his father's shop, an apothecary, surely served as a meeting place for political discussion. The wars of religion between Catholic and Protestant had been raging ever since Martin Luther posted his objections about the Catholic Church on a church door in Wittenberg.

One of the most gruesome chapters had its start just outside the family's house, in 1572, a few years before Louis' birth. Full of intrigue, conspiracy, murder, massacre and general mayhem, this chapter set in motion a chain of events that would lead to the opportunity for Louis to seek his fortune in the wilds of Canada. You can't make up a story like this: King Henry II, father of a number of princes and at least one princess, managed to get himself killed in a friendly joust just outside the Louvre, to start the latest round of trouble. His sickly and weak son became Charles II. Henry's widow, Catherine de Medici, was now the Queen Mother.

She was the daughter of an Italian banking family, disciples of Machiavelli, and well-known for their skill in inventive uses of poisons to kill off their rivals. Catherine was pulling the strings in the realm, and decided to marry off her Catholic daughter Margo to the Protestant King Henry of Navarre.

The wedding was scheduled to be held in Notre Dame and the Louvre in August 1572, and was ostensibly planned to put an end to the religious war by means of this mixed marriage. However, once the Protestant guests arrived for the uneasy matrimonial ceremony, Catherine and her son Charles launched the infamous Massacre of St. Bartholomew of August 25th, when the bells of St. Germain l'Auxerrois began tolling at midnight, the signal for Catholics to begin eliminating the Protestant wedding guests. Thousands died that night, just outside the doors of the Hébert household on Rue St. Honoré, and all over Paris.

Henry of Navarre, the groom, was saved only by his wise decision to convert to Catholicism, He and his new wife Margo, who despised each other quite mutually, left Paris for his kingdom in Protestant southern France.

Three years later, our ancestor Louis was born and baptized in the same church that announced the beginning of the massacre. He grew up during a time of pestilence, plague and more upheaval. Charles II had died within a year of the massacre. His brother became king as Henry III, a somewhat scandalous transvestite, who was, in turn, assassinated a few years later. This cleared the way for the return of Henry of Navarre to become Henry IV, one of France's most beloved kings, and a sponsor of Samuel de Champlain, whom some say was his illegitimate son. Like I said, you can't make this up!

So the stage was set. By 1600, Champlain, fascinated with the New World, was eager to explore that part of it called New France. He put together a crew, and needed a few specialists to help in settling and starting up a colony. He hired six stone masons, a tinker, a blacksmith, and an apothecary. Louis Hébert, having followed in his father's footsteps as a pharmacist, was the man for the job.

Louis was more than ready to leave his shop and seek adventures in a new land. He was recruited by Champlain to serve as doctor and maintain the health of the crew, and eventually to care for the well-being of the new settlement.

After a number of round trips with Champlain beginning in 1607, he settled in Port Royal (modern Annapolis) in Nova Scotia, and later in a remote site called Québec, with his family. He learned new herbal cures from the Amerindians, and took up farming, out of necessity to survive. For many years, Louis, his wife Marie Rollet, and his children were the first and only European family that survived in the harsh climate and long winters. His house and farm were located at the current site of the basilica of Québec.

There is a monument to Louis Hébert near the site, honoring him and his wife as the first family to be established in New France. His children produced many descendants who populated Québec, and down through the generations, some of us ended up in this small town in Massachusetts called Montague.

So it was with no little emotion that I read the plaque on Rue St. Honoré the other day, stating that this is where a part of the family story started. It did state that this is the house in which Louis was born. As for me, having completed the circle of a centuries-old voyage begun here, it might also have said: *"Enfant du pays, by the time you get back to read this, I will have been gone for 400 years."* There's the *future perfect tense* for you. I knew I'd get back to it somehow!

Postcard from Paris

A Quick Trip to the Guillotine – *(June 2010)*

Something in the newspaper caught my eye. A new exhibit at the Impressionist museum—*le Musée d' Orsay*—entitled Crime and Punishment, has just opened, with an authentic guillotine as its centerpiece. This I needed to see! This was the chance of a lifetime, after having taught the French Revolution for years, to actually have a guillotine experience, up close but, eh, not *too* personal. The article stated that several obstacles had almost stopped the undertaking: many considered it too repulsive and apparently, it hadn't been easy to actually find a working guillotine for the exhibit. Since the death penalty was abolished by the French in 1981, and given the powerful loathing inspired by this machine, they were all dismantled and sent to the dustbin of history. If you didn't already know, prior to the 1980, there was no trip to the "chair," nor lethal injection, nor gas chamber for those on Death Row; it was off with your head!

The article that triggered this excursion appeared in the International Herald Tribune, by Doreen Carvajal, and it covered the challenges of preparing such an exhibit. Trustees of the museum resisted the whole concept because they felt that including the guillotine was just too grotesque and macabre for the museum, which has on permanent display the light airy works of Monet, Renoir, Degas, and their contemporaries. However, Robert Badinter, the former Minister of Justice who succeeded in abolishing the guillotine back in the 80s, pushed hard for the exhibit and finally got his way. He was quoted as saying: "What does the world watch on television today? Crime, the police, the police commissioner, the judges, the lawyers. Crime is an enduring fascination for humans." He was right. There have been an average of 4000 visitors a day, and high schools have booked group tours through the month of July. The main problem in getting the exhibit up and running, however, was that no one could find a real guillotine. Once abolished, the French wasted no time in trashing the national supply of this infernal machine. Finally one was found, the last of its species in existence. Trailing *la Veuve,* the Widow, from museum to museum, they finally located the last one in a military fort outside Paris in a corner of a cluttered cellar. They were told they could borrow the guillotine, provided they never return it! This 1872 model, with its spring-action, push button efficiency was dusted off, refurbished, and set up in the exhibit room under a trailing black veil at the far end of the second gallery.

The article cites a certain repugnance among curators to actually include the guillotine in the show, but as the concept evolved, there was clearly no way to mount an exhibit on Crime and Punishment without giving the "Nation's Razor" its place. Unfortunately, the last executioner, the headsman, could not be present, having died (of old age) in 2008. He had guillotined the last criminal, Roger Bontems in 1972. The man who did the honors, a Monsieur Chevalier, had performed his task without knowing it was for the last time, and had brought his son to work with him to see how the job was done in the expectation that he would take over when the elder Chevalier retired. The executioner's position is typically a hereditary one, passed down through the generations from father to son. However, the younger Monsieur Chevalier was soon to be unemployed. The condemned man, Bontems, didn't actually kill anyone, but he did participate in a prison uprising that left two hostages dead, as Carvajal reports.

Monsieur Bontems, by the way, knocked back a cognac or two, was placed in the headlock, down came the blade, and it was over. Mr. Badinter, a young lawyer at the time, turned away at the last moment.

So there we were, on a beautiful morning in May in Paris, traveling by subway to the museum. We passed under the Place de la Concorde where the original guillotine had been set up during the French Revolution in 1789. Dr. Guillotin was its inventor, and had developed his machine as a more efficient and humane means of eliminating enemies of the new Republic. French social and political philosophers had had a great influence on pre-revolutionary thought in America, and the American Revolution of 1776 helped set the stage for the French Revolution of 1789. But whereas our revolution stopped at the point where relatively wealthy men, many of them slave-holders, consolidated power and framed the Constitution, the French Revolution spun out of control and led to the Reign of Terror. By the time Robespierre reached the climax of his power, thousands and thousands had fallen victim to the guillotine. The Clergy, priests, bishops, aristocrats, political moderates all made the quick trip to the Nation's Razor on the Place de la Concorde for public execution before cheering crowds. The severed heads of the more famous victims were held up for view. The heads really rolled during those bloody days, including King Louis XVI and Queen Marie Antoinette, followed a few years later by the very same ones who had sent so many others to the blade, and were responsible for the regicide, including Danton and Robespierre himself. In fact, capital punishment up until this invention by Dr. G. was quite medieval, featuring an ingenious variety of cruel tortures and beheadings by axe. So the guillotine was seen as actually humane. One wag of the period exclaimed that all you feel is *"une sensation agréable de fraîcheur"* (an agreeable sensation of coolness) as your head rolls.

Off the subway at the stop called Solferino, a quick visit to an irresistible pastry shop on the way, around a corner and there we were. A deep breath, and into the familiar Orsay we went. We entered a series of galleries to the side of the main exhibition hall. In the darkened first gallery, the fourteen-foot tall guillotine stands wreathed in a black veil, watched over by a portrait of Lucifer, with glowing red eyes. A quote from Victor Hugo faces Lucifer: *"One can have a certain indifference about the death penalty, not quite knowing whether to say yes or no, until one sees with their own eyes a guillotine."*

But this is an art exhibit after all, and this is France, so there are more than 400 works assembled around this theme of Crime and Punishment. The first paintings evoke themes from the Bible, and the 6th Commandment, "Thou Shalt Not Kill." One painting depicts the first criminal, Cain, who carries within himself his own punishment— culpability and crushing guilt. We are reminded of the first cousins of homicide: patricide, infanticide, regicide, genocide et al. From this point forward in the exhibit, the visitor views depictions of all of the above by some of the great masters: Goya, Blake, Prud'hon, David, Géricault, Daumier, Degas, right down to Andy Warhol. But it is the towering machine that lures you closer at the outset. It is remarkably simple: a plank where the victim is held in place face down, the wooden collar through which the head is placed, a copper basin to catch head and blood, a wicker basket in which the cadaver is placed. Efficient, as mentioned earlier: one second you're there, one second later, you're not there anymore. Standing there, various emotions flood over the visitor in quick succession: fascination, horror, revulsion, gallows humor. The Nation's Razor indeed. I'm reminded of the New Yorker cartoon: the condemned is placed with head under the guillotine blade, when the gracious executioner leans over, smiling, and says "paper or plastic?"

It's difficult to linger for long in front of the coldly efficient machine. Other rooms in the exhibit, 18 in all, covering different variations on the theme draw you further into this exhibit of macabre and artful mayhem. Severed heads, various body parts, death masks lead you from room to room as your sensitivities get dulled and revulsion grows. No wonder high-schoolers love this. There seems to be a particular fascination with maidens, damsels and bloody daggers. Women assassins like Charlotte Corday who killed revolutionary hero Marat in his bathtub are beautifully portrayed. Charlotte is in good company along with paintings of bloody crimes perpetrated by Salomé, Judith, Messaline, Lady Macbeth.

I quickened my pace, having seen enough. I lingered long enough to stand in front of a wooden Death Row door retrieved from a prison for this exhibit; I jotted down the graffiti of the condemned: *"Adieu, Frisette, adieu, adieu. 1889"*, *"Pas de chance , 1912"* By then, I really needed to get back to my familiar museum rooms with old friends like Monet, Sisley, Pissarro, and get back to celebrating life.

After a reassuring stroll through the bright, crowded rooms, I headed for the nearest bistrot on the corner. I needed to put things back in order. I stood at the counter and tossed back a cognac with an espresso for chaser, in memory of poor Roger Bontems, who holds the dubious distinction of being the last man to make the trip to the guillotine.

Irish Sketchbook

A Day in the Great Blasket – (*January 2009)*

Escaping to Ireland may be a good cure for what ails us in the last days of January, which has gotten us through three of the four seasons. Winter has stormed back after a peek at spring. The thaw melted away the snow we skied on the day before, and tricked one-year old pollywogs to the surface of the frog pond. They came up through a hole in the ice and swam coldly in the three inches of rainwater between sky above and ice below. Soon they would've been frozen solid, preserved like insects in amber, and not looking forward to ice-skating over their surprised and betrayed little bodies quick-frozen under our blades, we netted them all and dropped them back into the hole. They dove straight down into the pond bottom and debris, hopefully to sleep tight and safe until April.

Watching snow falling in the grey woods, dark sparrow shapes drifting in and out of the garden in the daylong dusk light, it came to mind that January and July would make for a rather nice symmetry. In the wink of an eye, I was time-traveling back to the 4th of July six months earlier, with the whole summer ahead of me and a trip to the Blasket Islands off the Irish coast just a step away from the quay to the ferry boat. I jumped onto the first boat crossing of the season.

To get this far, you're up early, over to the top of the cliff in Dun Chaoin, where the ticket office is secured by cables strung over the roof and bolted to boulders to keep it from sailing off the cliff and into the sea during the frequent gales, then a winding steep descent down a cement walkway that drops 75 feet rather rapidly to the stone quay to meet the boat *Tir na nÓg* (the *Land of Youth*, named for the fabled mystical land of Irish legend). Soft Kerry Gaelic mingles with shouted orders to travelers to *mind the step*! Graceful fulmars, seafaring whimsical birds, glide above us with nary a wing stroke; they come in here to the sea cliffs to nest. We catch a wave just right and the young captain picks his way out of the cove, avoiding jagged rocks just below the surface, and we're off across the Blasket Sound to the islands five miles away.

The Blasket Islands stretch out from the tip of the Dingle Peninsula of County Kerry: *An Blascaod Mór* - the Great Blasket - and several smaller islands, devoid now of permanent residents. They were home to the Blasket people for the last 500 years, but the Irish government evacuated the last villagers in 1953. The population had dwindled, the turf gave out, the fishing went "underfoot" as they say here, medical emergencies became tragedies too many times, and the treacherous Blasket Sound, which had kept the islanders safe from famine and greedy English landlords, finally brought to a close the chapter on the Blaskets.

However, before the last village turf fire went out, an extraordinary thing happened. By the early 1900s, anthropologists from Stockholm and Dublin discovered that the people of the Blaskets were living a language and a culture mostly unchanged for hundreds of years. It has been likened by linguists to the equivalent of finding a lost people still speaking classic Greek in versification by Homer! So a number of scholars made their way to the islands to explore, research, and document this unique time capsule of a society. Many came to learn the language, unchanged by English or modem Irish language reforms.

And even more importantly, they got the islanders to set down their stories. Some dictated them, some wrote them in Irish, with later English translations. Tomas O'Crohan was the first, and his *"The Islandman"* became an international bestseller in the 1920s and 30s. There were also Peig Sayers (*"An Old Woman's Reflections"*) and Maurice O'Sullivan *("Twenty Years A-growing"*), and many others. A tremendous output of literature and poetry from a small village just before it disappeared forever. It seems that at one point, so many villagers were trying their hand at writing down their stories and memoirs that many a jealous squabble arose among the 20 or so cottages in the village as to who should be the one to first write the story for the outsiders!

This brilliant flowering of Blasket Island literature lasted well into the 50s (and more new books about them have appeared in the past two years), but the harshness of the gale, the rip current of the Sound, and the lure of America caused the population to dwindle, and eventually leave for good. Interestingly enough, almost the entire population of the Blaskets that chose to migrate settled in Springfield and Holyoke, Massachusetts, where the memories and legends still thrive around Hungry Hill and the John Boyle O'Reilly Club.

Churning through the waves, the *Tir na nÓg* is tossed around like a cork, being a small boat, but slowly we draw closer to the strand of beach and the landing in among the rocks. The beach is full of seals and their pups sunning in the early summer morning, a dolphin and a curious seal circle and swim under the boat. They would soon get used to the comings and goings of the ferry, but this being the first of the season, it's something new to investigate. We are in all less than 20 passengers, and we wait our turn to be shuttled from the boat to the slip of a quay in a zodiac, the waves and the rocks being too risky for even the small *Tir na nÓg*. Setting foot firmly yet carefully on the slippery cement, I trudge up the rocky path, keeping a low center of gravity on the steep incline.

Once up to the village site, I wander among the ruins of the village, most stone houses still standing, minus the roofs whose timbers were scavenged long ago and brought out to the mainland. It is always moving to stand in Tomas' doorway, or to visit the hearth of Maurice O'Sullivan, now exposed to the elements, or to stand in the one room of the old schoolhouse. So many sites written about in the Blasket books, now just parts of a ghost town. Every path, every little portion of the island had its place-name, recorded in the memoirs of the islanders and scholars. The village is set on a steep slope, tucked under the shoulder of the island. You would think islanders would have evolved one leg shorter than the other just to keep their balance on such a slope!

After a wander through the village, the pleasure of a hike around the island is next in store, and off we go, striding up the open path, with all of the Kingdom of Kerry laid out on the horizon of a perfect Kerry blue sky.....

(January still, winter lurking outside the window, I get back to crossing to Ireland by armchair, snug in a corner near the glowing

Glenwood C, just the best thing this damp and grey Sunday. Outside, the blue jays swirl through the yard, their clan now numbering up to thirty, tree sparrows and juncos tune up their songs in this false spring morning. Inside, the stove ticks as its heat spreads into the room and the old dog shifts in his sleep.)

A far cry from a dark New England day, it's a sunny July 4th once again, six months back in time and I've got a day in the Great Blasket stretched out before me with nothing in mind but ramble on the island and do as I please.

The Great Blasket, the last parish in Ireland before America, is the farthest point west in Europe. It stretches from the tip of the Dingle Peninsula with a cluster of smaller islands trailing behind her in the foaming Atlantic.

After visiting the ruins of the only village, the broad path leading up and around the treeless island beckons. Hiking west up to the first shoulder of the island, the turf path switches back and heads off to the top of the island, but this will be my first stop. The island falls away just here, the grass close cropped as a golf course putting green by the sheep. The cliff edge is hidden by the steep curve of the island, down and away. Blue sea and white caps, a towering rock stack island in the distance - the Tiaracht - and nothing beyond but open sea and America, 4000 miles away.

This is a good spot to stretch out and lean back on an elbow, contemplate the scenery and reflect on the 364 days gone by since I last reached this precise spot on the planet. That's what vacations are for, and Ireland does strange things to the traveler. This is after all the land of the leprechaun, the *Tuatha De Danaan*, the Salmon of Wisdom, the singing stones, banshees and holy wells. Ages ago, Fionn Mac Cuhaill fought the King of the World, and helped decide the fate of the Irish peoples, just a few miles away from here, over on the other side of the mainland. Ireland draws the physical world in close to the spiritual world, and it's easy to fall under the charm it casts.

Time passes slowly when you're stretched out on your back in the warm grass, cap pulled over your eyes and the empty Atlantic rolling a hundred feet below the cliffs. However, the New Englander in me gets me up and pursuing the objective of the day, which is perambulating the island, following the path that angles around the Blasket like a belt. In spite of the warmth of July, lines from one of the island's writers, Tomas O'Crohan, come to mind: *"It's a winter's day and it looks it.... the grass that was green yesterday is withered today ... Sheep that have been blown out of their resting places in the hills are trying to force their way into the houses. The young woman who was as spruce as the swan on the lake, when she comes in with a bucket of water, the comb has been snatched from the back of her head by the wind, her hair is straying into her mouth, there is mud on her clothes, the water is half spilt, and she is as cross as someone who is out of tobacco ... there are many cures in fine weather and much harm in hard."*

Lucky for me, it is a rare, fine day, though even in summer gales can shut the island off from the mainland for a week at a time. The weather is bright and sunny, I'm far from the fireworks and cookouts of the 4th as well, celebrating the independence of the open path.

Once having rounded the far corner of the island, I find my spot on the landward side, where the sun shines brightest. The vast Bay of Dingle and all of Kerry stretches out in the sunshine. Time for a serious lunch and more lolling in the grass. Out of the backpack comes organic Dingle Bay salmon, soda bread from my B&B, and a bottle of Guinness. All of the principal Irish food groups. Feeling smug and fortunate on such a fine day, the thought of a letter received back in Millers Falls in the twenties comes to mind: my grandmother's aunt wrote asking for help, clothing, and mittens for the family's men out fishing on Dingle Bay that winter. A poignant letter kept in a drawer all these years until I found it, and I wonder what became of those men and their families, part of my extended family, who lived and fished just out there on the sparkling bay before me, with Kerry headlands on the horizon.

By sitting still and moving slowly, I blend into the hillside enough to reassure the dozens of rabbits living in the surrounding 100 yards, and before long they're out of their holes, preening and stretching, then sprawling out lazily full length in this rare sunny day. With no predators on the island, they breed, well, like rabbits! An occasional raven or black-backed gull glides by, and far out on the bay, brilliant white gannets plummet into the sea like javelins falling from 50 feet up, diving repeatedly into shoals of fish near the surface. You could feel like you've died and gone to heaven on such a day!

Eliminating that option, however, I'm back up on my feet and wandering downhill to the village, still out of sight around the curve of the island, then back down to the boat slip, the day's pilgrimage completed, soon to be leaving this western-most island on the *Tir na nÓg*. The young man who is piloting this bounding bark called the *Land of Youth*, turns out to be a college student from Cork who has lived most of his life in the village on the mainland. He has a great summer job running this boat. He sets his course through the Blasket Sound, attaches the wheel with a cord, and takes out his fiddle to practice as we churn through the waves. The schoolteacher in me rises up and I head to the pilot cab to help keep an eye on things while this seemingly carefree youngster nonchalantly steers with one foot while he fiddles. I ask him does he know the *"Mist-Covered Mountain,"* since just in the distance the line of mist is beginning to cause the top of Mount Eagle to disappear. He says he doesn't, but I do, and we make it a point to meet in Kruger Kavanagh's pub later on to swap fiddle tunes.

And in fact, that very evening, walking from my B&B to the village pub, the mantle of mist was hovering over the top of the island where I had spent my day, smoky and creamy in the moonlight. Resembling so stunningly I might add, the rich and creamy head on a fresh pint of Guinness, the inspiration came upon me to quicken my step a bit to get a little sooner to the glowing and beckoning pub over there in the soft evening distance.

Of Irish Wakes and Ancient Martyrs – *(October 2006)*

The Harp Pub--We held the wake last March, and a fine wake it was, even by Irish standards. We were all packed into Power's pub, the Harp, in North Amherst, and the stout, porter, whiskey and beer flowed by the gallon. And although there were neither coffin nor corpse (the two men who were being waked having died two hundred years before), that didn't keep the mourners from celebrating them in the time-honored fashion. The house was full of all manner of Irish professions: the judges, the lawyers, the teachers, the politicians, the poets, the bricklayers and the road-builders. Eulogies, stories, poems and toasts flowed, although there was no brawl nor miracle like there had been at the infamous Tim Finnegan's wake:

"Biddy O'Brien gave Biddy O'Connor a belt in the gob
And left her sprawling on the floor
Oh then the mighty war did rage
'Twas woman to woman and man to man
Shillelagh law did all engage
And a row and ruction soon began,
Then Mickey Maloney ducked his head
When a naggin of whiskey flew at him
It missed him, falling on the bed
The liquor splattered over Tim
Bedad he revives and see how he rises
And Timothy rising from the bed
Says 'fling your whiskey round like blazes
Thunder 'n Jaysus, do you think I'm dead?'

Wasn't it the truth I told you: lots of fun
At Finnegan's wake!"

So this wake at the Harp for the two men had been held appropriately near March 17th, but we didn't get around to the burial until this September, which could be considered macabre even by Irish standards. But all these events are symbolic anyway, given the 200-year delay. Actually, the celebration was more of a rising up or resurrection rather than a lowering down, since as I said, the deceased were not present, nor had they been for several hundred years. The two men who were not present at their own funeral were Dominic Daley and James Halligan, two Irishmen who in 1806 were in the wrong place at the wrong time in Protestant Massachusetts. Accused of a murder in Wilbraham that they did not commit, they got a speedy trial, and since thousands of people were waiting to see the public hanging, they were quickly strung up in a field in Northampton, victims of racial prejudice and hasty blind justice. The whole tale has been related in a book: *Garden of Martyrs* by Michael C. White, St. Martin's Press. They were eventually pardoned on Saint Patrick's Day in 1984 by Governor Michael Dukakis. I'm sure they felt a whole lot better about the misunderstanding upon hearing the news somewhere up there in Martyrs' Corner of the firmament.

So in honor of the two men, the Irish gathering at the end of September was billed as a *"Celtic Music Festival,* celebrating Tolerance, Justice and Equality." The Pines Theater was an excellent venue, with its gently sloping lawn going down to the stage and the towering pines as a backdrop. You couldn't have asked for a more typically Irish day than this: roaring rowdy music, Guinness, good food, and what they call in Ireland "a soft, fine day." In other words, it was wet, really *wet!* Unfortunately for the organizers, this *soft* day kept the crowds away, but those of us who were there had a great time of it. Many local Irish bands took a turn on the stage. The Greenfield-based group *Selkie* started the morning off, followed by *Spancil Hill, Tir Na nÓg,* with John Allen's band the *Big Bad Bollocks* kicking up the volume and the driving lyrics. *Murphy's Men* had flown in from rebel Cork with rousing ballads in the Clancy Brothers and Wolftones tradition, and tossed in some trademark Brit-bashing to the partisan crowd ("...we fought you for 800 years and we'll fight 800 more, give us our country back!")

The headliners were Craig Eastman, a local fiddling wizard who has made it big in Los Angeles and who always draws a sizable Valley crowd. His main man in the band is Bo Fitzgerald, a rock-jawed barroom and pub singer whose renditions of *"Brendan the Navigator"* and *"Eileen Óg"* generated enough heat to raise the fog from the pines. Just about then, a gangling Great Blue Heron winged through the trees, both bird and crowd were quite startled, just before it disappeared as quickly into the fog as it had appeared. He was surely sent by St. Columcille, a great Donegal holy man, who befriended a heron while in exile in fog-shrouded Iona. Birds do not appear to the Irish without a reason or a message involved. There's more to it than meets the eye, as they say. But what that is, who knows? After the heron came Maura O'Connell, formerly of the group *De Danaan*; she's now alive and well and living in Nashville. Powerfully talented, she belted out song after song, more like country soul than Irish ballad.

With her, the day in the Pines was drawing to a close, but it was early yet, and in true Irish fashion, Harpo Power, who runs the award-winning Irish pub where this celebration all began back in March, announced that the party was moving to the Harp where he was putting on a free spread. The day ended there, where the wake began in March: the stout flowed, the good-natured Irish *craic* continued non-stop, the fiddles, guitars and *bodhráns* launched another mighty session. So Daley and Halligan were given a grand send-off after all, even though it was 200 years late!

A Day in the Burren, Part I – (*March 2007*)

Corofin-- This is *the* time of all the year when the American Irish and those who wish they were Irish get misty-eyed, or pie-eyed in the pubs, in celebration of the feast of St. Patrick. Beer runs green, you must wear something green (never orange!), or at least stick a green shamrock somewhere. *B'gosh and B'gorrah*! (whatever that means), even the act of saying "corned beef and cabbage" has an authentic Irish ring to it, although our Irish forebears ate the stuff out of extreme necessity, definitely not for its delicate and subtle blend of flavors. Indeed, it's not a coincidence that the word for *to cook* in Gaelic is the same as *to boil*. That explains a lot about Irish cuisine.

At this time of year, some of us even hear echoes of somebody like Bing Crosby crooning:

If ever you go across the sea to Ireland
Then maybe at the closing of your day.
You will sit and watch the moon rise over Claddagh,
And watch the sun go down on Galway Bay..

The genteel longing and resignation in these lyrics have faded, to be replaced by more fierce head-banging anthems by the likes of the Pogues, Flogging Molly or Drop-Kick Murphy. True, a few thatch-roofed cottages still dot the countryside here and there in Ireland, although most of them can now be found in theme parks. The IRA has finally laid down its arms, the Brits are currently the good guys, and we even may see the time in a few weeks when the Protestants and Catholics will govern the lost Six Counties of Northern Ireland together. No indeed, with the Celtic Tiger all the rage, this is not your grandmother's Ireland any more.

However, there are places where the Ireland you imagined can still be found. For example, what wasn't mentioned in the Galway Bay lyrics was the landscape just across from Galway that defines this entire corner of Eirinn. This region is the Burren. Somehow, it would be hard to work such a blunt word as "burren" into a nostalgic song. Sounds too much like "barren, although there is no connection between the two words. The Burren in Gaelic is most likely *"bhoireann"* meaning "a stony place". The Burren is in fact a 300 square mile landscape most often compared to the surface of the moon. It's a limestone region, with parallel foot-deep crevices stretching off to the horizon. There are a few narrow roads that traverse this moonscape, but it's easy to get lost, and for some of us, that's just what we want.

A good ramble in the Burren starts with a good Irish breakfast to fortify you, which usually involves enough tea to float a battleship, along with a hefty dose of cholesterol and sodium nitrites—enough to keep you going until your lunch of Guinness and smoked salmon. To do this right, you have to spend the night in a lovely sounding village like Lisdoonvarna, Kilfenora, Corofin or Doolin. I always choose Corofin, an attractive village, made more intriguing by the fact that my ancestors, the *O hEifearnáin* (Heffernans in English translation, literally "demons from Hell" in Old Irish) were driven from this town in the early Middle Ages. Why, we haven't figured out yet, but we're having fun imagining. There is some sense of satisfaction that my DNA has made it back to town, although incognito, and none of the locals recognize me as a descendent of the banished demons. With breakfast settling, a good way to start the day is with a quiet drive on a narrow road (*bótharín*, in Irish) meaning a passage big enough for cows(*bó*). This particular one wends its way around Lake Inchiquin, just outside of Corofin. Easy enough to stop in the shade, because it's now really hot in Ireland: so much for the Irish Mist concept. No one else is on this wee road, so I leave the car where it is. Just below, beyond a grassy field going down to the lake shore, horses and cows mingle and wade knee-deep in the shallow lake, munching on water grasses, graceful swans glide by in their arched neck manner, accustomed as they are to spending time with the horses and sharing grazing rights. Wrens and wood warblers sing and move around me in the hedgerow.

It would be very easy to spend the rest of the morning here, but there are a few other things to see on this ramble on the way to lunch. Crossing from a green and shady border zone to get closer to the stony heart of the Burren, then turning left at the ruined church of Kilnaboy, it's a good custom to stop and look for the *Sheila-na-gig* carved in the church wall. Our *Sheila* is a pagan representation of Woman and Fertility, strangely enough, exposing the (ahem!) source of her fertility with both hands and a fierce smile; a sort of pre-Christian Vagina Monologue? How Sheila of the Pagans got to be carved a thousand years ago into the wall of this ancient Christian Church is something of a mystery, but not rare. There are many *Sheilas* represented on ancient stones all over the west of Ireland. Apparently, there was nothing wrong with mixing a little paganism in with your Catholicism. Irish contradiction is part of the charm of the country.

Further down the *botharín* you go, then taking an unmarked road to the right, without warning, you are in the middle of the lunarscape. Huge bare rounded hills called *mullough* rise up like the backs of whales rolling across the countryside, trees have vanished, temporary lakes called *turlough* appear or disappear monthly, seeping through the porous limestone that can't hold water for long. Beneath the surface however, water has formed fantastic subterranean rivers and grottos to the delight of cave explorers and spelunkers.

Right here in the middle of the Burren, if you look closely, you can see remnants of stone and mortar columns, and curious open spaces. Not some ancient ruins these, but rather a testimony to common sense and environmental protection triumphing over bureaucratic efforts to transform this area into another theme park. The locals organized protests and fund raisers and lawsuits, and finally the government, with its European Community subsidies, gave up, tore up the blacktop, never built the invasive hotel and visitors' center, and moved the whole concept to the nearby village of Kilfenora. The heart of the Burren was preserved, and it's still a place where, according to those who live here, you can hear the sound of stone and ancient music on the wind.

On the other hand, the stomach has a music of its own and it's saying something that sounds like "lunch!" Monk's Restaurant in Ballyvaughn is just the place, where the moonscape abruptly meets the seascape on the Clare shore of Galway Bay. Guinness, seafood chowder, smoked salmon, lamb stew, all manner of fish and pub grub await. After lunch, it'll be a good idea to get walking again, but there's no rush. With the daylight lasting until close to midnight this far west, there's plenty of time ahead for a hike along the Famine Road, some bird-watching at the Cliffs of Moher, and an evening of music in Doolin. But for now, time to lay into a meal at Monk's, to sit and look out over Galway Bay, and feel pretty smug about being in this place, lost for the time being, in the West of Ireland.

A Day in the Burren, Part 2

If you're lucky, you're sitting at an outside table at Monk's Pub in Ballyvaughn, your pint of Guinness optimistically half full (you can count the foam rings formed with every gulp taken), you've spent the perfect morning drifting through the limestone scenery of the Burren, the sun sparkles on Galway Bay, even through your closed eyelids, and the Irish gods are in their heaven. Luckily, there's no concept of *siesta* in Ireland, even for the lazy traveler in this slow-moving country, otherwise I'd be here for hours! I've been told by the

Irish they've also rejected *manana, manana,* another Spanish-language concept, because it conveys far too much urgency to suit them! So, keeping the 'don't rush, don't bother' rule in mind, a plan slowly forms to continue the ramble through the Burren, making sure there's a pub at the beginning and at the end of each ramble.

Reluctantly leaving Monk's, a drive along the Coast Road brings you past the Black Head (headland) where shortly you turn left and up the Caher Valley to a secret little spot known mostly to the birds and a few hill-walkers. Up here there's a little stream that trickles out of the Burren, a green oasis of running water in the rocky landscape. This shallow laughing brook is home to finches and wagtails, and became part of our Burren routine when we were bird-watching and botanizing up this way a few years ago.

A stony slope rises up behind us bearing on its shoulders what is called a 'Green Road', impassible by car even though it's ten feet wide. Stone walls border each side, marching off in both directions as far as the eye can see. These green roads lead nowhere. The true Irish name is Famine Road, as the bilingual signs will tell you: one name in English, the real name in Gaelic. The starving Irish were forced to build these roads during the Famine by the occupying British, in order to justify the doling out of a few pennies a day. Somehow it galled the British to give the native people of this land any kind of welfare support for free. They were made to earn the pittance by building useless roads that went nowhere. The Brits often complained of the Burren that "there wasn't enough water to drown a man, nor a tree to hang him on, nor enough earth to bury him."

Nevertheless, off we go up the hill, scrambling over the shale surface of the so-called road, peeking into crevices for wild flowers. Through a series of quirks of geological history, the Burren is a rare spot where exotics like orchids and other Mediterranean flora share some of the same terrain with alpine flowers, where the gentians give this desert stone a blue hue in May.

Here and there in the slab-stone walls you see a deliberately constructed little doorway, a bit more than ankle-high. The builders knew that the Little People travel along certain paths and to disturb that would certainly bring down serious misfortune and evil upon the thoughtless one. The fairy people were not to be trifled with, so allowances had to be made. You must still remember to turn your jacket inside out before you enter any one of the fairy circles that dot the landscape, otherwise, you'll be carried off and not be heard of again. Or at least that's what I've been told.

A forty minute hike leads to the top of the hill from which you can spy another headland, the Cliffs of Moher, about 20 miles away. We'll get there in due time. But there's some back-tracking and one last stop in another lost corner of the landscape before reaching the coast.

The ringfort at Caher Chómain is invisible most of the time. You approach it from a road that leads you past wedge tombs and dolmens dating from 4000 BC. Soon you see a little lay-by, big enough for two to three cars. It's through the cow-gate with you, and you're off on a short mile-long hike along a path through the hazelbush and furze woods. The path leads down to a little glen, one of the most peaceful spots you'll find in this peaceful country. The glen glows in the late afternoon light. There's a swale of meadow grass and wildflowers that sweeps in a crescent along the base of a curving one hundred foot cliff, partly hidden by groves of small oak and hazelnut shrubs. The path turns upward to the top of the hill and soon you're picking your way through a rocky grassland of tumbledown walls. You first reach the outermost walls of the ringfort. which is beginning to materialize before your eyes. This wall is 8 feet thick and still about 5 feet high, and encloses another ring and another. These rings are really semi-circles that end at the edge of the cliff. Safe from attack up the cliff, and with these concentric defenses, the inhabitants were quite secure here. Just to be sure however, there were a series of tunnels that led to escape routes far down the cliff. It's estimated that an extended family of about 60 to 70 people lived on this site around 400 AD and for several centuries.

Sitting on the edge of the cliff, quite safe from your enemies, out comes the soda bread and Irish Cheddar that's been riding around in the backpack. Sun is moving at an angle but there's still hours of daylight left. Trees rise up the cliff, their top leafy branches softening the atmosphere here. A small falcon with a reddish hue, a kestrel, hovers on the updraft and hunts for supper. He does have a fierce look on his darkly hooded face, and a sharp glint in the eye. Suddenly you're floating with him over the tops of trees and down the glen, with trees rushing past, and your knapsack left far below! Good God, it could be the fairies, you think, and in a wink the spell is broken, and you're back sitting near your cheese. Thank goodness it was just a reminder to turn the jacket inside out! Suddenly, a donkey brays in the wind in the distance, but otherwise, silence again, except for the trees swaying in the light breeze.

Ignoring one of the basic rules of the rover in the Irish landscape, it's time to formulate a plan and a time-frame. Get over to the cliffs the other side of Doolin, before the light fades too much. A short jaunt in the car, and by timing it right, you arrive there after the last tour bus leaves around 6 PM. The cost of parking has risen from a reasonable one euro to about 12 euros over the past few years. You can't park without paying, unless it's after hours, so by shrewd calculation, at this hour you don't have to pay for the privilege of walking up a paved path leaning into the constant gale blowing up the cliff face from the crashing sea hundreds of feet below, to look at the Cliffs through wind-seared watery eyes.

Birds however, are what bring some of us here; you can see waves any time. Not too far below are numerous rock stacks where you can watch thousands and thousands of sea birds. Puffins, guillemots, murres, fulmars and gulls glide, wheel and scream, carrying on with their lives in this raucous seabird colony. This is the kind of sight you would need to travel for hours by boat Stateside in the North Atlantic to witness. Here, it's a ten minute walk to the bird rocks. Sadly, the Celtic Tiger, the chance to make millions off this natural attraction, and too many deaths when nonchalant tourists allowed themselves to be swept off cliffs by the fierce winds, have changed the visitor's experience. The government has launched a mammoth project to do a massive reconstruction of the viewing areas and walkways. Apparently soon one will view the Cliffs from *inside* a hollowed-out, artificial hill facing the cliffs, the access to which you'll pay for mightily with your hard-earned euros.

Ah well, surely the birds will keep up their racket all night, and the waves will roar as they have for millions of years here. It's high time to be rolling down to the musical town of Doolin through the twilight. In the distance you see the lighthouses on the Aran Islands, turf smoke rises up the chimneys into the gathering evening along the down-turning road. You can almost already hear the fiddle and tin whistle lilting up from celebrated pubs like O'Connor's, Mc Dermott's and McGann's. The sun will be back up again before we see the end of this perfect day in County Clare! But then, as they say here, "ah there's no rush, won't we all be sleeping long enough one day?"

Séamas Begley and the Captain – (*August 2007*)

Coumeenoule--Séamas was a hard one to get to know, a fierce-looking Kerryman, yet short enough, with a tangle of hair the color of the weathered hay stacked in mounds in his field. He lived alone out here on the edge of Western Europe. The headland that was his home and field faced the uninhabited Blasket Islands, considered the furthest-most western point of Europe. Séamas lived on the mainland, but it was his house that was the furthest west in any case. Considering that he most likely slept in the west end of the house, with his feet in the east as is the traditional Irish custom among country people, his own head was the one the farthest west of any of the hundreds of millions of Europeans living behind him in the rest of Ireland, the British Isles, and the Continent! Sort of like standing out over the bow of a ship plowing through the North Atlantic, like the Queen Mary, or the Titanic. But I don't think he ever thought much about that. This bachelor farmer thought mostly about his hay, his sheep and his land, way out here on the western tip of Europe.

I got to know him, in an indirect way, thanks to John Crohan. These things take time in Ireland, as does this story! John Crohan was an elderly gentleman who at the end of his life, stayed with Séamas, and the two old gents probably fixed their simple meals, and watched the sea just beyond their kitchen window. However, whereas Séamas rarely smiled and usually had a stern look on him, old John was gentle and poetic. We first met John when he appeared out of nowhere on the cliff above Coumeenoole beach and warbled a sweet song in Irish to Monique while she waited for me to come back along the cliff where I was off walking. I heard a bit of it; he had a fine thin and reedy voice like old people do, but it was as clear as limpid water. He told us who he was, and how the government moved him off the Blasket Island in the 50s. He was glad to go, but still longed for the deserted village across the Sound. That's why he was finishing his days in Séamas Begley's house, where he could see his island every day. It was he who took us down to the strand and showed us how to find Kerry diamonds twinkling in the cliff, and he introduced us to the seal who came along the shore, a dark gray shape underwater, every evening. I'm sure there was a connection between the seal and the old Islandman, but when he spoke to the seal, his ancient Gaelic was too hard for me to follow. So whatever had gone on between the seal and him, I could never make out, but there was a connection.

Well, after five years of my spending a week or two in the B&B next to Séamas' house, I came one June and there was no Old John. I asked Séamas about it, the first words we'd exchanged in five years, other than nods and grunted hellos. He seemed surprised that I was asking about John, and he explained to me that the old man was now over in the cemetery of Dun Quin, facing the islands, not far from Peig Sayers, the legendary storyteller from the village. I uttered in Irish *"Tá brón mór orm dó"* (There is great sorrow on me for him.) A quick light came into Séamas' fierce little eyes and he said something like, "You know a bit of our language, do you?"

"Only a little bit," I answered in Irish, concerned that he would break into a flow of words that I could never fathom. Instead, he smiled briefly and said goodbye. And off he went up to Dun Mór Head. The Head, rising up from a field at the edge of the sea, resembles the head of a whale, the sloping back humping up like the hills do in Kerry and coming to an abrupt round crown overlooking the Sound and the islands like a big green Moby Dick. This headland was the pride and bane of Séamas Begley. It belonged to him through his family, going back into the ages, except for the time of the English landlords. He hayed the foot of the head and he grazed sheep on the rest of the slope. It was a bane to him because tourists often trespassed there, knocking down the old stone walls, letting their city dogs chase his sheep, and sometimes those sheep broke their legs in the furrows and rabbit holes in their panic to get away from the dogs. I always asked him if he minded if I went up there for an evening walk to watch the seabirds coming through the Sound on the way home to roost. He said he didn't mind. But every time I was up there he'd appear out of nowhere, apparently examining a sheep or looking at the sea, but he'd be watching me out of the corner of his eye. And he never went anywhere without The Captain. You see, The Captain was his dog. Black and white of course, but bigger and calmer than the hyperkinetic border collies we see here in Massachusetts. I loved the Captain at first sight. I'd been a long time without a dog and I began calculating how to get one like him back to the States. That never happened, but every summer for years I did visit Séamas and The Captain, watching them work their sheep and walk the hill, silhouetted against the sunset and shining sea facing the Blaskets.

Then one year, the inevitable happened. I got there a week after Séamas had been put in the ground, a too-early death from cancer. On my first evening walk going west along the road past Séamas' empty house, I heard a bark. I had to look hard. But there was the muzzle and forepaws of The Captain. He was peering out through a space under the shed door where he had been locked up. Was he calling me? I had had my share of old dogs dying one by one back home, and here I was, faced with another old dog, an old acquaintance, locked up and abandoned in the dark for all I knew. The Captain, who had spent a life time running free in these hills and fields in this corner of Kerry, proud of his work, was now locked up in the dark with barely any room to stretch his legs, only a few feet from the doorway where his master should be. Now this was a dilemma. Why had all those years come down to this? Was this some kind of destiny that I was supposed to be here to help The Captain escape? Was this part of some inexplicable plan the Irish fates had conjured up? I called to him and he just barked. Maybe he recognized me, or maybe he was half crazy with fear, grief, hunger or was he going to protect his home until his master got back? I promised him I'd come back that night with a plan to get him out of there, but it turned out I was never able to help him escape. My landlady at the B&B, Columba, told me that some farmers up the road were looking in on him. That wasn't good enough for me, but not being from here, I wasn't sure that I could free him, and if I did, then what? Columba was sure he'd attack me, but I didn't think so. Be that as it may, I never got to find out. The next day he was gone, and although I asked around, I didn't get a straight answer from anyone. I'd like to think he lived out his days working the sheep, and lounging in the sun, but there's no knowing.

That western-most house is still there but abandoned, like many of the houses of the Old Ireland, and in a few more years no one will remember the little story of Séamas and The Captain except me, and now, you.

The Hills of Donegal – (*March 2008*)

"Come by the hills to the land where fancy is free
And stand where the peaks meet the sky and
The loughs meet the sea
Where the rivers run clear and the bracken is gold in the sun
And the cares of tomorrow can wait till this day is done"

North Amherst--Sean's voice rises up above the din in the Harp pub; the Friday night gathering of the Irish diaspora in this corner of Massachusetts is picking up steam, and patrons are partying as only the Irish and near-Irish can, especially at this time of year. Yet the poignancy of the words and the clarity of the voice reach to the back of the house where even the loudest voices drop silent. Pints posed on the bar or still in midair, patrons turn their attention to the singer or peer deeply into their frothy glasses finding somewhere in the foam of the stout the start of a collective memory and yearning evoked in the phrasing of the song. Soon there won't be a dry eye in the house. The singer and the song continue.

"Come to the hills to the land where life is a song
And sing while the birds fill the air with their joys
All day long,
Where the trees sway in time and even the wind sings in tune,
And the cares of tomorrow can wait till this day is done."

Now the spell is cast, and many of us are thinking about hills. In the Irish frame of reference that this week requires, you could think about the hills of Kerry or Kildare, Cork or Kilkenney, Glendalough or Armagh. For some of us, it's the hills of Donegal. And luckily for us who love Donegal, it isn't easy to get there. You have to leave most tour buses behind, forget about the paddy-whackery of the Killarney stereotypes, and the leprechaun tea cozies. Donegal is way up in the Northwest corner of Ireland, and you need a good reason to go there. And as in everything, there's the easy way and the hard way. I always prefer the hard way—that is, a meandering road that has me going a half a day west, in order to turn slowly north on my way through Connemara, Mayo, Sligo, lovely Leitrim, to Donegal. It's always best in this country to get off the main roads, to see what'll happen. Otherwise your visit here will be like a drive down the Interstate. This trip and this story are taking us to the village of Glencolumkill on a far western peninsula in Donegal. This Glen is isolated enough so that you have the feeling of being on the edge of the world. Which in fact, you are. The roads get progressively smaller until you're sharing them only with sheep, who are not particularly impressed by your need to get anywhere anytime soon. Another factor in your sense of isolation is that English has disappeared from the road signs several hours ago, because this is the Gaeltacht, a Gaelic-speaking region where most inhabitants grew up speaking Irish, and prefer to keep it that way. The small road leads through rolling moor land and stacks of turf cut and set in rows to dry. The village of Glencolumkill is set in a valley created by a wee river that flows down from the highlands just to the north and reaches the sea at the edge of the village. In addition to being home to a folk park project begun in the fifties to help locals find employment here, it's also home to a thriving Cultural Center called *Oideas Gael*, that specializes in Irish-language workshops, classes in weaving, pottery, local dance and song, archeology and hill walking. This has been very successful in attracting visitors interested in an intelligent option for an Irish learning vacation and in participating in Irish culture during their stay.

The Glen gets its name from a famous saint who was born not far from the village, who spent enough time here praying and being a hermit to lend his name to the spot. In fact the places he frequented as a holy hermit are recorded in the local lore, and a pilgrimage every April takes place here: the faithful walk the length of the various stations, oftentimes barefoot, beginning at midnight and finishing a little after dawn at the holy well. Columbkill (the Dove of the Church) was an Irish saint born in Donegal in AD 521. Like St Patrick, he's one of the best-known Irish saints, but unlike St. Patrick, he was a truly Irish native, born into the great northern O'Neill clan who ruled this part of the country at the time. Columbkill, like most Irish saints, was the focus of many adventures and legends. One of the favorites being the Battle of the Books, which people still tell in the pubs in these parts if the mood is right, like now. It seems that Columbkill had a great love of books, as would any holy man, and that his teacher St. Finnian had recently made the pilgrimage to Rome and had procured a new translation of the Psalms. When Columbkill learned of this he asked to borrow the book, and St. Finnian agreed, on the condition he not copy it.

As it turned out however, Columbkill did spend many nights copying it before returning it, more than likely rationalizing that he was serving God by being able to spread His Word through the new translations. Being suspicious, St. Finnian sent a spy to find out what Columbkill was doing late at night with the book. The spy peered into the saint's cell through a keyhole to catch him at his copying. Luckily for Columbkill, he had rescued a great heron who now lived with him in his room. Unluckily for St. Finnian's man, the heron saw the eye at the keyhole and with one lightning-fast thrust of his beak, the heron quickly turned the intruder into a one-eyed spy! St Finnian however was not about to let St. Columbkill get away with the copying. He appealed to the high King Diarmaid. Not only did Finnian want his book back, but he also wanted the copy. The king ruled in his favor and ordered the book and its copy returned. Columbkill refused, got his northern clan of O'Neills to march against the high king and the clan of the southern O'Neills, and eventually after much death and destruction at the foot of Benbulben in Sligo, Diarmaid was defeated by the northerners. Within two years Diarmaid was killed in another battle and the northern O'Neills took over as the high kings of Tara for centuries to come.

But the Battle of the Books took an unexpected turn. Columbkill got to keep his copy, but he was filled with remorse at the huge number of dead, over 3000, and vowed to leave Ireland in self-imposed exile. He left in AD 563 for exile on the island of Iona, off the coast of Scotland. He apparently returned once to Ireland before his death, but under strange circumstances. Since he had sworn his feet would never again touch Irish soil, nor would his eyes see Ireland again, he apparently arrived home blindfolded, sitting backwards in the boat, and when he stepped on shore, he had clods of peat attached to his feet so that it could be said that his feet didn't actually touch the earth of his homeland. Or at least, that's what they'll tell you at Biddy's Crossroads pub in Glencolmkill, in between the jigs and reels, the pints of stout, the turf fire and the Irish whiskey, in the hills of County Donegal.

> *"Come by the hills to the land where legends remain*
> *Where the stories of old fill the hearts and yet come again,*
> *Where the past has been lost and our future is yet to be won*
> *And the cares of tomorrow can wait till this day is done."*

Lá feile sona Naombh Padraig daoibh! Happy St. Patrick's Day!

Music in the Glen – *(March 2009)*

Glencolumkill-- If ye be at all like myself, as the calendar dates start marking off the countdown to the 17th of this month, ye feel the need to get back by hook or by crook, by *Aer Lingus* or by armchair, to that distant Shamrock Shore. And if you've at all paid attention to these articles over the years, you know I like to linger a day or two in County Clare. Just long enough there, as Seamus Heaney puts it:

> *"...along the Flaggy Shore, when the wind*
> *And the light are working off each other,*
> *As big soft buffetings come at the car sideways*
> *And catch the heart off guard and blow it open."*

Well, once I'm after getting the wind into my lungs in the ancient Burren, I'd be off up the winding tar road to Sligo and to Donegal beyond. Sometimes I drift up there in a round-about way to the northwest corner of the Republic, other times it's a bee-line I'm making to escape the tour buses, the shamrockery and the jig-dancing leprechauns. Way up in Donegal it's rare enough to see a tour bus, and there's definitely nary a one off the main road. So it's the small roads for me, the *bóthar,* officially, a road the width of a cow standing sideways and measured from tip of nose to tip of tail, roads where you often have to argue with the sheep as to which one of you should move out of the way first.

Up you go to the Glen, its full name being *Gleann Cholm Cille*, the Glen of the Dove of the Church. You may remember I've spoken of this truly Irish-born saint (St. Patrick you must know, was not born in Ireland!) Good Columcille started out on his saintly ways here in these parts, before he got himself into trouble and exile. A fairly common fate of high-spirited Irish I might add. Our glen of Columcille is tucked away as small valleys are wont to be, and is easily overlooked, although songs have been written about it and poems dedicated to it. But I'm always up here not only for the Gaelic isolation and untouched beauty of it all, but also for the music. There's a wondrous fiddler here, a true Irish national treasure by the name of James Byrne, a sweet simple man and a fiddler with no equal. I'll get back to this Fiddler in the Glen in a bit.

For the isolation I'm talking about, to get deep into it, you need to drive through the small village, which doesn't take long. A short 200-yard main street with a church, a grocery store, and three pubs which you have to avoid if you're going to get anywhere at all this day. You could drive the rugged tricky road out of town by passing the empty golf course (not only a victim of overly grandiose plans to attract golfing tourists way up here, but also victim of the gales that are constantly causing golf balls to hook and sail far over the sea cliffs into the crashing surf below). You could also take the road north, being more direct. Either way, once out of town you soon arrive at a fork in the road in a grove of small oaks. If you bear right it'll take you all the way to another hidden valley where Ardara is tucked away, if you bear left where the faded sign indicates the road to Port, then it'll lead you up through a treeless valley dotted with occasional cottages. The *bóthar* has become a *bótharín*, a road big enough for only little cows you would suppose, and once you leave the few cottages behind, you are winding along and alone, down a long twisty road through an empty landscape, on the way to the deserted fishing village of Port. All is rocky out-cropping and rolling peat-covered hills and moors here, as far as the eye can see. The bog road follows the stream valley down to the cleft in the cliffs at the sea edge. Four stone huts, in ruins, their stone walls slowly tumbling down to the rocky ground from which they came, make up the deserted hamlet. Men, having gone out to sea from here to fish on the churning North Atlantic, finally gave up their centuries-long struggle years ago and faded away. The place is now abandoned to a few birds, the lonely rocks, and occasional visitors like me. It is too melancholy for many, but I come time and time again, for the wildness and the isolation of it all. However, a few hours in this place is usually all it takes to be ready for some human company and the friendly warmth of any one of those three pubs I mentioned to you earlier.

On the way back at two miles an hour up the long road, in a sheltered curve behind a mountain of turf I stop to take out my fiddle, and tune it up to see what it sounds like in such a lonely place like this. The violin, so much like the human voice, can express the feelings that are in your mind or draw inspiration from the surrounding empty hills such as these. I try a merry jig that fades away, and more slow stately waltzes and lonesome airs are drawn forth, as if from the landscape. It's definitely high time to get myself to a pub.

After that short fiddle stop I'm up the road to town ten miles away, and before long in the evening I'm snug in the pub called Biddy's Crossroads. I'm enjoying the fiddling of our man James whom I mentioned earlier, when he gives me a sign. He asks, "Now weren't you the Yank who was driving out on the road to Port in the little red rental car? And did you bring the 'whistler' you were playing out on the road?" Decidedly, news travels fast in these parts, and I go out to the little red rental car to get my "whistler"—what they call a fiddle around here. That was my introduction to the fiddler from this glen, and we remained musical acquaintances for years. The epitome of the Donegal fiddler, he was born in a cottage with no electricity in the wee valley through which I had just driven to get to Port, and he had learned his music from his father and uncles, and played with all the legendary fiddlers from towns nearby: Johnny Doherty, Francie Byrne, Con Cassidy, Tommy Peoples. A slightly built man, yet stocky enough, weathered face from the years of farming and haying and turf-cutting, his fiddle is always not far away hung on a hook on the kitchen wall, dusty with rosin. He often played with the whole family, his wife and three mischievous daughters, who made the kitchen or the pub ring with the wild reels, the Donegal highlands, and the exquisite slow airs. When James played he had a distant look on him, his eyes were far away, a look you get if you've stayed out in deserted Port too long, all the while his fingers chasing each other over the strings with a mind of their own.

Once the session gets roaring, the custom up here is for everyone to take a turn, to do their piece to entertain the others. Old gents from out of the hills come to do their bit of a poem, there's a heart-wrenching song about the martyred Michael Collins, an off-color music-hall tune from a visiting bawdy middle-aged Dublin woman, some fancy step-dancing from the local teacher, who later actually had us all outdoors and dancing Kerry sets in the very crossroads at Biddy's! And the night goes on. The shades are drawn and the doors locked so that no one can come in, but inside the *craic* is mighty, the fiddles are aglow with the jigs and the reels as the pints come around, and the smiles get deeper.

Well then, this is where I go, when March comes around, to The Glen far away, the three pubs and the wild music. And as for you, if you've got a craving to get away to Ireland before it's too late, and if you've got an ounce of adventure in you, you'll get up to the hills of Donegal and drop in at Biddy's where there's surely a fiddler near the fireside, a glass of Jameson's, where a pint of stout is your only man! And a song and a hearty laugh are never far away.

RIP James Byrne 1945-2008

Isle of Inishfree – *(March 2010)*

> *"I've met some folks who say that I'm a dreamer,*
> *And there's no doubt there's truth in what they say,*
> *But a man's bound to be a dreamer*
> *When all the things he loves are far away.*
> *And precious things are dreams unto an exile.*
> *They take him o'er the land across the sea—*
> *Especially when it happens he's an exile*
> *From that dear lovely Isle of Inishfree."*

The voice of our singer Seán Burke rises above the drinking din and the clatter of the Harp pub this St. Patrick's week. His song, sung many the time each year, has special meaning during this season, for it evokes the aching longing some of us feel for the Emerald Isle. And wouldn't you know that this story has strands that tie into our Spring Street bridge project and the swans we see on the lovely river that flows through our town? Since we Irish and near-Irish have the freedom to weave all manner of tales this month, and the Irish surely don't need an excuse to tell a story, we will here explain how Seán, the bridge and the swans work their way onto this page.

> *"And when the moonlight peeps across the rooftops*

Of this great city, wondrous though it be,
I scarcely feel its wonder or its laughter.
I'm once again back home in Inishfree."

Our man is no sweet-singing Irish tenor, he has the working man's voice, plaintive, lonesome and lyrical and it can cut through the noisy crowd in the bar, and stop the blathering pub-talk in its tracks. The singer is a man from *Maigh Eo* (County Mayo), a region up towards the northwest of Ireland. You'd take a left off the road to Sligo and Donegal to get there, and you'd better brush up on your *cúpla focal* (your few words of Irish) because it's a grand Gaelic-speaking region. Mayo has produced many generations of stout-hearted road-builders and heavy construction men over the years. And it turns out that when this man Seán is not singing, bringing a tear to every dreamer's eye, causing us to carefully study the lingering froth in our pints of Guinness, well, he's up over our wee town of Turners Falls overseeing the re-building of the Spring Street bridge, so long closed and separating the two sections of Prospect Street. Now not only does the street provide a picturesque view of the village rooftops, but a bit further along, as the street curves slowly around the hill's contour, it does indeed give a prospect out over the river, and this is where the swans come in. Upon this lovely river and the nearby cove, on any given day neatly sail wondrous white swans as graceful and light as any three-masted sailing ship. Since we have the liberty and time to evoke Inishfree this week of weeks, you mention swans to an Irishman, and it's going to bring to mind the Children of Lir, this tale weaving into the song:

"I wander o'er green hills through dreamy valleys
And find a peace no other land could know.
I hear the birds making music fit for angels
And watch the river, laughing as it flows.."

Fadó, fadó, long long ago, up near County Mayo in fact, in the Kingdom of Lir, there were four children who were the light of the King's eye: Aodh, Fiachra, Conn, and Fionnuala. Now, Fionnuala

217

was the sister to the three boys and it's said she was as beautiful as the flowers of summer. But of course, all was not well because their stepmother Aoife, with no children of her own, was jealous of the King's love for them. So when she saw her chance, she coaxed the children into Lake Dairbhreach for a swim, and with a wave of her magic rowan wand, changed them into swans. Her curse was a severe one, with a riddle at the end which no one seemed to be able to solve. She commanded them to remain as swans for three hundred years on the lake, then to be sent as swans to the Sea of Moyle for three hundred years, and on top of that, another three hundred years on the western ocean. The only event that could break the spell would be for the Man from the North to join the Woman of the South. But she did allow them the gift of song, so they could sing with human voices.

When the King heard of this, he rushed to the lake shore but he could not change Aoife's spell. The evil stepmother was banished forever to be a demon spirit of the air, but there seemed to be no way to join the Man from the North and the Woman from the South, which were two mountains on different sides of the kingdom. Three hundred years went by, during which the fame of the swan children and their beautiful mournful singing spread throughout the kingdom, even reaching the wild swans. When the children told them their story, the wild swans of course wanted to help, but no one could solve the riddle that would break the curse. During the first three hundred years, the king, strangely enough, did not seem to age, but he was deeply worried about his swan children having to soon face the fierce weather on the Sea of Moyle, between Ireland and Scotland.

When it came time to leave for the northern sea, all the kingdom assembled to say goodbye, and everyone was in tears. Suddenly, the story goes, something blocked the light of the sun and everyone looked up to see a great flock of wild swans gathering in the sky. They joined in a line high up in the air, forming a bridge that went right across the kingdom and joined the Man from the North to the Woman from the South. That's when the children turned back into humans and left the lake to join their father on the shore. And of course, they all lived *uaidh sin amach,* happily ever after.

So you should keep that story in mind, the next time you stroll along the riverside, or catch a glimpse of the seemingly unconcerned swans floating quietly upon our river. You never know, you may need them someday! Keep in mind too, that Seán and the lads are working on joining the east and west of prospect Street, so long separated!

As for the swans, there is certainly magic in the birds, and in the people who could weave such a legend, and besides, it's probably all *true*. Indeed if you go up to County Meath, and if you look hard you can find four white stones on the lakeshore under the moss, marking the spot in that magical isle, where the children came back to their father.

"Ah," continues Seán,

"But dreams don't last—
Though dreams are not forgotten—
And soon I'm back to stern reality.
But though they pave the pathways here with gold dust,
I would still choose the Isle of Inishfree."

Lá Fhéile Pádraig Sona Daoibh! Happy St. Patrick's Day!

CPSIA information can be obtained
at www.ICGtesting.com
Printed in the USA
EDOW021144271212
314ED